TIME LOST

A TIME TRAVEL NOVEL

by

Elyse Douglas

Broadback Books

COPYRIGHT

DEDICATION

For Annie, who loves to look at the stars.

QUOTATION

"Like a master illusionist, time conjures visions of what was, what is, and what could be, leaving us in awe of its magic."

~Dexton Collier

TIME LOST

ELYSE DOUGLAS

PROLOGUE

S ally Anne D   and
  mother of   : of
October 5, 1953.

A newspaper ar   .d in
the local paper, *The Rosemont Chronicle.*

**Mysterious Disappearance Rocks Our Town!
Local Woman Vanishes without a
Trace, Leaving Police Baffled!**

Days and weeks of searching by police, friends, volunteer groups, and even the FBI had produced not one shred of evidence. Sally Mason had simply disappeared.

Sally Anne Davis was first featured in *The Rosemont Chronicle* at the age of eighteen, having been voted first place in the Miss Rosemont Queen contest of 1944. The article read,

Amidst a spectacle of beauty and elegance, Sally Anne Davis, a captivating 18-year-old, was crowned the esteemed Miss Rosemont Queen of 1944. Her raven black hair, blue eyes, radiant smile, and unwavering poise enchanted not only the judges but also the entire community, who eagerly cheered for their new queen. In a momentous ceremony at City Hall, Sally Anne was crowned by Mayor Fassbender, an honor that marked the beginning of her year-long reign. Filled with a contagious enthusiasm and natural charm, Sally Davis addressed the crowd, stating, "I want to bring hope, joy, and a positive impact to the people of our beautiful town, the State of Indiana, and the entire nation."

On October 5, 1953, Mrs. Sally Anne Mason was driving her 1951 Chevy Styleline Belair along Route 9, a blacktop two-lane road. She was about four miles from home. The night was clear, with a dazzling display of stars and a crescent moon hanging low on the horizon.

When it happened, Sally's car was the lone vehicle on the road. She had just completed the first night of an eight-week shorthand course at Rosemont High School, her old alma mater, and she was proud of herself for her courage and initiative, even if she hadn't done well on her first night. But her teacher, Sybil Brown, had spoken encouragingly to the five women. "It's your first night. You'll get it, girls. Don't be discouraged. Just practice. Very few take to it right off."

Watching the fragmented yellow lines on the road blur by, Sally felt a surge of nervous excitement. She was back in school, rediscovering the joy of learning and the potential for expanding her skills and, hopefully, her horizons.

The occasional glare of headlights stabbed her eyes as cars from the opposite lane zoomed past. Was she driving too fast? What was the speed limit? She'd driven that road so many times, but she couldn't recall.

She switched on the radio and found WQMI and

dialed into the Rollin'-with-Folen radio show. As Frankie Lane crooned, she snaked a hand into her purse, feeling for her pack of cigarettes. A cigarette would help calm her nerves. Ahead, a black-and-white road sign loomed out of the darkness.

SPEED LIMIT 35

Sally glanced at the glowing speedometer. Too fast. Her dial read 43.

Using the car cigarette lighter, she lit her cigarette, blowing a feather of smoke toward the windshield.

There was comfort in Frankie Lane's song, and in the familiar hum of the Chevy's 6-cylinder 92 horsepower engine. She was well aware of the horsepower, a detail her husband Ronnie had intentionally kept from her. With a sneering grin and a smug expression, he'd said, "Women don't know nothing about cars, and they don't need to. They can barely drive as it is, and most should be kept off the roads."

One day, to spite him, she'd snatched the car manual from the glove compartment and looked it up. Yes, 92 horsepower. Not stopping there, she'd also memorized "Spark-ignition 4-stroke engine," whatever that was. She'd be prepared the next time he said women knew nothing about cars. And, of course, he'd repeat the line because it was one he frequently used, along with, "I love you, baby, but I think you must have flunked Home Economics."

Well, now she knew something about cars, and

she was going to learn shorthand, and nothing or no one was going to stop her, not even Ronnie.

Then she saw it. A bluish white light flashed across the road ahead, at tree-top level. Thinking it was a reflection from her headlight beams or from another vehicle, Sally leaned her head forward over the steering wheel, stared out the windshield, and scanned the sky. She saw nothing, but she slowed down, sensing danger.

The night grew as black as a cave. The moon was gone. The stars were gone. Growing uneasy, she stubbed out her cigarette in the ashtray, staring out the windshield, her eyes round, scared, and watchful. She thought of Ronnie, and she wished he was with her.

Her quick eyes darted about, and she saw it again—a bluish white light ahead, descending from the dark sky like a puff of smoke, expanding. Sally watched in horror as the blue, boiling cloud morphed into a massive, glittering spacecraft, hovering ominously above the road, emitting a low, eerie throb that drummed deep in her chest.

Sally's breath came with pain as the saucer-shaped craft advanced, its dome lights flashing and whirling.

It crept ahead, heading straight for her.

CHAPTER 1

S ally didn't believe her husband Ronnie was a bad husband, or a mean one, even though he had struck her a few times during heated arguments. Much of what he said and did he'd learned from his father, who treated most women, including his wife, as servants.

But Sally was certain Ronnie loved her, and he was a good provider, and, most importantly, he loved their two children and they loved him.

The latest ongoing argument concerned Sally taking a night school shorthand course. Ronnie was vehemently opposed to it, and after dinner the evening before the course was to begin, the argument grew heated.

"You've got two kids and me to look after, Sally. That's your job," Ronnie had said, pointing a sharp finger at her. He was of medium build with broad shoulders, a lean face, and a flattop haircut.

"You don't need to be out fooling around at night when you're needed here, at home."

Sally had agonized for weeks about whether she should take the course, but once she'd registered and paid the money out of her allowance, she was determined.

"I keep telling you, Ronnie. I keep saying over and over that it's only one night a week for eight weeks. Then after I pass, maybe I can work part time. Bonnie can pick Mary up at kindergarten, since she picks Jimmy up anyway, and I'd be home before the bus drops Don off from school."

Ronnie shook his head, his voice edged and strong. "I won't have it, Sally. I don't want my daughter picked up by a neighbor. The next thing I know, you'll be working late and you won't have time to shop and cook my supper. No. I'm putting my foot down on this one."

His strident voice rose, and from the living room, 7-year-old Don cranked up the volume on the radio, as he and 5-year-old Mary, sprawled on the living room carpet, listened to *The Mickey Mouse Theater of the Air.*

Sally held up a hand like a stop sign and then crossed to the kitchen door and closed it.

Ronnie continued, his face flushing red. "When we got married, we agreed you'd be a housewife. Yes, ma'am, we agreed to that. That's why you didn't go to college, remember? We wanted to start a family. So, now, I just don't get all this. Why do you suddenly want to become some kind of working woman? We don't need you to work, Sally. I'm the breadwinner, and that's the way I want it to stay."

Sally folded her arms to keep her hands from shaking, looking directly at him as she struggled for courage. "Things change, Ronnie. People change. I want to change. Sometimes, I just want to get out of this house and meet people. Maybe I have dreams, Ronnie. Dreams that I keep to myself."

"What kind of dreams? What are you talking about?"

She swallowed, dropping her arms to her sides. "Maybe I dream about working at *The Rosemont Chronicle*, and when I learn shorthand, maybe I can work there as a secretary or something."

Ronnie stared at her as if she'd just lost her mind. "Are you nuts, Sally? Are you completely nuts?"

"Don't you have dreams?" she countered.

"No, I have my kids, my work, and a wife. At least I had a wife. What the hell, Sally? You're talking a lot of crap here. You'll never work at *The Chronicle*. Never. You're a woman, and you're not smart enough, and they'll never hire you, anyway. Forget it, okay? And forget about all this night school business, and just be a housewife, like your friends. They don't work, and they seem happy to me. None of them have these crazy ideas and want to run off and leave their kids to work at some nothing of an office job."

Sally squeezed her hands into fists, trying not to provoke her husband. "I want more than they want, Ronnie. I've never been out of this town except for vacations in Tennessee."

"So, is working as a secretary going to take you, I don't know, to Paris or something?"

"Of course not," she said, but even as she spoke the words, an image of Don and Mary romping about a small Parisian garret apartment, while she sat behind a typewriter, flitted through her mind.

"Then what the hell are you saying?" Ronnie

asked. "I mean, just tell me, what in the hell are you saying?"

Sally struggled to control her frustration. "I'm just trying to explain how I feel, Ronnie. I want to do things. I need to feel like I'm doing something besides housework and cooking. I can do those things, too, but I want to do more than that. And besides, we could use the extra money, maybe for a nice vacation in Florida. I'd like to see the ocean."

Ronnie pointed another finger at her face, his eyes wide with a threat. "Well, I say no, Sally. That's what I'm saying, all right? It's not right that you want to break your promise to me and the kids."

Sally huffed out a sigh. "What promise? What are you talking about?"

Ronnie's eyes flared with anger. "I'm saying it's not right. That's what I'm talking about, Sally. I'm saying, I don't want my kids growing up without their mother."

"*Your* kids? They're my kids, too, Ronnie. I had something to do with them being born, remember?"

"Don't get sassy-mouthed with me, Sally. I don't like that, and I won't take it."

Sally backed off, her eyes pleading. "Ronnie, I'd only be working when the kids are in school and you're at work. Nothing's going to change for you or for them. I stayed home when the kids were babies, but now that they're growing up, I need to get out. I have to do this."

Ronnie's posture tensed. He shook his head and jammed his fists into his trouser pockets. "This is how it happens, Sally. This is the kind of thing that happens."

"How what happens?"

"Couples start busting up over things like this. So, maybe you want us to bust up, is that it?"

"No, Ronnie, of course not. You're missing what I'm saying."

And then Ronnie had a startling thought, and his accusing eyes narrowed on her. "Are you mucking around with someone else? Is that it? Is that what's really going on?"

Sally stared, incredulous. "What? Don't be ridiculous. I just want to take a night school course, Ronnie, and maybe work part-time. My mother worked part-time when I was growing up. I'm not running off to Paris or anything. And no, of course I'm not seeing anyone else. Who would I see? Who haven't I known and seen in this town since I was a kid?"

Ronnie took a step closer to her, not appeased. "Didn't you take shorthand in high school?"

Sally took a step back. "No, they didn't offer it then. They offer it now. I took typing, sewing, cooking and home management, but not shorthand."

His face tightened. "Don't push me, Sally. I don't like it when you push me. It's not right. I told my mother about this night school thing, and even she said it's not right."

And then Ronnie wheeled about and stormed out of the kitchen.

Sally turned to the sink, piled with dirty dishes. Her spirit and her shoulders sagged as she fumed and swiped at a dinner plate. If only Ronnie was more like her father, understanding and patient. But he wasn't, and she'd just have to maneuver around him. She heard them in the living room shouting with laughter. If she couldn't go to college, then for heaven's sake, she was going to night school to study shorthand, no matter what Ronnie did to her.

Late the next afternoon, Sally wanted to get out of the house before Ronnie arrived home at 5:30. She hastily scribbled him a note, telling him of her decision to attend night school. She left the note on the kitchen table, gathered Don and Mary and loaded them into the Chevy. This was one of the two days a week that Ronnie caught a ride to work with his father and left her the car, so she could run errands.

Sally dropped the kids at her parents' house, told her mother what she'd done, and then she left the house, hurrying to her car. Her mother, Ruby, stood in the front doorway, twisting her hands, calling after her.

"Ronnie is not going to like this, Sally."

Sally called back over her shoulder. "Yeah, well, if he doesn't like it, he can just lump it. I'm going to night school."

After her first class, Sally slouched away from the school to the parking lot and made her way over to the Chevy. It was time to drive home and face Ronnie. Her stomach was already in knots and she had a blurry headache. She felt sorrow and fear, but she accepted them, as she started the car and drove off into the night, hoping to regain some of her fragile courage before she arrived home.

It was anybody's guess what Ronnie might do to her. Curse her? Slap her? Take the car keys away?

CHAPTER 2

When Sally was about two miles from home, she needed a distraction from her anxious thoughts, and she switched on the radio. In a raspy over-adrenalized voice, the DJ shouted, "Hello, all my friends and neighbors, this is Rollin'-with-Folen with you until the magic midnight hour, right here on WQMI. Okay, now, let's not wait for grandma to struggle up those steep stairs. Let's not wait until dear old dad puts the cat out. Let's not wait for Sister Sue to get back from her date with Backseat Charlie, but let's get right to it. Yes, with the one and only Frankie Laine and his heartfelt runaway hit, let us spin into action with his new song, *I Believe*."

While the car's headlights tunneled into the night, and the car went winding through the dark trees, Sally lit a cigarette, eased back, and listened to Frankie's lusty, rough-edged voice. Being alone in the cocoon of night didn't frighten her. It gave her much needed time to recharge her mental and emotional batteries before she had to face Ronnie's anger and threats.

When the song ended, and the DJ rattled on about some commercial, Sally thought the road seemed endless. She couldn't remember it taking so long to drive home from the high school, and there were so many twists and turns that the yellow lines seemed to jump out of the darkness.

Then she saw it. A bluish white light flashed across the road ahead, at tree-top level. Thinking it was a reflection from her headlight beams or from another vehicle, Sally leaned her head forward over the steering wheel, stared out the windshield, and scanned the sky. She saw nothing, but she slowed down, sensing danger.

The night grew as black as a cave. The moon was gone. The stars were gone. Growing uneasy, she stubbed out her cigarette in the ashtray, staring out the windshield, her eyes round, scared, and watchful. She thought of Ronnie, and she wished he was with her.

Her quick eyes darted about, and then it happened —a blinding burst—like a massive flashbulb going off. It left spots swimming in her vision. She squinted, her pulse rising. What was that? The light —a stabbing glare so intense, it had the brilliance of ten noonday suns. She shielded her eyes with one hand, the other hand tight on the steering wheel. With a sick pitch of her stomach, she yanked her foot from the accelerator, disoriented, fighting to keep the car on the road.

In a hot panic, she banged down the door lock knob with the flat of her hand. Was the Chevy still in motion? Where was the road?

Straining her eyes, she saw something ahead, and goose pimples rippled up her back. She slammed on the brakes, and her head jerked forward.

A silvery, gleaming, saucer-like craft, disc-shaped with a dome center, emerged from a smoky blue fog, like something dreamed. It drifted over the road toward her; stopped about twenty yards away and hovered.

Sally was frozen, her eyes wide, a hot electric current lifting the hair on her arms, her heart thundering in her chest. The craft was small, only ten feet across, a few feet tall. It pulsed and was as silent as a whisper. It was a thing of wonder. A thing of beauty, with whirling, dazzling blue and yellow dome lights, and a shiny gray surface the color of wet tin.

She watched, and her breath stopped. The space craft wobbled, flashed red and bold, and, impossibly, it expanded, becoming an immense thing. It was a child's crazy toy turned gigantic monster, dwarfing Sally's Chevy.

She screamed, but it was a silent scream, caught in the tightness of her throat. A blinding flash of blue light engulfed the car like a towering ocean wave. Sally threw up her hands as a shock-wave of heat struck her, bursting the breath from her lungs.

Seconds later, the road was dark and still. A speeding car approached, the motorist taking the curves like a confident racecar driver on an empty track, speeding past the spot where Sally, the Chevy, and the spacecraft had once been.

The driver was George Perry, who owned the Rosemont Roxie Theater that was currently featuring *Gentlemen Prefer Blondes*. George had just downed a few beers in town and was on his way home. He cranked down his car window and glanced up, smiling at the buttery, crescent moon and a sky glittering with stars. As he drove through the quiet night, he heard croaking frogs and singing crickets, and he thought to himself, *What a beautiful night.*

CHAPTER 3

S heriff Ray Connell and Deputy Mike Benson saw the car resting on the narrow shoulder of Highway 9. Connell slowed the patrol car down and drove toward it.

They'd been alerted to its presence by forty-year-old Karen Spivey, who lived in the Sunrise Condo Complex. She'd spotted it in the early morning and had called the police.

"There's an old type of car across the road aways, and it's just sitting there, and it's been sitting there for about an hour now. I wake up early. Anyway, somebody might be dead in there. I can't see if anybody's inside, but the car's back end is kind of sticking out, and I notice cars have to swerve around it. And we all know about drug deals going on. I hope it's not some dead drug dealer. Anyway, I'm not going out there. You should send some cops."

Ray Connell was forty-one and balding at the crown. He was a bit stocky, a bit paunchy, and a bit bored. He'd skipped breakfast and then managed to spill half the Dunkin' caramel-favored coffee that Mike Benson had bought for him. That had raised his grouchy meter to a near ten.

"Should have grabbed a couple of jelly donuts," Mike said. "What was I thinking, anyway?"

Ray slapped his gut. "Donna's put me on a diet. More fiber. More fish. No friggin' donuts."

"Well, Donna is thin," Mike said, with a shake of his head.

"Yeah, as she keeps reminding me."

Ray Connell had been with the Rosemont police force since he'd been discharged from the Army at twenty-three. He'd risen to the rank of Sheriff when he was thirty-two, and he was next in line for chief of police. But Chief Kennie Gosser would have to retire first—if he ever did—and then Ray would have to get elected, which he thought he probably could.

Ray didn't enjoy being stuck at a desk like a potted plant. He preferred being outside the office, and Chief Gosser was flexible, as long as the paperwork got done, and as long as Ray kept the four male deputies and two women deputies in line. All were in their late twenties or early thirties. Two of the male cops liked to party, and one liked his gun too much. One female deputy, Linda Baxter, was as serious as a funeral, never smiling and never admitting a mistake, and the other female deputy, Jill Webber, was perky, chatty, and had recently married a guy who sang and played guitar in a country western band. In Ray's mind, Mike Benson was the best of the lot. He was smart and level-headed.

"Keep them off those damn cellphones," Chief Gosser repeated, like a mantra. "And make sure they don't do any of that vaping and smoking weed. And I don't want to see any of them coming to work drunk or getting drunk on the job. You watch them, Ray, because I'm just too damn busy and getting too damn fat. And you know how I feel about regular firearms training. At least three times a year."

Ray and Chief Gosser didn't share a particularly close friendship, but they held a mutual respect and a professional fondness for each other. They also shared their spouses consistently urging them to adopt healthier eating habits and engage in physical activity, behaviors that both cops actively attempted to avoid.

Ray was happily married to Donna, had two sons, two dogs, two cats, and what Ray jokingly referred to as "too many in-laws."

Deputy Mike Benson was twenty-eight, tall and thin, with a mass of right arm tattoos and a saucy-mouthed girlfriend named Pink, who tended bar at Fat Wannabe, a trendy bar in town.

Mike's father worked for the railroad, but his maternal grandfather had been a cop. After attending two years at the community college and not taking to business courses, it was Mike's grandpa, Benny Buck, who'd talked Mike into being a cop.

"It's not the kind of policing I did back in the day," Benny Buck had said, a cigar clamped between his teeth, "but it's still a good job for a man, and it's still an honorable one, no matter what silly words get batted around these days."

The road was damp from an overnight shower, and the early morning traffic was light. Sheriff Connell tapped the brake as they approached the retro parked car, both men peering ahead, curious.

"Look at that," Mike said, leaning forward, placing his half-drunk Dunkin's coffee cup in the coffee holder. "That's an old beauty, isn't it, Sheriff? How old is that thing?"

"It's an old Chevy," Ray said. "Maybe a 1953 or even earlier. Damned thing looks new."

The patrol car parked behind the Chevy, with Ray activating the flashing blue dome lights.

"And what's with the license plate?" Mike asked, his eyes squinting. "It's yellow with black numbers."

Ray moved his lips from side to side as he went into thought, a habit he'd formed in the Army, waiting in the endless lines.

The radio crackled, but Ray didn't hear it. "Do a license check. There's somebody in that car, slumped over the wheel. I don't like the looks of it. After the check, stand at the rear of the car."

Ray emerged from the patrol car into the overcast and chilly October morning. He closed the door, pulled on his cap, straightened it as he always did, another habit, and sucked in a quick breath. Ray's chocolate-brown uniform was pressed and crisp, his stride was confident, and his curiosity was piqued.

Mike stepped from the police car and straightened, calling out. "Nothing on the license plate yet," he said, pointing at the Chevy's plate. "The license plate says '53. It's says 1953."

"I saw it," Ray said, keeping close to the road and away from the traffic. He thought, *A vintage, beautifully restored antique car? What does that say? And with 1953 license plates? A show-off? Somebody with over a hundred grand or more to throw away on a toy? Somebody shot dead? A drug deal gone bad?*

At the driver's window, he peered inside.

Just then, a car crept by, the driver leaning toward the passenger window, gawking at the Chevy. Ray turned sharply. "Move the friggin' car," he shouted, waving a hand. "Go on, get out of here!"

The driver slid back behind his steering wheel and drove away. When Ray peered into the Chevy's driver's window, he expected the worst, and maybe that's why he thought of Donna and the kids. Things can happen fast, and your life can change in a flash.

The window was rolled up. Ray's mouth turned sour when he saw a woman slumped over the steering wheel, her left arm dangling. He stilled. Yes, it was a woman. A sickness rose in him as he stared. Instinct and experience told him it wasn't a drug hit. Most likely, it was a domestic. A rich couple. They'd had an argument. One or both of them had had an affair. Maybe it was sudden money troubles, and now they couldn't afford the retro toy. Maybe she had stolen his love, his money, and his toy, and he'd killed her.

She wore a floral-patterned dress, a pink sweater, black pumps, a green scarf around her neck and a pink headband. No jeans. No trendy top. Since Ray couldn't see her face, he couldn't estimate her age.

Ray hesitated, and then he ran a hand across his freshly shaven jaw.

"Anything?" Mike called.

Ray didn't answer. He pondered, as another car

crept past, the driver gaping, rock music thumping. Ray turned an angry face and waved the car off. "Move!"

Why was he hesitating? A flutter in his gut told him something wasn't right. Maybe the woman was asleep, sleeping off too many vodka martinis or cosmos. Maybe she'd driven half the night and pulled over to catch forty winks.

Ray sighed, lifted a hand, and rapped on the window.

No movement. Dead?

He knocked again. Her shoulder moved. Slightly.

Ray's lips did the twist again, back-and-forth. With two knuckles, he tapped the window.

Her head gently lifted, then settled back down, her forehead resting on the top of the steering wheel.

Ray stiffened. She was alive. He tried opening the door, but it was locked.

As if in slow motion, the woman raised her head, leaned back in the seat, and stared ahead, her eyes wide open. They looked haunted. Frightened.

Again, Ray rapped on the window. "Miss? Miss, please open the door."

She didn't respond.

"Miss? Please roll down your window. Open the door, please."

With a slow turn of her head, she faced him, her eyes screaming. Ray moved around the front of the car to the passenger side, and tried the door latch. It opened. He leaned down and peered in.

"Miss? Are you all right? Do you need help?"

She seemed fragile, easily broken. She turned to look at him, her eyes still round.

Ray saw a trim, pretty woman with glossy black hair, in her middle-to-late-twenties. "Can I help you?" Ray repeated.

She cast her eyes about, fear holding in them. When she spoke, her voice trembled. Her hands trembled. "What...? What happened?"

"It's okay, Miss. Everything is all right. I'm Sheriff Connell. Are you hurt? Are you in pain?"

She opened her mouth as if trying to scream and covered it with a hand. "Light... There were those lights."

"Are you injured? Do you need medical assistance?"

She stared as if she didn't understand the question, and then pointed at the windshield. "Over the road... Out there, over the road. A flying thing... a flying saucer. So big. Right out there."

Still leaning in, Ray followed her gaze. "It's okay, Miss. There's nothing out there. Nothing at all. What is your name?"

She blinked once, then closed her eyes. Ray noticed her long lashes. He noticed she was a very attractive woman, and he noticed she was scared to death.

He spotted her purse on the seat next to her. "Can I call someone for you?"

Her eyes opened, and she searched ahead, left, and right. "My husband..."

"Yes," Ray said. "I can call your husband. But please tell me if you are injured. Are you sick?"

Her eyes rolled up, she swayed, wilted, and her head sagged left and struck the window.

CHAPTER 4

"WHAT THE HELL'S GOING ON?" Chief Kennie Gosser asked, standing, adjusting his black-rimmed glasses. "Is this some kind of joke? She said she saw lights and a flying saucer? Was the woman drunk? Did she take fentanyl-laced pills?"

Ray lifted a hand. "There's no toxicology report yet, and I didn't smell alcohol on her breath."

Chief Gosser's neat office had polished gray floor tiles, white walls, and overhead fluorescent lights that made the men look stark and washed out. Ray sat in a sturdy wooden chair facing the chief's gray metal desk, with a paper cup of lukewarm coffee in hand.

Chief Gosser stared out the window for a time, his back to Ray. He finally turned and eased down in his high-backed leather chair, a laptop on one side, two wire baskets stacked with papers on the other.

"What else do you have?" the chief asked, leveling his eyes on Ray. "Did you find her cellphone?"

"There was no cellphone. We searched the car. We'll search again."

Ray thought that the chief's bushy graying eyebrows seemed bushier than usual. They arched, then relaxed, and he sighed. "So, there's no one to call?"

"We found an address book in her purse."

"And?

"It contains names and phone numbers, but the phone numbers only have three digits."

"I don't get that. What are you saying, Ray?"

"I'm just saying that the phone numbers are not seven-or ten-digit numbers. They are three digits with a letter, like, 210J, and 345M."

The chief pressed his chin down into his neck so that his jowls bloomed. "Well, what am I missing here? I mean, it seems to me that somebody is playing some kind of stupid joke. But why?"

Ray stared at the back wall, at the framed certificates and awards, and the photographs of two retired chiefs of police. Both men seemed to stare back at him with authority and a challenge. He could almost hear them say, "Hey there, Sheriff Connell, what's the matter with you? Get with it."

A large whiteboard mounted on a wall to the right displayed schedules, duty rosters, and important announcements, some of them out of date.

Ray took a sip of coffee. "I told her attending, Dr. Taylor, to call me as soon as Mrs. Mason wakes up. By then, I'm sure she'll have some answers. Meanwhile, Deputy Benson is busy going through motor vehicle databases, historical archives, old newspapers, and public records from the early 1950s. He's good at that kind of thing, and he likes it."

"Well, what are we looking for here, Ray?"

"I don't know, sir. I'm following the evidence I have, and we'll see where it leads. Deputies Bob Haynes and Jill Webber have checked out Mrs. Mason's address listed on the driver's license."

"Mrs. Mason, you said?"

"According to her driver's license, she's Sally Anne Mason of 223 North Maple Street. She's five feet six inches tall, a hundred and twenty-eight pounds, hair black, eyes blue."

The chief lifted his chin with mild surprise. "North Maple?"

"Yes... I know. There is no such address anymore. It's all condos over there, and the golf course. The bungalows built after World War II were knocked down in the late 1990s."

Chief Gosser's heavy forehead wrinkled. He ran a hand over his gray brush cut, and inclined forward, his meaty hands folded on his desktop. "And you said her driver's license was issued in 1953?"

"Yes, sir."

"And the car is a 1951 Chevy Belair?"

"Yes, and in mint condition. We had it towed to the lot next door."

"I assume you examined her purse?"

"Yes, along with Officer Jill Webber."

Ray hesitated, glancing out the rain-beaded window at the courthouse clock tower. It was 3:20. He was tired, and his shift was officially over, but he wasn't about to go home. He'd already called Donna and said he'd be late, without going into details.

Chief Gosser reached for his half-eaten Milky Way bar, bit off a piece and chewed, waiting for Ray to continue.

"We found cash and coins, totaling twelve dollars and thirty-seven cents. There was a receipt from the

Rosemont Beauty Salon for ten dollars and twenty-two cents. Officer Webber knows of two hair salons in town, but she's never heard of the Rosemont Beauty Salon. We found a library card, a Social Security card, a half pack of Kent cigarettes, lipstick, a compact mirror, and a photo in a photo sleeve. No credit cards."

Chief Gosser grew eager. "A photo? Talk to me, Ray."

"It's a black-and-white family photo. Mrs. Mason stands next to a man, surely her husband, with two kids in front of them. They're all wearing their Sunday best, man and boy in suits and ties, Mrs. Mason and the girl in dresses, and old-fashioned hats with veils. All the clothes are retro style. And the family is standing close to a 1951 Chevy that looks exactly like the one we towed this morning."

Chief Gosser blinked twice, sniffed, and pulled on his nose. He removed his glasses and turned aside, and the room fell into silence. He tugged a tissue from a tissue box and polished the lenses of his glasses while he thought things over.

Ray broke the silence. "Besides her purse, we found a paper bag on the back seat, with two sharpened pencils, a stenographer's notebook, and a copy of *Gregg's Shorthand*."

Chief Gosser's attention returned to Ray. "Does anybody even do shorthand anymore?"

"I don't know, but the book looks new, and it was published in 1949."

Gosser tapped his fingers on the desk. "Okay, Ray,

something is really messed up here," he said. He slipped his glasses back on, then jabbed a pointed finger at his closed office door. "You told them all out there to keep their mouths shut, right?" Gosser barked. "No talking cops to each other. No talking cops to reporters, girlfriends, husbands, or wives. No talking to anybody. Right? I'll kick ass if I have to."

"Right. I had a meeting with the deputies and staff. I made it clear that nobody talks. Those not present were texted, then they were called in, and I spoke to them directly."

"And the medical center staff?"

"She was admitted as Mrs. Sally Anne Mason, DOB and insurance status unknown. No one at the Medical Center has seen her driver's license or Social Security card... or anything from her purse or car, for that matter. I told them to put her in a private room, and we'd work out the insurance."

"And the doctors? I want no doctors talking to other doctors or nurses. No nurses talking to orderlies. Nothing."

"When I spoke to Dr. Taylor, I told him to keep Mrs. Mason isolated. I told him if she wakes up, he's not to talk to her about anything other than medical. The nurses or aides either."

Ray frowned. "Out on the road this morning, cars stopped to snap photos. People take photos of every damn thing, and I'm sure they've posted that vintage car and me standing next to it on *Instagram* and *Facebook*."

Chief Gosser pounded a fist on his desk. "Dammit,

Ray, how am I supposed to lose weight when a thing like this jumps up and bites us in the ass? Lights and a flying saucer? It doesn't smell right, it doesn't sound right, and it doesn't feel right."

Gosser reached for his candy bar, peeled back the wrapper, and stuffed the last piece into his mouth. He chewed with vigor, then swallowed before speaking, waving a hand in the air.

"And all this UFO business is in the news now, Ray. It's all over the internet, with these military whistleblowers and pilots shooting off their mouths about UFOs, here and there, and under the damned water, if you can believe it. My wife's even talking about it and asking me questions, as if I know anything. As if I want to know anything. I've got a bad feeling about this, Ray, and at my age I've got to watch my blood pressure."

CHAPTER 5

C hief Gosser cursed again. "Wish I had a cigar, Ray. I need a cigar on days like this."

"I understand, Chief. I'm concerned about social media."

"Well, social media won't matter unless this, whatever it is, gets out. Then, here will come the bloggers, and the conspiracy theory assholes, and the whackos, and then we're in the shit, okay? Clear this thing up, Ray. Whatever this is, just clear it up and let's get back to our business."

"Yes, sir. Deputy Webber and I are going to head back to the medical center. I'll hang around until Mrs. Mason wakes up."

"And no one else has spoken to Mrs. Mason, right? No doctor or nurse?"

"No. She was unconscious when EMS rolled her into the ER. She briefly woke up, looked about, and then began screaming. She was sedated, and the last report from the doctor said she was sleeping."

Ray's eyes wandered toward the bookshelf that contained law enforcement reference books, manuals, and legal codes. He thought, *There's nothing in that bookshelf that references this.*

Chief Gosser looked straight at Ray. "I don't know, Ray, we're both old cops. Can we talk about this thing?" He waved a hand through the air as he searched for the right words. "Can we talk about weird lights, and a flying saucer, and a vintage car in perfect shape, with 1953 plates? And what about her driver's license issued in the 1950s?"

Ray drained the last of the coffee, gripped the cup with both hands and stared down at the tile floor. "She was scared... the fear was big in her eyes. And the way she was dressed. The fine dress, the scarf, the headband. It fit with the car, the clothes, I mean. Like from an old movie... a fifties movie, I guess you can say. And then there was her stop-light red lips. Hard to forget them, with her mouth open as she tried to scream."

A knock turned the men's attention to the door. Gosser called out, "Come in."

Deputy Benson entered and pulled the door closed, his face set in solemn concentration. At first, Gosser was annoyed with the interruption, but a closer look at Benson's face, and the pages clasped in his hand, made the chief shift in his chair.

Ray spoke up. "What is it, Mike?"

Deputy Benson took three steps closer to Gosser's desk, extended a hand with the papers, and Gosser accepted them. Mike kept his eyes down as he spoke. "It's from Motor Vehicles. The Chevy was registered to a Ronald David Mason at 223 North Maple Street. I followed up his name and found a match with Sally Anne Mason. I found a marriage certificate. A copy is included. Sally Anne Mason's maiden name was Davis. They were married on May 19, 1945, soon after the Germans surrendered in World War II."

Ray's lips twisted. Gosser sifted through the

pages, his eyes hard on them.

Deputy Benson continued. "I ran a detailed search for Sally Anne Davis Mason for Rosemont, checking *The Rosemont Chronical* that closed in 2010."

Mike's hands were busy at his sides, as if he wanted to put them somewhere. "Well, you have the newspaper articles there, Chief."

Gosser read the words, scratching his cheek twice. His left eye twitched. When he finished reading the newspaper article, he rose and handed the three pages to Ray, his expression grave.

Ray stood, took the pages, and began to read.

Miss Rosemont Queen of 1944.

Amidst a spectacle of beauty and elegance, Sally Anne Davis, a captivating 18-year-old, was crowned the esteemed Miss Rosemont Queen of 1944. Her raven black hair, blue eyes, radiant smile, and unwavering poise enchanted not only the judges but also the entire community, who eagerly cheered for their new queen.

Ray lifted the page and read the next article, and he felt the heavy fist-force of a sucker punch.

Mysterious Disappearance Rocks Our Town! Local Woman Vanishes without a Trace, Leaving Police Baffled!

In startling local news, Mrs. Sally Anne Mason, wife of Ronald Mason and mother of two, has mysteriously vanished, leaving friends, family, and authorities searching for answers. The sudden disappearance of the former Miss Rosemont Queen of 1944 has sparked deep concern and confusion among residents, who anxiously await any information that may shed light on her whereabouts.

Mrs. Mason was last seen at approximately 8:30 p.m., as she left Rosemont High School, where she was enrolled in a night course in shorthand.

Sheriff Tom Widmeyer has launched an extensive investigation, concentrating his department's efforts on retracing Mrs. Mason's steps and gathering any leads. The police are reaching out to the public, urging anyone who may have witnessed anything unusual or had contact with Mrs. Mason around the time of her disappearance, to come forward with information that could aid in solving this case and locating Mrs. Mason.

Mrs. Mason grew up in Rosemont, and her history as Miss Rosemont Queen of 1944 has brought added attention to her disappearance. It has sparked an outpouring of support from friends and residents, who have joined forces to organize search parties and distribute flyers throughout this and neighboring towns.

Mr. Ronald Mason, a partner in his father's construction business, has been questioned by the police, but Sheriff Widmeyer said Mr. Mason is not a suspect at this time. It is noted that Mr. Mason suffers from asthma, a medical condition that kept him from serving in the armed services when he turned eighteen in 1944. Mr. Mason was admitted to the hospital for that condition when he learned about his wife's disappearance.

The police are currently following several leads, and if anyone has any information that could assist them in locating Mrs. Sally Mason, please contact the Rosemont Police Department at the confidential phone number listed below.

Chief Gosser looked stricken. Mike stood rigid. Ray eased back down in his chair, staring blindly ahead.

A long moment later, Gosser said, in a low, shaky voice. "I'm going to call... what's his name? That psychiatrist, Dr. Sweeny. I don't know what we've got here, but I don't want this in my town, or on my watch. I don't want any part of this, whatever the hell it is."

Ray slowly returned to his feet, pulling on his lower lip.

Deputy Mike Benson cleared his throat. "Chief, I think this could be a national security thing. I know it sounds crazy, but if Mrs. Mason was alive in 1953 and did encounter what used to be called a UFO —what they're now calling an Unidentified Aerial Phenomenon, or UAP—then maybe that spacecraft was out on Highway 9, like she said. I mean, maybe it's still out there somewhere."

Ray said, "Highway 9 used to be Route 9. It was changed over twenty years ago. Well, I guess that doesn't matter, does it?"

Deputy Benson shrugged. "Well, I don't know, maybe Mrs. Mason was just beamed here like in *Star Trek* or something, but ... Well, it's possible somebody at the CIA or FBI might want to interview her. I mean, I'm just saying, you know?"

The men considered it, their expressions sullen.

Gosser pushed up, throwing his hands to his hips, exasperated. "I'm not going there, okay? What the hell am I supposed to do with this? I don't believe it, and nobody else is going to believe it unless they're nuts. It's like a damned silly *Netflix* movie. We've got to get to the bottom of this without making up Sci-Fi stories."

Ray looked at Mike. "Mike, in that database, in the old Rosemont newspaper, were there any follow-up articles? Was Mrs. Mason ever found?"

Mike shook his head. "There was a follow-up article in the same paper about five years later. The sheriff had asked the FBI for help, and they did for a while, but Mrs. Mason and the car were never found."

Chief Gosser focused on Ray. "Ray, go ahead and call Dr. Sweeny. Before I call anybody else or do anything else, call him, and let's get a complete psychiatric evaluation of this woman. Let's interview her and find out who she really is and what she knows."

Ray thought about it. "Chief, I'm thinking a woman psychiatrist might be a better choice."

Gosser threw up a hand. "Okay, whatever. I don't care. Who?"

"There's a Dr. Stanley. Meg Stanley. She helped us out on that drug bust a few months ago, when that girl went crazy on us with the knives. Dr. Stanley lives near Bloomington."

"Okay, fine, call her, but tell her she's got to do this ASAP. Today. Tonight, whatever. Tell her it's an emergency. I'll okay the budget, somehow, but tell her to drop everything and come. The longer this goes on, the more it could blow up in our faces, and maybe it already has."

CHAPTER 6

S ally Mason's eyes fluttered open. Her vision was blurred, her head pounding. A sterile smell hung in the air, and there were beeping sounds. *What are those beeping sounds?* she thought. She was lying in a bed, covered by a sheet and a beige-colored blanket. Her head rested on a soft, deep pillow.

A tube snaked around her arm, leading to a clear bag of liquid suspended above her. She squinted, her mind dull, straining to comprehend her surroundings and remember how she got there. Accident? Car accident? Seconds stretched into eternity. Her body seemed made of stone, heavy, punished.

Muffled voices came from somewhere, and a police siren quickened her pulse. With effort, she moved her head left. Blinking monitors emitted soft beeps, and the hum of machines made her tense. A flickering florescent light overhead made a low, staticky sound and colored the room in a weird light. Privacy curtains enclosed most of her bed. A hospital bed. A hospital room.

Sally struggled to sit up, but her muscles were weak and unresponsive. Her children's faces flashed by her inner mind like windblown leaves, and Ronnie's face was wet and wavy, as if under water.

A flare of memory widened her eyes. She saw

the night road, a burst of light, a nightmare of something descending—a spaceship hovering, casting an eerie glow across the road.

Sally's scream was a hollow wheeze.

A woman appeared.

"Mrs. Mason... Mrs. Mason. I'm Nurse Harden. Please relax. I'll give you a sedative. Just relax now."

Sally found her voice, her chest heaving. "No... No sedative. No. Just help me. Where's Ronnie? Let me see him. I want to go home. How are my kids? I just want to go home. I'll be okay. Just let me go home so I can see my kids."

Nurse Harden kept her soothing voice low. "Yes, all right, Mrs. Mason. I'll talk to Dr. Taylor, but please just try to relax."

Sally struggled to sit up, noticing she was wearing a blue hospital gown. "Where are my clothes? What happened?" she said, panic just below the surface. "There was this light and a big... thing... flying thing over the road and..."

Nurse Harden touched her shoulder, urging Sally to lie back. "Please, Mrs. Mason, the doctor will be here soon. Just rest."

"Where's Ronnie? Shouldn't he be here? How long have I been here? Does he know I'm here? Has someone called my parents?"

Nurse Harden felt her patient's jagged emotions. "Yes, yes, Mrs. Mason. It's all good. Just relax."

And then Sally seemed to see Nurse Harden for the first time, and she squinted at her. "Who are you?"

"I'm Nurse Harden, Mrs. Mason."

"But… you're a Negro. You're a Negro nurse."

Nurse Harden tried to smile. "Yes, Mrs. Mason, I am an African-American woman."

Sally kept her stare. "What hospital is this? Why am I here? Where's Ronnie?"

Just then, Dr. Taylor appeared, gently sliding back the privacy curtains, a smile on his lips, a helmet of silver hair adding distinction, his smooth face making him appear younger than his fifty-eight years. He wore a white lab coat and had a stethoscope draped around his neck.

"Good morning, Mrs. Mason. I'm Dr. Taylor. How are you feeling?"

Reflexively, Sally finger-combed her hair with her free hand. "Where's my husband? I want to see Ronnie. I want to go home."

Dr. Taylor's smile faded. He knew little about Mrs. Mason's history. Over the last two days, he and Sheriff Connell had talked on the phone three times. The Sheriff told him that Mrs. Mason had suffered some sort of trauma, that she was found on Highway 9, and that she would be seeing a police-appointed psychiatrist. At the present moment, Sheriff Connell was outside with that psychiatrist, a Dr. Megan Stanley.

"Yes, of course, Mrs. Mason," Dr. Taylor said. "Did you rest well last night?"

"I don't know. I'm confused. I don't know what day it is or how long I've been here. Can you please let me see my husband? He must be eager to see me.

He must be worried sick. I want to go home and see my kids. How long have I been here?"

Dr. Taylor forced a reassuring smile. "Not long, Mrs. Mason. Now, the good news is you have no injuries, and your blood work is good."

Sally didn't seem to hear the doctor or care about what he'd said. "Is Ronnie outside?"

Dr. Taylor slid his hands into his lab coat. "Well... no, Mrs. Mason, but there is another doctor who wishes to speak to you, if that is all right with you?"

"No. No, it's not all right. If there's nothing wrong with me, then I want to leave. Call Ronnie, for heaven's sake. Why isn't he here? I don't understand. Where are my parents?"

Dr. Taylor looked at Nurse Harden and nodded toward Sally's I.V. drip.

"We're going to remove your I.V. drip to make you more comfortable," the doctor said.

The nurse moved to the other side of the bed, removed the I.V., and then left the room.

Dr. Taylor met Sally's eyes, and he spoke in a firm voice. "Mrs. Mason, there are no physical concerns, but we believe you have experienced a shock. As such, we think it would be beneficial for you to speak with Dr. Meg Stanley, who is a female psychiatrist."

Sally's eyes moved, her expression a strange, fixed grimace. She rolled her head away from his intruding gaze. "Psychiatrist? I don't need a psychiatrist. I want to go home."

"We believe that having a conversation with Dr. Stanley would be beneficial. Engaging in dialogue with a professional might provide valuable assistance and help you put things into perspective."

Sally glanced about, twisting her hands. "I don't know... I'm fine. You said I'm not hurt or anything. I just need to get out of here and go home. I need to see Ronnie. Get my husband, Ronnie, Doctor. Just let me see him and my kids. Please?"

Dr. Taylor gave a slow nod. "All right, Mrs. Mason," he said, growing uneasy. He didn't even know Sally Mason's date of birth, never mind her medical history or what had happened on Highway 9. He could smell a medical malpractice lawsuit in the making, and the entire situation was making him very uncomfortable.

"Mrs. Mason, there is a policeman outside... the man who found you in your car two days ago. He and Dr. Stanley wish to speak with you."

Sally jerked her head to face the doctor, her eyes wide with shock. "Two days? I've been here two days?"

"Yes, Mrs. Mason. You fell unconscious and when you awoke, you were in great distress. That's why you were brought here. We have done a thorough physical examination and now, with your permission, we would like to conduct a psychiatric one."

Sally squeezed her eyes shut, willing the images of the bright eerie light and the spaceship to fade, fighting a volcano of terror that threatened to erupt and engulf her. She couldn't give in to it. Couldn't. These people would never let her out of the hospital if she couldn't control herself.

Paranoia arose. Maybe they were in on it? Maybe the doctor was an alien? Maybe she'd been abducted? She'd heard about such things at the beauty parlor, and in church a few weeks ago, Mrs. Gainer had said she'd read in *The Indianapolis Star* about a man who'd been taken aboard a flying saucer. Sally had laughed. She didn't believe it. Of course, she didn't believe it. None of it.

A few seconds of clarity sharpened her mind. Yes, why not speak to another doctor? A woman? Why not? She might understand better than the male doctor, and Sally could fake calm. Deny anything had happened. Lie. Whatever it took to convince the woman doctor that she was fine and could go home. Yes, why not?

Sally's eyes opened. She swallowed down another wave of panic and said, "All right... I'll talk to the doctor. Not to the policeman, but I'll speak to the doctor."

ΔΔΔ

Sheriff Connell and Dr. Meg Stanley sat in the second-floor lounge in yellow plastic chairs, waiting for Dr. Taylor to appear and give them the okay to see Sally Mason. Dr. Stanley had been on call for almost two days, and Chief Gosser had grown impatient and agitated.

"I don't care how you do it, Ray," the Chief had said, "but get that psych evaluation from Mrs. Mason

ASAP. I don't want to call in the Feds until we've done that, at least. But we can't sit on this much longer. Rumors are flying. I know they are."

Ray thought Meg Stanley's looks favored the British actress Emma Thompson, except, of course, Meg Stanley was an American. Meg was forty-eight years old, a trim short-haired blonde, with quick, intelligent eyes and a pleasant manner.

"So, do you believe Mrs. Mason was transported here by aliens?" Dr. Stanley asked.

"What do I know about this stuff?" Sheriff Connell answered. "I've never watched that movie *E.T.*, or the other one…"

"*Close Encounters*?"

"Yeah."

"Those are classics."

"Never interested me."

"Well, you saw Mrs. Mason first," Dr. Stanley said.

"But as I said, I haven't actually spoken with the woman since then, since she was pointing and talking about bright lights and a flying saucer. She screamed and fainted. So, what's to believe? I follow the evidence."

"And…? Are you going to tell me everything—all of it—and not just the bread crumbs you've been throwing at me for the last two days?"

Sheriff Connell hunched forward, folded his hands, and sighed. "No, I'm not, because I can't. Not yet anyway. I've told you all I can tell you. We just want you to talk to Mrs. Mason and give us your professional opinion. Just ask the right questions, whatever those questions are."

"Right questions?"

"She's been out of her head... Oh, forgive me, that's not the proper speak these days, is it?"

Meg smiled. "Might be. I was out of my head the other day when some kid plowed into my new Mercedes because he was on his phone with his girlfriend."

"But you weren't hurt?"

"No, but I went out of my head and blasted the kid. I think I called him a son-of-a-bitch, and some other colorful things. He thought I was a crazy woman, and I was. A cop had to pull me away. I wanted to slug that baby-faced college boy."

Ray straightened and grinned at her. "That's what I like about you, Dr. Stanley. No charm school stuff. No B.S. degree hanging on your office wall."

"I was tossed out of three schools before I was sixteen."

"Well, ain't that something?" Ray said, holding his grin. "How did you become a head doctor?"

"Sad story. Long story."

"I think we've got time. Dr. Taylor's nowhere in sight."

Dr. Stanley angled her body toward Sheriff Connell, looking him dead in the eyes. "My mother shot and killed my father when I was fourteen."

Ray's face fell. He turned away, looking down the hallway. An orderly guided a wheelchair out of a room; the elderly man sat slumped and staring.

Ray turned back to Dr. Stanley. "Okay, Doctor, I

didn't see that coming."

Meg shrugged. "I had to testify at the trial. He was abusive, and she was just trying to protect us both. But she still got put away. Later, after fits and starts, and cops and shrinks, I met a guy and, as they say, a good man is hard to find. Paul came from a good family and, for some reason, he fell in love with me. He got me through some dark times and encouraged me. He said I'd be a good shrink. I said, 'How do you know? You're a lawyer.' He said, in his most charming way, 'You're a little nuts, and nuts can help nuts.'"

Meg's and Ray's eyes connected, and Meg spread her hands. "So, here I am, ready and willing to talk to a woman who believes she saw a spaceship and probably some nasty little aliens. Your run-of-the-mill delusion. See what an education can do?"

Ray scratched his cheek. "I like your sarcasm, Doctor. Yes, I do."

Dr. Taylor came striding down the hall, and Ray and Meg rose to meet him.

"So?" Ray asked.

Dr. Taylor kinked his neck. "She's delicate. She wants to see her husband and kids."

"What did you tell her?" Ray asked.

"Nothing, since I don't know anything about her husband or kids. I suspect that's your job, Sheriff. Or perhaps it's Dr. Stanley's job? In any case, she will see you now, Doctor, but only you. Not you, Sheriff."

CHAPTER 7

D r. Meg Stanley stepped into Sally Mason's hospital room and proceeded straight to the bedside, offering a warm, friendly smile. "Hello, Mrs. Mason, I'm Dr. Meg Stanley but please call me Meg."

Sally didn't speak.

Meg said, "Do you mind if I open the blinds? It's a lovely blue-sky day, and I think it would be nice to let all the sun in. Is that okay?"

"Okay," Sally said, watchful and nervous.

Meg pulled the cords, and the room glowed with sunlight. She noticed no one had sent Sally flowers. Meg grabbed a metal chair, placed it near the bedside and sat, holding her smile. "Thank you for agreeing to see me."

"Do I have a choice?" Sally asked.

"Yes, and you still do. If you want me to go, just say so, and I am out of here. No argument. No questions asked."

Sally frowned. "You're a... psychiatrist?"

"Yes."

"Why aren't you wearing a doctor's uniform?"

"Psychiatrists are lucky. We can wear whatever clothes we want. Though we *are* medical doctors."

Sally checked out Meg's side-part hairdo. "Your hair style is different."

"Does that mean you like it?"

"Yes... But I've never heard of a woman

psychiatrist. I don't know of any female doctors, not in Rosemont anyway."

"We're around. More than you think."

Sally gazed at the door before responding. "What do you want to know? Do they think I'm crazy?"

"It sounds like you had a rough time out there on Highway 9. Maybe things got a little confusing, and maybe we can talk about it."

"I don't know."

"It's your choice."

Sally bit her lip and shrugged. "Okay... If you want to."

Meg lowered her voice. "I'm truly sorry you've had a difficult time, Sally. *May* I call you Sally?"

Sally nodded.

"And you can call me Meg."

"All right."

"So, let's just have a conversation, like we're having coffee at Starbucks. Talk about whatever you want to talk about. Ask whatever you want to ask. Will that be okay with you?"

Sally sat up, propped a pillow, and leaned back against it. "What is Starbucks?"

Meg laughed at the joke, but then realized from Sally's questioning eyes that there was no joke. "Oh... It's just a coffee place."

"Like a coffee shop?"

"Yes, that's right. Let's talk as if we're sitting in a coffee shop on a beautiful sunny day like today."

"I'd love a cigarette, Meg. It would help calm my nerves. Do you have one? I don't know where my purse is. I think they locked it up somewhere in the hospital."

"I don't smoke, Sally, and there's no smoking anywhere in the hospital, anyway."

Sally put a hand to her a cheek. "Oh…"

Meg asked, "So you're married?"

"… Yes, I am, to Ronnie, and I have two kids. Do you know why he hasn't come to see me?"

"No, Sally, I don't."

"And no one has sent me flowers, or a card or anything, and Dr. Taylor said I've been in the hospital for two days. I don't know, I'm just confused or something."

Dr. Stanley smiled with compassion. "I understand."

"And we have a family doctor, but the nurse said she couldn't contact him."

"I'm sure the medical staff are looking into things, Sally. So, tell me about your husband and your kids."

Sally's shoulders relaxed, and a faint smile formed. The words came staggered at first, but the longer she talked, the easier it became. She and Ronnie married about a year after they graduated from high school. He had been the high school quarterback, and she had been a cheerleader. Sally also worked on the school newspaper, sang in the choir, and played on the girls' softball team.

"I don't want to bore you, Meg," Sally said, her face softening. "My life is boring, and I guess it's always been kind of boring."

"Well, I'm not bored at all, Sally. Please continue."

There was a longing on Sally's face when she described her children, Don and Mary. "They're such good kids, you know? Don is seven and he's so, well, rambunctious, and he loves crawling under things, the kitchen table, and our bed. He hides under there, and I have to yell at him or he won't come out. But he's sweet and cute, too, and he loves tossing the ball with his dad. Mary is five, a little shy, but she's so smart, and such a pretty little darling. I call her my Mary Sweetness. She likes to get underfoot when I'm cooking dinner. She wants to help."

Meg crossed her arms, trying to assess Sally's mental state. She sounded like a normal, caring mother.

"Do you have children, Meg?" Sally asked.

"I have one son. But what I really want to talk about is you. If you're comfortable, please tell me what you experienced a couple of nights ago when you were driving along Highway 9."

Sally stiffened. Her jaw clenched. "You mean, Route 9?"

Meg waited, lowering her arms. "Yes, all right. Route 9. You told a policeman that you saw lights, or a light over the road?"

Sally lowered her gaze with a gentle nod. "Yes."

"Anything else you want to tell me?"

Sally licked her lips. "My husband, Ronnie, laughed about it."

"Oh... Did he see the lights, too?"

"No... I mean, not that night. A week or so before, people in town saw lights in the sky.

Some said they were spaceships. Flying saucers. At dinner one night, Ronnie said it was the military putting up weather balloons and such. He said they were working with the local weather bureau out of Indianapolis. He said people were stupid for believing in spaceships. 'They just love to get all riled up about nothing, and make a mountain out of a mole hill,' he said.

Sally continued. "And then Don asked his father something like, 'Are those flying saucers from Mars, Daddy?' Ronnie said, 'No, Don, the only men from Mars are in the movies, and in the science fiction magazines they sell at White's Drug Store.'"

Sally smiled at the memory. "'But I'd like to see them,' Don said. And I remember exactly what Ronnie told Don. 'You won't see them, Don, because they're not there. It's all made up in crazy people's heads.'"

Meg folded her hands in her lap. "But you saw lights, Sally?"

Sally looked toward the window into the sunlight. "Yes. I saw them, and then a..." Sally stopped talking, and her breath caught.

"It's all right, Sally. You're safe. Perfectly safe, and you can say whatever you want to say. We are all here to help you. Just take a few deep breaths and if you want to continue on, it's fine. If not, that's fine, too."

When Sally looked at Meg, her eyes twinkled with tears. "I was so scared."

"And who wouldn't be?"

"It's just that, I don't remember much after that. It's hard to talk about it... to explain it. From this bluish, kind of spinning light, this big, I don't know, spaceship came down from above and..." Sally faltered again. "It sounds so... You know, like I'm crazy, but I'm not crazy. I know Ronnie would say I'm crazy and I made the whole thing up, but I didn't make it up. I know what I saw."

Meg didn't stir. "And then what happened, Sally?"

Sally shook her head, tears trickling down her cheeks. "I don't know. I guess I just fainted. But since then, sometimes when I'm sleeping, I see this face."

A box of tissues sat on the bedstand. Meg reached for a tissue and handed it to Sally, who blotted her eyes.

"Do you recognize the face?" Meg asked, absorbed.

"I don't know. I just don't know."

"What does the face look like? Can you describe it?"

Sally balled the tissue in her hand and sniffed. "It's a man's face. It's like chiseled from stone, from rock. Lean, and strong features. The hair is short and white, but the face isn't old. It's... how do I say it? It's masculine."

"I see. Anything else?"

"He talked to me, but I don't remember what he said. He's appeared in my dreams and talked to me, but I don't understand. I've tried to remember the words... his words, but I don't. I can't."

"It's all right, Sally. You will. When you're ready to remember, you will."

"I don't want to," Sally said, frightened. "I don't. I don't want to remember anything. None of it. I want to see Ronnie. I just want to go home. Why can't I go home?"

Sally burst into tears, covering her face with her hands. Meg rose, pulling more tissues from the box.

"Let it out, Sally. Let it all out."

Seconds later, Sally dropped her hands, her face stark and pleading. "Do you believe me? Do you?"

Meg nodded. "Sally, I believe you're having a very difficult time and that things are confusing. We want to try to understand what happened."

Sally took the tissues from Meg and wiped her eyes, gasping out the words. "And then I woke up in the car, and a policeman was knocking on the window, and I looked around and I didn't know where I was, and I didn't know what happened, and I was so scared."

"It's okay now, Sally. It's over and you're safe."

Sally's sad eyes took Meg in fully. "Will you help me, Meg? I want to see Ronnie and my kids and go home. Will you help me? Will you call Ronnie? I want to go home and see my children. They must be so scared and confused. Help me. Please?"

A long, hanging moment later, Meg said, "I'll do everything I can to help you, Sally. We'll work all this out, and it *will* work out, I promise." She paused. "Sally, have you ever had this kind of experience before?"

"No."

"Have you ever had treatment for depression or

anxiety?"

"No. I'm not crazy, and I'm not depressed, and I'm not anxious."

"Okay, and on the night you saw lights, had you been drinking, or had you taken any kind of drugs, even prescription medication?"

"No! I was coming home from night school. Ask the teacher. She'll tell you I was there. I wasn't drinking."

"All right. And are you on any kind of medication now?"

"No. I told the doctor. I don't take anything."

"Well, that's good. Very good news."

Meg turned from her and picked up the pen and the clipboard she'd brought into the room to record Sally's answers on an evaluation form. "Now, I just need to ask you a few basic questions," she said.

Sally nodded, squinting through her blurry tears.

"Sally, what is your full name?"

"Sally Anne Davis Mason."

"And what is your date of birth?"

"March 16, 1926."

An experienced professional, Meg did not react. She repeated her answer, emphasizing the year. "You said March 16, 1926?"

"Yes."

"Okay…" Meg wrote that down. "And where were you born?"

"Right here in Rosemont."

"A local girl. Very good. And Sally, who is the current President of the United States?"

"Dwight D. Eisenhower."

Meg nodded as she recorded her answer. She glanced up when she asked the next question.

"And Sally, do you know today's date?"

Sally thought for a moment. "Well, I've been in the hospital for two days, so I guess it's October 7. My first shorthand class was on October 5, so it must be October 7."

"And the year?"

With a tissue, Sally touched the corners of her eyes. "1953."

Meg forced a smile, struggling to show no alarm. Sheriff Connell had not prepared her for this level of confusion.

CHAPTER 8

S heriff Connell, Dr. Stanley, and Dr. Taylor gathered in Dr. Taylor's recently painted white and beige office for a conference, its lone window open to dissipate the lingering smell. Dr. Taylor occupied the seat behind his L-shaped mahogany desk, while Meg and Ray took their places in leather chairs with metal frames.

"We need to get this patient into a psychiatric facility as soon as possible," Meg Stanley said, with an inflection that suggested a command. "As I told you earlier, Sheriff Connell, Mrs. Mason is delusional. She firmly believes she had an encounter with a spaceship and is dreaming about someone associated with it. She told me he talks to her in her dreams, but she doesn't understand what he's saying. Since this happens only in her dreams, I would say they are not true auditory hallucinations, but we'll have to probe further to make sure. She is also disoriented to time. She's convinced that she was born in 1926, that Eisenhower is President of the United States, and that it's 1953."

Meg unscrewed the cap from a bottle of water and took a sip. "She's clearly upset that her husband and parents haven't visited her... and why is that? Has anyone tried to contact them?"

Ray scratched his head, struggling with the situation and the unfortunate reality he found himself in. "We have not contacted them, and the reason for that will be clear as soon as I give you all the facts about Mrs. Mason," Ray said. "In the meantime, please continue. I want Dr. Taylor to hear what you told me."

Dr. Stanley turned to Dr. Taylor. "Mrs. Mason claims she's never experienced this kind of thing before, but we don't know if we can believe her. Maybe she was drunk, or on PCP or crack, although she denies that and, I must say, she doesn't look like the type."

"Her blood work came out clean," Dr. Taylor said.

Meg nodded, then continued. "So she's experiencing some kind of psychosis, and we don't know why. It could be schizophrenia or delusional disorder, or I suppose it could be a kind of dissociative disorder. I rarely see that, but she may have created this elaborate fantasy as a way to cope with trauma or a distressing life event." Meg leaned forward in her chair. "Look, we really need to talk to her husband and parents, explore her background and medical history, and find out if there's any family history of psychosis... in other words, we need to do a full evaluation."

Sheriff Connell lifted a hand, massaged his forehead, and straightened. "Doctors, Chief Gosser gave me orders to keep certain information secret until Mrs. Mason was examined by a psychiatrist. Well, I talked to the chief a few minutes ago and shared with him what you told me earlier, Dr. Stanley, and he has now given me permission to tell you both everything we know about Mrs. Mason. Of course, it *will* stay in this room, and it will *not* be discussed with spouses, friends or colleagues."

Meg angled her body to face him, and Dr. Taylor eased back into his chair, his face showing a slight anxiety, as he mentally braced himself for what was to come.

Sheriff Connell fell into a kind of grudging meditation as he presented a detailed list of everything that had occurred since he and Deputy Benson had parked behind Sally Mason's 1951 Chevy Belair. He described Mrs. Mason's deeply emotional condition, her precise mention of "lights" and "a flying saucer," and her subsequent fainting spell. Ray itemized the contents of Mrs. Mason's handbag, including her 1950s driver's license with an outdated home address, and a partially used pack of Kent cigarettes, displaying the phrase "famous micronite filter" on the front.

Ray looked at the doctors with a sideways grin. "I mention this little fact, that is, the cigarette filter, because according to our research, the company widely publicized the micronite filter from March 1952 until somewhere around May 1956, when it was discovered that this 'famous' filter contained compressed carcinogenic blue asbestos. After a number of lawsuits were filed, and a number of cases of mesothelioma were believed to have been caused by smoking the original Kent cigarette, the filter was changed in 1956."

Meg Stanley turned to stare out the window with

a poker face, trying to make sense of what the Sheriff had just told them. Dr. Taylor tapped a finger on his desktop.

Sheriff Connell cleared his throat and proceeded to list more evidence, which included the family photograph, which he passed around. He noted the apparently identical 1951 Chevy that he and Deputy Benson had discovered on Highway 9. And then he mentioned Sally's address book that contained outdated phone numbers, the 1945 marriage license, and the two newspaper articles: the first featuring Sally Anne Davis as the Miss Rosemont Queen of 1944, and the second recounting the disappearance of Sally Anne Davis Mason, a wife and mother of two, along with her car, in October 1953.

Dr. Taylor's phone rang, and he reached for it while he handed the photo of the Mason family back to Sheriff Connell. Meg checked her cellphone for messages, distracted, struggling to absorb the new and startling information.

Ray sat still, feeling a new chill in his bones. Retelling the story had manifested it, put more flesh on the bones of the thing, and made the impossible sound not only possible, but probable.

Dr. Stanley lowered her cellphone, and Dr. Taylor whispered something into the phone and then hung up. He grasped a pen and looked at it as if it were a lab specimen.

Dr. Stanley pursed her lips, considering her words. "What is clear is that Mrs. Mason is in a highly emotional state, and if what you are saying is true—that she is not mentally ill, but that she really did experience some sort of time travel with the help of a spaceship—as unbelievable as that seems —then she is going to need a lot of help in the next year. She wants to see her husband and her children. Someone is going to have to deal with that, tell her the truth and help her accept the loss of her family —and the loss of her entire previous life, for that matter. My professional recommendation is that we engage in a multidisciplinary approach to provide all the appropriate support she will need." Meg took another swallow from her bottle of water. "And I can't believe I'm saying this, but we should probably also consult with experts in the field of anomalous experiences or UFO-ology, if such a thing exists."

"Interesting idea, Dr. Stanley," Sheriff Connell said, sighing.

Meg said, "I can't be the only one holding her hand. The bottom line is, Sally Mason is going to need a lot of help."

Dr. Taylor sat forward. "Obviously, something is going on here that none of us have any experience with, and we can't keep Mrs. Mason in this hospital indefinitely. She's going to have to go somewhere."

"I've put a call into the CIA," Sheriff Connell said.

The room went silent, as Dr. Taylor and Meg stared hard at him.

CHAPTER 9

D r. Taylor stared down at his desk. "What in the world will the CIA do about this?"

Sheriff Connell offered Dr. Stanley a smile that barely reached her, and then fell.

Meg said, "Just last week, I skimmed an article about UFOs that my stepson forwarded to me. I thought they—the government—don't deal with this kind of thing anymore. Didn't they wash their hands of the whole UFO thing and pass it on to... I don't know... Who?"

"You're right," Ray said. "The government doesn't do this kind of investigation anymore. But I put some feelers out, anyway. I have an old contact from a few years ago who worked for the CIA. I leveled with him, and he put me in touch with an intelligence officer. I told him everything I just told you. He listened."

"I can't wait to hear his response," Meg said.

Ray ran the tip of his tongue along his top teeth. He hadn't had time to brush his teeth after breakfast. "He said he'd be in touch."

"So he was interested?" Dr. Taylor asked. "He didn't just hang up on you?"

Ray deflected the question. "Deputy Benson, who was with me Tuesday morning when we found Mrs. Mason, is into UFOs or whatever they call them now. He and his girlfriend follow the trends. This morning before I called the CIA, Deputy Benson came into my office and told me that recently, there has been an alleged deep-state cover-up of a retrieved extraterrestrial craft, including the corpses of pilots and other crew. Now, before you both respond as I did, let me finish. Deputy Benson said the allegation comes from a respected former intelligence officer who often worked with..."

Ray stopped, reached for his cellphone, logged in, and tapped playback on his recording app. "It's easier if you listen to a conversation with Mike that I recorded," he said, boosting the volume.

The two doctors inclined forward as they listened to Deputy Benson's recorded voice.

"Is the recorder turned on, Sheriff?" Benson asked, on the recorder.

"Yes, go ahead, Deputy Benson," Ray had said in response.

"Okay, so this intelligence officer worked for The Pentagon's All-domain Anomaly Resolution Office. Among other things, they're responsible for identifying unidentified objects near military assets. They also oversee operating areas, training areas and secret airspace. They moderate any threats to military operations and national security, and what they call trans-medium objects, which are UFO-related phenomena, or UAPs, Unidentified Aerial Phenomena. So, here's the thing I remembered when we started investigating Mrs. Mason. This former intelligence officer talked to a seasoned reporter about his personal knowledge of extraterrestrial craft, corpses, and contacts. She wrote an article, based on what he'd said. He wanted to blow the top off the whole UFO deep state thing. *The Washington Post* and *Politico* passed on the story, but it was eventually published on a respected science and defense site called *Enigma.*"

There was a pause on the recording before Deputy Benson continued. "So, I'm just saying, Sheriff, that maybe we should call somebody at the All-domain Anomaly Resolution Office and let them know what's going on here."

Sheriff Connell tapped his cellphone screen and stopped the playback.

Dr. Taylor sighed, turning his head aside. "This is way beyond my paygrade, Sheriff. If all this UFO stuff is true, I don't care. I don't believe it, and it doesn't interest me."

Meg Stanley sat on the edge of the chair, processing Ray's information. "I'm stuck on the words 'alleged deep-state.'"

Ray shrugged. "Now I know this is going to sound like a spy movie, but supposedly, according to Deputy Benson, believe it or not, there are dark agencies within the CIA, and he says that most senators and congressmen don't even know about them."

Meg stood up. "All right, gentlemen, I'm late for appointments. I recommend that Mrs. Mason be admitted to Richard Clarke Medical Center in Indianapolis. The psychiatric department there offers a range of services and treatments, including life counseling, psychotherapy, medication management, and other interventions that will be tailored to her specific needs. Our goal will be to provide comprehensive care and support for her while ensuring her safety and well-being."

Sheriff Connell rose. "And who's going to pay for the treatment, Dr. Stanley? By all accounts, this woman, Mrs. Mason—whether we like it or not—believes she is living in 1953, and all the evidence, so far, bears that out."

Meg reached for her black leather purse. "I've given you my recommendations, Sheriff, and I'll send a written PDF and hard copy report to Chief Gosser, marked personal and confidential, of course."

Meg inhaled a quick breath. "Sheriff, whoever breaks the news to Mrs. Mason that she is living in 2023, and has no husband or children, better be prepared for a mental breakdown. Good day, gentlemen."

As Meg Stanley started for the door, Sheriff Connell said, "Oh, by the way, Mrs. Mason's husband, Ronald, died in 2002 at seventy-six years old. He had remarried in 1959 and had two more kids, both daughters. But Sally Mason's daughter and son are both still alive."

Meg turned sharply, her eyes expanding on him, and Dr. Taylor looked on with a pale despair.

Sheriff Connell squared his shoulders. "Her son, Don Mason, is seventy-seven, and he lives in Fort Pierce, Florida. Her daughter, Mary Mason Donovan, is seventy-five years old, and lives in St. Louis. Unfortunately, she has Alzheimer's and is living in a nursing home near her daughter."

Meg took a step back into the room, her expression grave. "You have actually located her children? And they're in their seventies?"

"Yes... It's just another part of this wacky puzzle."

Meg consider the new information, lowering her head, her eyes moving. "Okay, someone has to be on her side. I'll help Mrs. Mason all I can. But I'm very concerned, Sheriff. Somebody out there in this great, big, crazy world will want to get their hands on Sally. God only knows what will happen to her mind, and to her life, if they do. When you called the CIA, you kicked open a Pandora's box. Protect Sally Mason if you can, Sheriff Connell. She's going to need all the friends she can get."

Dr. Taylor paused, carefully considering his words. "I'm a scientist. I deal with evidence and facts, not some occult world I know nothing about. Besides, Mrs. Mason has no physical symptoms I can treat. Will I sound too insensitive if I wash my hands of this situation?"

Sheriff Connell kept his eyes on the doctor, but said nothing.

Meg gave the men a twist of a smile. "Occult or not, it's what's before us. As the poet William Blake said, 'In the universe, there are things that are known, and things that are unknown, and in between, there are doors.'"

Sheriff Connell looked at Dr. Taylor and shrugged.

He had no idea what that meant, and he didn't want it explained to him.

CHAPTER 10

TOP SECRET

Subject: Operation ShadowShield 2

Interview Request for Sally Anne Mason

To: Kara Gonne - Counterintelligence Officer

Pentagon

From: Morgan Compton. CIA Operations Officer

Date: October 5, 2023

Officer Gonne,

I am writing to request your immediate attention and action regarding an intriguing incident involving a civilian, Sally Anne Mason, who claims to have encountered an unidentified aerial phenomena (UAP) on October 5, 1953. This incident may have significant implications, and it is imperative that we thoroughly investigate Mrs. Mason's claims.

Background:

On Tuesday morning, October 2, 2023, in Rosemont, Indiana, local authorities discovered Sally Anne Mason in the breakdown lane of a highway, sitting behind the wheel of a 1951 Chevy Styleline Belair, bearing 1953 license plates. She was carrying a valid driver's license issued in 1953.

Sheriff Ray Connell and Deputy Mike Benson were the first on the scene. Over the course of Sheriff Connell's investigation, and after Mrs. Mason's cursory psychiatric evaluation by Dr. Megan Stanley, there is supporting evidence to suggest that Mrs. Mason may have experienced an alien teleportation from 1953 to the present day 2023. Please see attached, to review all the evidence, as well as the psychiatric evaluation.

Objective:

I hereby request your presence and assistance in conducting an interview with Sally Anne Mason at the Rosemont Medical Center in Rosemont, Indiana. This interview aims to gather crucial information and firsthand accounts of the incident she claims to have experienced. Your expertise in legacy programs, in working with the UAP Task Force, and in counterintelligence, as well as your familiarity with handling sensitive information, make you the ideal candidate for this assignment.

Action Required: Travel to Rosemont, Indiana

Contact: Chief of Police Kennie Gosser, Rosemont Police Department

Departure: ASAP

Destination: Rosemont Medical Center, Rosemont, IN

Conduct an Interview:

Interview Subject: Sally Anne Mason, twenty

seven years old. (Also see attached for her biography, newspaper articles from 1944 and 1953, and names and brief biographies of her husband and two children.)

Gather Information:

Review all evidentiary materials and document Mrs. Mason's account of the encounter with the UAP in as much detail as possible.

Inquire about any physical evidence or personal experiences related to the incident and interstellar alien craft.

Assess Mrs. Mason's credibility and mental state during the interview.

Report Findings:

Compile a comprehensive report summarizing the interview and any findings of significance.

Include an analysis of the credibility and feasibility of Mrs. Mason's claims.

Highlight any potential national security implications and recommend further action.

Please keep me updated throughout the process and provide a detailed report upon completion of the interview. Given the sensitive nature of this operation, discretion is of utmost importance. Handle all information and findings with the utmost care and ensure their confidentiality.

If you have questions, or should you require any additional resources or support during your mission, please do not hesitate to reach out to me directly.

Thank you for your prompt attention to this matter. Your expertise and dedication are crucial in shedding light on this intriguing incident.

Best regards,
Morgan Compton
CIA Operations Officer

Thirty-eight-year-old Captain Kara Gonne sat in her third-floor pentagon office, staring into her secure laptop computer screen. She read the memo and the attachments three times before standing and performing a full body stretch, an action which usually allowed her mind to process such a memo's contents.

The walls were a pale gray; the furniture made of dark wood; her desk arranged in the center of the room. A small window let in natural light, and a bookshelf held books on counterintelligence, military history, and national security.

Kara's short, midnight-black hair was swept back neatly, allowing her attractive, sharp Russian features to take center stage, features she'd inherited from her half-Russian mother. She was taller than average, with an athletic build, a dancer's elegant neck, and perceptive, deep blue eyes.

Kara Gonne was born in Colorado Springs, Colorado, to an Air Force colonel who'd served in Vietnam, and a mother who ran her own successful accounting firm. Kara had been an exceptional student and a star athlete in high school, lettering in track and field.

She studied international relations at West Point, where she graduated at the top of her class, and was commissioned as a second lieutenant in the Army.

For several years, Kara served as a counterintelligence officer in Germany, where she investigated potential threats to American troops and installations. Later, she worked in Washington, D.C., helping to develop counterintelligence strategies, and she was then assigned to the Pentagon, where she worked as a case officer. She was part of a team responsible for investigating potential threats to national security and developing strategies to mitigate those threats.

Kara was promoted to captain in her early thirties, spending the last two years in collaboration with the Director of National Intelligence, helping establish the Airborne Object Identification and Management Synchronization Group (AOIMSG), a successor to the U.S. Navy's Unidentified Aerial Phenomena Task Force.

The AOIMSG synchronized efforts across the Department and the broader U.S. government to detect, identify and attribute objects of interests in Special Use Airspace (SUA), and to assess and mitigate any associated threats to flight safety and national security.

Kara was currently not married, although she'd been married to an older intelligence officer for a little over a year, in 2015, before a mutually agreed-upon divorce. She dated occasionally but was known to be "married" to her work, and she didn't apologize for it, even if her mother expressed disappointment that she'd never have any grandchildren.

Kara paced her office for a time, then returned to the laptop and read the memo twice more. She reached for her secured cellphone, found Morgan Compton's number, and tapped it.

He picked up on the third ring. "Kara... Thought you'd call."

"You didn't say if you got clearance for this."

"I didn't."

"I figured."

"They give you a long leash. Another reason I contacted you. Anyway, you're right for it, and I knew you'd want to," Morgan said.

"I do, but can you keep '*they*' away from me?"

"I can, and I will."

"You have the power, Morgan."

"But, alas, no glory."

"You don't want glory any more than I do. Glory is for suckers. Isn't that what you always say, Morgan?"

"We're mutt dogs, Kara."

"And we love it. So, I read the memo. What else is there?"

"The cops are nervous, and they're housing and buying clothes for Mrs. Mason, all on the county's dime. Chief Gosser doesn't like it. He's a smart cop and, from what I've read about him, he doesn't like glory either. He's a family guy who likes Milky Way candy bars, and cigars. My kind of guy. Anyway, he has to justify the budget, and he wants to get reelected. And then there's Dr. Taylor, who's been treating Mrs. Mason. He's got gossiping nurses, probably because he told them not to speak to Mrs. Mason any more than they have to."

"Mrs. Mason seems delicate," Kara said.

"No one's told her yet that she's not breathing 1953 air, and she's demanding to see her husband and kids. She's sedated, and not happy."

"What about the shrink, Dr. Stanley?" Kara asked, pacing her office.

"She's supposed to tell Mrs. Mason the cold truth today. This afternoon."

"I'd like to be there."

"So go."

"Can't. I've got reports. Some cleanup before I can flee. How secret are we talking about?"

"Think ShadowShield. Downed craft. Two aliens dead, secret."

"How many are in on this?" Kara asked.

"The UAP Task Force. You."

"And if Mrs. Mason checks out?"

"Move her to Area 86. Safe house. Can you clear your calendar and do the debrief?"

"Yeah… for a few days. There are a lot of noses sniffing around because of that *Enigma* article."

"Thank God for disfunction in all things government. They can't even find the legacy programs."

"Funds?"

"Got'em," Morgan said.

"Security? Man in black, in case I need help?"

"Mark Ravic."

"Fine and dandy. He's good, and he's scary," Kara said.

"He's on his way to Indiana. He'll be around."

There was a pause before Kara said, "This is new stuff, Morgan. Never seen this before."

"Yeah. Should we label it teleportation, 'beam me up, Scotty,' or time travel?"

"Are we assuming?" Kara asked.

"Sure, why not? You saw the evidence from Chief Gosser. You read those old newspaper articles. And you've seen an extraterrestrial or two. So, let's play 'spin this mad and infinite universe' and assume there are extraterrestrials out there who can beam a car, and a mother of two, seventy years ahead in time."

"But that's big power, Morgan. Big stuff. And why do it? For what purpose? Why send her into the future? Random?"

"Doubt it. Maybe you'll find out."

"Has she been hypnotized?" Kara asked.

"No... But she's had dreams. She saw a face," Morgan said. "Ever seen one like this in your encounters?"

"As I said, no... Where is Dr. Meg Stanley on the trust meter?"

"Quite a rocky background, but on paper she looks smart, edgy, and solid, I think. The police officer, a sheriff, who found Mrs. Mason, isn't too shabby, either. His name is Ray Connell. He was an MP in the Army. Has a good record. Also, a family man, with two kids, and he and Chief Gosser get along."

"I like him already."

"Keep me posted," Morgan said.

"I'll be there tonight."

"Why does this one make me want to kill a bottle of single malt Scotch, Kara?"

"Because it's a first, and there's no roadmap. There's not even a road. Just thin air."

CHAPTER 11

L ate Friday morning, October 6, 2023, Sally Mason sat slumped in a comfortable armchair in her hospital room. Her eyes were glazed with sadness as she stared listlessly out the window into the glowing autumn morning. She was waiting to see Dr. Stanley. They were going to have another talk, or so Dr. Taylor had said.

Earlier, Sally had tried to leave her room, but when she'd opened the door, a beefy broad orderly stood there, his muscular arms crossed, like some kind of genie.

"You can't leave the room, Mrs. Mason," he said, with stern authority.

"Why? I want to walk. I'm going stir-crazy in this room."

"Doctor's orders."

Sally stiffened her spine. "Can I see the doctor? Can I talk to him?"

"I'll tell the nurse to get him for you, Mrs. Mason, but you can't leave the room."

"Can you please get me a newspaper or some magazines, then?"

"I'm sorry, Mrs. Mason. They're not allowed."

Furious, Sally slammed the door and marched back into her cell, as she now thought of it.

The evening before, she'd had a shower and a shampoo. They had helped. Without curlers, she'd had to improvise a soft bob hairstyle with rolled curls. If only she had some makeup and lipstick. As she stared at herself in the bathroom mirror, she thought she didn't look completely insane. She just had the blues, and who wouldn't have the blues if they'd been locked away, unable to see or speak to family and friends? She tried a smile. It lifted with hope, then fell and drooped.

After she'd had her meeting with Dr. Stanley, some burly, balding guy, with a lot of tattoos on his arms and neck, and looking like an escaped prisoner, had entered with a male orderly, and they had removed her TV. That was okay. She didn't know how to turn the thing on, anyway.

Ronnie had promised he was going to buy one, but he kept putting it off. "Hey, what's wrong with the radio?" he'd said, with a smirk. "Just because the Johnsons have a television set, doesn't mean we have to get one, too, does it? And they aren't so cheap, you know. And everything is going up, groceries, cigarettes, heat."

Later, a nurses' aide and a different orderly came bursting into Sally's room with excitement. They told her they were going to make her room seem less like a hospital room. "We want you to feel more at home, Mrs. Mason," the aide had said.

Sally barked out a laugh, filled with contempt. "The only way I'm going to feel at home is if I actually go home."

The transformation of Sally's hospital room had little effect on her low mood. The orderly hung three tasteful, store-bought paintings: a glittering lake, rolling fields, and a forest of vibrant fall colors.

A comfortable armchair was delivered, the private screen was taken away, and a policewoman, about Sally's age, arrived with new clothes packed in two plastic bags. The labels inside the clothes said they were made in Indonesia, India, and Peru. The question lingered: Why didn't they just bring her own clothes from her home? Nothing was making sense.

Sally was five foot six inches tall and weighed 128 pounds. She normally wore a size ten. All these clothes were marked medium, and they fit strangely. The underwear and bras were too big, and the slacks were loose, but the slim jeans felt tight across the tummy and hips. The two tops looked odd on her, showing too much and clinging too tightly. One of them had a V-neckline, cut low, and Sally thought, *Ronnie would never let me wear this, except maybe in the bedroom.*

The blue sweater fit well enough, but it was cheaply made. Happily, the electric blue and white sneakers felt great, like she was walking on a lush carpet.

Two vases of fresh flowers appeared—one on the nightstand, the other on a round table by the window. Their fragrance lifted her mood, but when she asked who had sent them, Ronnie, her parents, or friends, she was told that Dr. Stanley had ordered them.

Sally knew something was very wrong, and it

wasn't just the chaos of the last few days. There was more to it than that. She couldn't find a logical, mental, emotional, or physical explanation for what she was seeing and feeling. She was rattled, her mind muddled like her Grandma Myrtle's had been. When you talked to her, she was often distracted or mixed up, just as Sally was distracted and mixed up.

Thinking about it scared her: the dark road, the bright lights, the hovering spaceship. And then there was the hospital room filled with beeping machines, the nightmares, Dr. Taylor's wary glances, the nurses' nervous whispers, and Dr. Stanley, a psychiatrist.

The nurses wouldn't talk to her. Dr. Taylor kept reassuring her, with a pasted-on smile and a nervous twitch of his left eye, but no one would tell her where Ronnie, her kids or her parents were, and why they hadn't visited.

Sally slouched in the chair, arms crossed, mouth drooping. She had on the new dark slacks, the cozy blue sweater, and sneakers. Dr. Taylor would soon arrive for his morning check-in, as usual. This time, she was going to insist that he contact Ronnie, the police, a lawyer, or, at the very least, bring her a phone so she could call Ronnie herself. She wouldn't delay it any longer. If she was truly losing her mind, then she wanted an explicit confirmation. Then she'd discuss it with Ronnie and her parents, and they'd all decide how they should proceed with her care.

Sally got up and went to the window. At least

there weren't bars on the window, and it wasn't locked. Maybe she wasn't as crazy as she thought. She saw a grove of brown and yellow autumn trees, heard the moan of a train whistle, and viewed the distant tall white spire of the Methodist church, the same church she and her family had attended for years. For minutes, she stared at it with a sad longing, and her mind was filled with echoes.

Lowering her gaze to the parking lot, she found it intriguing. It bustled with activity—people, ambulances, cars coming and going. Strangely, she couldn't name a single car model. There were no Fords, Chevys, Buicks, Cadillacs, or Packards. No pickup trucks. The cars appeared to be mostly the same model, with no sense of style or uniqueness, as her Chevy had. They were blocky and big, like from the military.

Sally was suddenly flushed with a now-familiar panic. Had she been abducted and brought to this weird place that looked like home but wasn't?

She left the window and dropped back down into the chair. She was medicated, that much she knew. At first, she had refused to take the pills, but then her mind was burning with fear, and her nerves began to fray. At least the pills calmed her agitated mind for a time. She glanced at the clock. It must be time for another one.

The night before, she'd awakened sweaty, gulping in breaths. In her head, she heard whispered questions. *Was that spaceship real or a mirage? What happened when I passed out? Did I die? Did some aliens take me someplace I don't remember? Whose face do I see in my shadowy dreams? What really happened on that dark road in that flash of bright light?*

CHAPTER 12

Just after eleven in the morning, Dr. Meg Stanley knocked on Sally's door, then entered with a pleasant smile. "Good morning, Sally. Can I come in? Is it a good time to talk?"

Sally nodded. "I guess I should thank you for the flowers. They are beautiful."

"Then I guess I'll accept your thanks, Sally," Meg said, with a little wink.

When a motorcycle outside revved its engine, sounding like an angry snarl, Sally snapped a look toward the window, startled, throwing a hand over her heart. "Oh my heavens, that scared me."

Dr. Stanley said, "So much for a quiet hospital zone."

Meg grabbed a chair, placed it opposite Sally, and sat. "How are you, Sally?"

"I want to get out of here. I'm a prisoner in this room, and I don't know why."

"You'll be leaving soon."

Sally perked up. "When?"

"It won't be long. That's one reason I'm here today."

Sally shook her head, color deepening in her cheeks. "The sooner the better. I'm sick of this. Sick of not being able to see my husband and my children. It's not right, and I know I have rights. You people can't keep me locked away like this."

Meg sought to change the mood. She cast her eyes about the room. "Nice change, but it still smells like a hospital, doesn't it?"

Sally ignored the question. "Is this the day you tell me I'm crazy and I'll have to go to a nuthouse? Is that where I'm going?"

"No, Sally. No nuthouse. I promise."

Sally blew out a sigh. "What then? Just tell me what's going on. I can't take this anymore ... not knowing. I can't."

Meg had thought long and hard about her approach. Though she'd wanted to discuss Sally's case with someone else, she'd been sworn to secrecy, and she had kept her promise. Instead, she had reviewed all her therapeutic tools and decided to try one she had been trained in but rarely used.

"Sally, I need to know more about your experience, so I want to begin by doing a little exercise. It's nothing difficult. It's just a little exercise for relaxation and visualization. Okay?"

"I can't relax," Sally said. "My stomach's in knots. My head is all confused."

"I understand. Just try to see if you can relax. Okay?"

Sally exhaled a frustrated breath and nodded.

Meg reached into her blue business suit breast pocket and withdrew her cellphone. She held it up. "This is a kind of receiver and tape recorder I sometimes use. Do you mind if I record our session?"

Sally tilted her head left, thinking about it. She picked a piece of lint from the sweater and glanced away. "I don't know."

"It's up to you. I find it helpful to go back over things later. The recording will be confidential. No one else but you and I will ever listen to it, I promise. And I erase them after a time. But if you're not comfortable with it, I won't."

Sally sighed out resignation as she stared at the cellphone and pointed at it. "I've never seen anything like that."

Meg sought to downplay it. "It's just one of those silly modern gadgets we doctors use."

Sally looked away again and shrugged. "Okay... It's okay. I guess it won't hurt. I don't think anything I'm going to say will be all that important, so why not?"

Sally watched as Meg tapped the recording app and then placed the cellphone on her lap.

"All right, Sally, let's begin. Put your feet flat on the floor about shoulder-width apart and rest your hands in your lap. Now close your eyes, take a few deep breaths, and then silently tell yourself to relax."

Sally did so, sitting up, closing her eyes. But after a few seconds, she opened them again, looking frightened.

"It's okay, Sally. You're safe. It's just you and me. Now close your eyes and take a few more deep breaths."

Meg watched as Sally closed her eyes and breathed deeply. Moments later, Sally's face lost its frown, her shoulders settled, and her body eased.

Meg continued. "Now, in your mind, I want you

to imagine a photograph, a snapshot. It can be real or imagined, whatever comes to you. Either way, imagine you are seeing an actual photo that you can recall with clarity."

Meg observed Sally's soft breathing. "Do you see one?"

After Sally dug into her watery memory, a snapshot rose to the surface of her mind, and she smiled. "Yes... I have one. It's a photograph of Ronnie and the kids at Aurora Lake last summer. Ronnie's in the knee-high water, grinning. He's handsome, just like he was in high school. Don has climbed on top of his shoulders and he's waving at the camera. Little Mary has this cute little swimsuit and sunhat on, and she's sitting on the shore crying because she's afraid of the water and she wants me to come and pick her up. I took several snapshots that day, but this one was my favorite. It was such a beautiful day, and we had so much fun. Later, Ronnie grilled hotdogs and hamburgers, and the man next door to our cabin brought some of his homemade ice cream. I loved that day. It was a perfect day."

"Good, Sally. Very good. Now keep your eyes closed, and this time, I want you to gently... very gently... walk your mind back to the night you were driving home from your night school class."

Sally's smile vanished. "No... I don't want to."

"It's okay, Sally. I'm here. Nothing and no one is going to hurt you. I promise. Please just try. Will you try?"

Sally swallowed, her body tensing up.

"Relax, Sally. Take some more deep breaths and relax."

Sally moved in the chair, inhaling two deep breaths, and letting them out slowly.

"All right now, in your mind, go back to that night and pretend you have that same camera you used to take photos of your family on that perfect summer day. With that camera, take photographs of what you saw the night you saw the bright light. Not what you felt when you saw the light, but only what you saw. I want you to pretend that you are just watching. You're a witness to the events, but you're not emotionally involved in those events. Not at all. Do you understand?"

Sally's voice dropped to a relaxed whisper. "Yes…"

"Good. All right. Now, relax, step out onto that road, lift the camera, and when you see something, press the shutter button, and take the photo. Okay? Is that clear?"

Sally's face softened. "Yes."

A minute passed.

"Have you seen anything, Sally? Have you taken a photo?"

Sally nodded.

Meg leaned forward, earnestness in her eyes. "Okay. Pretend the photo is developed. Hold it up into the light. What do you see?"

Sally's lips trembled. "No… Oh… God. What…?"

CHAPTER 13

Sally's expression changed. She trembled, and fear radiated from her. Her hands made fists and her eyes squeezed shut.

Meg said, "Breathe easy and relax, Sally. Relax your face and hands. You're safe. There's absolutely nothing to fear. You're just watching. You're just taking photos and then looking at the snapshots. There's no danger from looking at a photo, Sally. It can't hurt you. No fear, and no danger at all. What do you see, Sally?"

Sally's hands lifted, then slowly came down, and her fingers grabbed the chair's armrests and tightened, as if to brace herself.

"Snap the photo, Sally. Now hold it up and look at it."

Sally spoke slowly, carefully, as if she were mentally stepping barefoot across broken glass. "It's like a movie... Yeah, more like a movie than a photograph."

"Okay. That's fine, Sally. Tell me about the movie."

"A white light flashes across the road. Then another. I slow down. The road is dark. My headlights are on. I see the beams lighting up the road. But then the car engine goes dead, and the headlights shut off. The glowing dashboard blinks out, then on, then out again. I'm in the dark. I'm surrounded by darkness."

Meg's voice was soothing. "Relax. I'm here with you, Sally. I'm right in front of you and no one is going to hurt you. Just take photos, or watch the movie, and tell me what you see."

"I see myself in the dark. I'm so scared. I look around, but I'm really scared to look around. I think some killer is out there. I'm panicking. I lean right and I'm going to lock the passenger door, when... Oh, heavens. Good heavens!"

"What is it, Sally? You're not there. You're just watching. What do you see?"

"There's this bright flash of light. Very bright, like a bunch of flashbulbs from reporters' cameras flashing all at once. I hold my hand up over my eyes. I'm screaming. I'm so scared."

"We're safe. Completely safe. What do you see next?"

Sally's face opened in a slow wonder, her eyes fluttering, her mouth opening in surprise. "Oh... my... Oh... I..."

"What, Sally? What do you see?"

"It's so big... It was small, but then it grew in size like magic or something. I saw this bluish foggy light, and then this small circle-like thing appeared from that fog and took shape, and it grew, and it got bigger, and it's like a... I don't know how to describe it. It's like one of those spaceships I've seen on the covers of... drugstore magazines and science fiction magazines."

Sally sat rigid, her mouth moving, but nothing came out.

"Go on, Sally. Tell me what you see."

"It's dim at first, and silvery. I don't hear anything except my breathing. My heart is beating so fast it hurts. Oh, my heavens. I see it better now. It's like a flying disc thing, with a spinning dome, with a search light or something shooting out bluish sparks in all directions. It's shiny... like wet steel gray. It's lowering... and I see some kind of letters written on the body of the thing, but I can't read it. The letters look like Egyptian writing I've seen in books. Figures and symbols. I'm so scared I think my heart's going to jump out of my chest. But that thing is so... I don't know how to say it. It's so beautiful, like something I dreamed, but forgot I'd dreamed. Oh my... Now it's changing colors. Oh... my heavens. Yes, it's green, then blue, then red, lighting up the road and the trees. Now it's shiny gray again, and now I hear a kind of low humming sound, and I feel a vibration. The whole car is vibrating. I'm vibrating. And now I see myself screaming. I'm so scared. I'm praying. Praying so hard, and then..."

A scream caught in Sally's throat. Meg cut in, her pulse rising. "Okay, Sally, you can stop now. You can stop taking photographs or watching the movie. Come back to the hospital room."

Sally's face stretched in shock, her eyes fluttering. She tried to speak, but only squealing sounds wheezed from her mouth. Her breath caught.

"Relax, Sally, relax," Meg said. "Drop the camera and come back. Listen to the sound of my voice and come back to the hospital room. Please. Come back now."

Sally gasped. "I see it! I see... Yes. I see him. He's standing twenty feet in front of the car. Oh, my... my God! He's there, right there in front of the car. He's tall. Taller than Ronnie, and he's just staring at me."

Meg sat motionless, her heart drumming as she felt the palpable impact of Sally's words. Sweat popped out on her forehead. "Sally? Sally? Can you hear my voice? You're safe. It's okay. Just witness the scene. Just watch it, and then come back. Follow the sound of my voice and come back to the hospital room. I'm here. You're safe."

Sally leaned her head forward, eyes squinting, lost in an inner vision. "He's wearing a one-piece suit of some kind, and white, glowing shoes. The suit is gray and blue, and it shimmers. It's so odd how it shimmers. So lovely, how it shimmers like that. Oh... Now it's blinking on and off like someone's flipping a light switch. And his hair is snow-white and short, but he's young, with refined features, like he's from a foreign country, like he was carved from white marble. I don't know how to describe it. I don't have words to describe his eyes. They flash and glitter like wet rubies. Oh, my heavens, he's coming toward me. Oh, no... He's coming... and there's a kind of ghostly glow around him. I can't move."

"Sally, does the man take you anywhere? Does he force you onto his spaceship?"

"No! He's just standing there staring at me, and then... I don't... I start to shake and I look down at my hands and it's like I can see right through them!

I can't move and my whole body is shaking, and he's coming towards me ... Help me!"

Meg jumped to her feet, and her cellphone went flying from her lap onto the floor.

"Sally, come back now. Focus on my voice and come back. Now."

Sally stiffened and sucked in a sharp breath. Her mouth opened, her eyes popped open, and she wilted. Meg rushed over, grabbing Sally's shoulders in time to stop her from tumbling forward out of the chair and onto the floor.

Meg gently eased Sally back into the chair. Her body was limp, her head bent to one side. When Meg was certain Sally was secure, she hurried to the door, opened it, and asked the guard to help her carry Sally to the bed.

CHAPTER 14

Fifteen minutes later, Drs. Stanley and Taylor were standing by Sally's bedside when her eyes opened. She blinked twice, then shifted her head left and right. Meg had pulled the window curtains closed, the overhead lights were dimmed, and the room was quiet. An orderly and Nurse Harden were outside in the hallway, waiting, in case they were needed.

"How are you feeling, Sally?" Dr. Taylor asked.

Sally stared up at the ceiling. "I don't know. Like I'm living a nightmare."

Meg said, "Sally, I'm sorry you were frightened, but you did very well."

Sally ignored her. She sat up, Dr Taylor adjusted her pillow, and Sally leaned back against it. Her gaze was stuck in the distance, as if something lingered out there in the room.

"Do you remember what you saw, Sally?" Meg asked.

Sally nodded.

"Can I get you anything? Can we do anything for you?" Dr. Taylor asked, feeling inadequate to the bizarre situation. Meg had shared some of Sally's experiences.

Sally looked at him with cold eyes. "Yes, you can release me from this hospital so I can go home."

Dr. Taylor and Meg exchanged a concerned glance.

Meg had decided not to disclose the peculiar details of Sally's situation to her before their hypnotic session, believing it would have traumatized her, diverting her attention from the session. Meg was now obligated to tell Sally the truth.

Meg smoothed back her hair with a hand, cleared her voice and said, "Sally, we have kept you here in the hospital for your own protection."

Sally stared at Meg with dull patience. "I don't need protection. I need to go home."

The words left Meg's lips before she could stop them. "You can't go home, Sally, because you have no home to go to."

Dr. Taylor glanced at Meg, worried.

Sally and Meg stared eye to eye.

"What do you mean, no home to go to?" Sally asked, her voice cracking with emotion. "Is my family dead?"

"Things have changed, Sally."

"Was there a nuclear war or something? Is that what happened? Is that what's going on? Was that the flash of white light I saw?"

"No, Sally."

Sally's eyes opened fully. "Was I abducted?"

"No, you were not abducted."

"Then is this really Rosemont, or am I somewhere else?"

"This is Rosemont, Indiana."

"Then I don't understand," Sally said, her eyes pleading. "Tell me. Just tell me what's going on."

Meg gathered her thoughts, and tried again. "Sally, you have experienced something extraordinary, something unthinkable. As far as I know, it is completely unique and it is perplexing. During our first session, when I asked you the date, you said it was October 7, 1953, right?"

Sally nodded, anxiety rising. "Yes… Of course."

Dr. Taylor stared down at the floor, preparing himself.

Meg swallowed. "Sally, this is not 1953. Something happened out on that road that none of us can explain. We have no answers whatsoever, and we have kept you here because we hoped we could find the answers for what happened to you. Sally, it is not 1953. You are not living in 1953 right now. You are living in 2023."

Sally made a small sound of fear, her eyes blinking rapidly. When she thought of her kids, the pain was sharp, like a spike driven through her heart, and she struggled to pump out the words. "My children… What are you saying?"

Meg continued, fumbling the words. "We don't know… I mean, we didn't believe… but as fantastic and frightening as it sounds, all the evidence points to the fact that you encountered an alien spacecraft out on that road in 1953, and, by some means that no one yet understands, you and your car were transported from 1953 to the same spot on the road in 2023."

Sally seemed to become a smaller person as she processed the words, as if she wanted to shrink and to hide.

"We're going to help you, Sally," Dr. Taylor said. "We're going to support you every way we can as you transition into a new life."

Sally stared at them, her face a mask, first of shock, and then of vivid despair. "No... No. How?" And then her voice trailed away, and tears pooled and spilled over, and ran down her cheeks. "No..."

Meg handed her some tissues. "We don't know how or why, Sally. But our priority is to ensure that you are protected, supported and safe. Dr. Taylor and I are committed to seeing you through this transitional period, and I am confident that once you get through the understandable shock of all this, you'll be able to adjust and begin a new and rewarding life."

Dr. Taylor said in a soft voice. "Mrs. Mason... Sally... I can give you something to help you sleep. Right now, rest is the best thing. Then, once you've had time to rest and think about things, we'll all sit down and discuss your future options."

Sally fell into choking sobs, her shoulders rolling, her hands covering her face. "My family? Where is my family? Where are my children? What happened to my children? Ronnie? God in heaven, what's happened to me?"

CHAPTER 15

Kara Gonne tapped her temple with an index finger as she gave Chief Gosser and Sheriff Connell a focused stare. And then she turned her full attention on Dr. Meg Stanley. "I've been here for almost forty-eight hours, and I still haven't seen Mrs. Mason. I need to see her," Kara stressed. "I can help her. You people can't. Not anymore. It's over your head."

"And it's not over your head?" Dr. Stanley asked. "It's not over everybody's head?"

Kara ignored the comment. She saw resentment in Meg's face and that surprised her. When they'd spoken over the phone the day before, she'd thought they'd get along. Now Kara noted a conspicuous air of overprotectiveness. Weren't shrinks supposed to be detached? W*ell,* Kara thought, *Sally isn't one of the doctor's usual patients, is she*?

They sat in Chief Gosser's office, the door closed, the air stuffy, the atmosphere tense, a late afternoon rain tapping the window. Kara and Sheriff Connell sat before Chief Gosser's desk. Dr. Stanley stood near the bookshelf to their right. She'd said she couldn't stay long.

It was late morning, two days after Dr. Stanley had told Sally Mason she'd time traveled from 1953 to 2023.

Kara wore a dark business suit, black pumps,

and unexpectedly large, gold hooped earrings. Her makeup was light, her lipstick was pale pink, and her black hair was swept back from her forehead, giving her a severe look, a look she liked. It suggested "all business."

"She's under the treatment of Dr. Stanley," Chief Gosser said, reaching for a half-consumed bag of peanut M&M's. He tossed two into his mouth and chewed.

Dr. Stanley said, "Sally isn't stable enough for you to see her yet, Ms. Gonne, and she's certainly not ready to travel to wherever you'll take her. She's fragile. Most people who'd undergone what she has would be broken to pieces."

Kara was undaunted. "You can't protect her. I've been monitoring social media. Her name is getting out there. There are crazies out there who live for this kind of thing. Have you read the comments on *TwitterXverse* and *Threads*? Or seen the *TikTok* videos?"

"Nobody believes them," Sheriff Connell said with irritation.

"Who has to believe anything these days?" Kara replied. "But Sally Anne Mason's name is out there, and so are the pictures of her 1951 Chevy Belair, which should have been quarantined immediately. Forgive my self-righteous tone, but the longer Sally Mason stays in that hospital, the more stories about her and her car will spread on social media. Someone will remember her from 1953 and make a connection and start spreading rumors. That will lead to conspiracy theories about government cover-ups and more reports of spaceship sightings. You just said that the nut-job calls to the police station are increasing."

"All the talk on those damn sites is mostly made up," Gosser said, his eyes flashing with irritation. "Nobody knows the truth anymore. We don't even know the truth, and maybe we wouldn't know it if it kicked us in the ass all the way to Indianapolis and back."

Chief Gosser resettled his shoulders, offering a meek smile. "Pardon my language, ladies. But I'm sure you know what I mean. When the calls come in, we tell them it's all a big hoax."

"But the evidence in this case is there," Kara said, spreading her hands, "and you all know it. Sally Mason must be removed from that hospital room before someone finds a way in there to kidnap her."

"There's a cop at her door twenty-four hours a day," Gosser said.

"And all of this is costing the county a pretty penny, right?" Kara added. "And the bills must be piling up, Chief."

The chief scooted his swivel desk chair closer to his desk and leveled his eyes on Kara. "You let me worry about the bills, Miss Gonne..."

"... Call me Kara, Chief Gosser. I like straight-forward, I like fast balls, and I like M&M's. Can I have a couple?"

Chief Gosser grabbed the package and extended a hand. "Be my guest, but leave the red ones. My favorite."

Kara rose, took the bag, rolled two into her palm, and returned the bag to the chief.

"The name M&M stands for Mars & Murrie's, after the company's founders, Forrest Mars and Bruce Murrie," Chief Gosser said. "Did you know that, Kara?"

"No, I did not, Chief Gosser."

He shrugged nonchalantly. "Well... My daughter loves trivia, and she's always sharing things like that. She's a smart girl."

Dr. Stanley and Sheriff Connell traded impatient glances.

Kara smiled and popped an M&M into her mouth, munching it thoughtfully as she sat back down. "The sooner I see Sally, the better it will be for her and for your town. The longer we wait, the more she could be compromised, and if you think she's fragile now, wait until reporters, bloggers and bad actors get to her, and they *will* get to her. Some bad actor will slap a wad of cash into an orderly's or a nurse's hand, pardon my cynicism, and you don't have enough police in this town, or in all the neighboring towns, to handle the tidal wave that will come. And it *will* come. This is too good a story. Alien spacecraft, the return of a woman thought to be dead, aliens visiting the town... it could be a gold mine for social media and the press."

Chief Gosser and Sheriff Connell frowned at each other.

"Kara," the chief said. "I don't want any part of

this, and the sooner Mrs. Mason leaves town, the happier I'll be. But I gave my word to Dr. Stanley that I wouldn't let you see Mrs. Mason until she thinks she's mentally and emotionally ready. I'm old school, Kara. I keep my word."

Dr. Stanley broke in. "I have built an excellent rapport with Sally. She trusts me. We've discussed her children and her husband. I've started introducing her to 2023 things, like cellphones and TVs. We've talked about historical and current events. But it will take time. I'm willing to take responsibility for Sally. When we decide to discharge her, I'll find her an apartment away from here, and I'll continue to work with her, so she has time to adjust."

"Not a good idea, Dr. Stanley," Kara said.

"And handing her over to you, and to the government, whoever that government is, is a good idea?" Dr. Stanley asked, her chin lifted in defiance.

"I can help Sally Mason in infinite ways that you cannot, Dr. Stanley," Kara said. "You don't have the experience or the secure facilities. You must know that. If you take Sally to some house, no matter where it is, she will be found, and she will be confronted and attacked in ways you can't even begin to imagine. The press will trace her to you, Dr. Stanley, to you, Chief Gosser, and to this town. You'll have a nightmare on your hands. All of you."

Chief Gosser reached for his package of M&M's. He shook two out into his palm, studied them as if they might speak comfort, and then he lobbed them into his mouth without saying a word.

Meg's expression held a challenge. "So much drama coming from a counterintelligence officer, Ms. Gonne. And what exactly will you do with Sally?" Meg asked, crossing her arms. "I think we all deserve to know. I certainly want to know."

Kara looked at Dr. Stanley frankly. "Let me speak openly. Sally Mason, her ordeal, and her remarkable experience have shaken you all. I see it in your faces, and I understand better than you think I do. I bet there is a part of you that still doesn't believe Sally encountered a UFO, as most people call them. I bet you're having a hard time believing she was beamed from 1953 to 2023, and that she actually met an extraterrestrial. Sounds like the stuff of fiction, doesn't it? Maybe it sounds like a free movie on *Prime*?"

Chief Gosser stared down at his desk. Sheriff Connell twisted his lips, and Dr. Stanley held her hard gaze on Kara.

Kara continued. "Sometimes, something just comes from out of the blue—excuse the pun—and it completely rattles our notions of who we are, and what we understand about the world and the sheer immensity of the universe. Based on recent estimates, there are approximately two trillion galaxies within our observable universe. Within our Milky Way Galaxy alone, there are about four thousand solar systems, which means there are about four thousand stars, like our sun, with planets orbiting them. So this naturally begs a question that's hard to ignore: If the cosmos contains such an unimaginable number of galaxies and solar systems, then how many potentially livable planets might be among them?"

From the room's hush, Kara knew she had their attention. "And how inconceivable is it that entities from those planets might visit Earth? These are questions that truly give one pause, and these are questions that my agency has experience dealing with."

CHAPTER 16

Kara rearranged herself in the chair. "We will take care of Mrs. Sally Mason. She will be protected, and she will have the best of care. Beyond that, there is nothing more I can say."

"Sally wants to see her children," Dr. Stanley said, her eyes not wavering.

"Please tell me that the kids, the adult kids, haven't been contacted," Kara said.

"No, they have not," Sheriff Connell said.

Outside, thunder boomed, and Kara glanced out the window, then back to Dr. Stanley.

"Doctor, it won't help anyone to contact them—not Sally, and not her kids. Because no matter how hard you try to keep it a secret, it will get out. Again, there are some very bad guys and girls out there, and many are just plain cruel and crazy. Sally needs to leave this town, be protected, and begin to learn the skills of moving on with her life as it is now, in 2023. She needs a new name and a new identity. She needs to know that, as far as she, and anyone else, is concerned, Sally Anne Mason died in 1953. The police said it was most likely foul play, that she was probably murdered, and the car and her body dumped into a lake where she'll never be found. Best to leave it at that."

But Dr. Stanley still wasn't finished. "So, Sally will never get to see her grown-up kids, and they will never truly know what happened to their mother all those years ago? Can you imagine how terrible it was for them, growing up thinking their mother had either abandoned them or was murdered? Sally has the chance now to change that. I think it could be very healing for them all."

Kara placed the second M&M into her mouth, and she worked the chocolate candy from one cheek to the other. "Pardon me, Dr. Stanley, for being blunt. Are we talking about Sally and her background, or are we talking about you?"

Meg's eyes flared and heat shot to her cheeks. "Who the hell do you think you are?" she snapped.

Chief Gosser held up a placating hand. "All right, all right, this isn't helping anybody. We've talked this up and down, and back and forth, until it's talked out. Okay, so Kara, if Sally Mason goes with you, what will happen to her?"

Sheriff Connell broke in. "Will she go into witness protection?"

Kara shrugged.

Chief Gosser leaned back in his chair and made a pyramid of his fingers, holding them to his lips. "Let me ask you something, Kara. Is Sally Mason a first for you? Have you ever come across anything like her predicament before? UFOs and time travel, or whatever you want to call it?"

Kara swallowed the soft, sugary M&M and stared him in the eye. "Well, Chief, as the British astronomer, physicist, and mathematician, Sir Arthur Eddington said, 'The universe is not just stranger than we imagine, it is stranger than we can imagine.'"

Dr. Stanley's cellphone bleeped. Kara's secure phone dinged a message. Chief Gosser's phone rang.

There was a knock on the door, and Deputy Benson entered, his face tight with stress.

Dr. Stanley answered her phone, turning away from the group. "What did you say?" she asked with surprise.

Kara glanced at the text from Mark Ravic, her security agent and spy. Her man in black.

Chief Gosser answered his phone, and his eyebrows shot up. "What?"

Sheriff Connell sat up, alert. "What is it?"

Chief Gosser shouted into the phone. "Get out a BOLO and find her! Deploy all on-duty units and get hospital security personnel to review surveillance footage. We need a positive ID on that orderly son-of-a-bitch."

Gosser slammed down the phone and rose. "Dammit, she's gone. Sally Mason left the hospital with some orderly."

Meg Stanley squeezed her cellphone so hard that her hand turned white. She faced the group, still staring at her phone as if it were an enemy. "That was Dr. Taylor. He said the orderly's name is Kyle Fisher. He's twenty-five. He pulled a gurney into her room and told the hospital security cop that Sally was going downstairs for tests. The cop didn't check that out with anyone. Then they took the back staircase and ran for it."

"Where's he taking her?" Sheriff Connell said, standing.

Kara was calm as she stood and reread Ravic's text. *Target in car with orderly Kyle Fisher. Following them on Highway 9. Heavy rain. Traffic. I'll have her soon.*

Chief Gosser stared at Kara, whose face was oddly placid.

"You seem calm, Kara."

Kara swung her purse over her left shoulder and went to the standing wooden coat rack and retrieved her blue trench coat. She shouldered into it, then faced the group. "It was nice meeting you all. Thanks for your help."

As Deputy Benson turned aside, Kara walked briskly from the office.

Dr. Meg Stanley glared at Kara's retreating figure, and Sheriff Connell looked at Chief Gosser.

"I'll get going," Connell said. "We'll find her."

As Sheriff Connell exited the room, Dr. Stanley hurried off after him, a growing sorrow on her face. It had occurred to her that Sally might have had an additional occult experience after she fainted, an experience that she wouldn't or couldn't recollect. Meg had hoped to use actual hypnosis during a session to probe a little deeper, assuming Sally consented.

Of course, Kara Gonne would have medical experts examine Sally from head to toe, from mind to soul, whether Sally agreed or not. And then who knew what would happen to Sally Anne Mason, and where she'd end up?

When he was finally alone, Chief Gosser eased down in his chair and reached for the bag of M&M's. He tossed one into his mouth and sighed out relief. Kara Gonne would take it from here. She'd have Sally Mason in a dark SUV and out of town within the hour. He was sure of that. No need to worry. Maybe Kara had even set up the entire event. Isn't that the kind of thing the CIA did?

A smile tugged on the corners of his mouth, and he thought he'd have a cigar and a beer when he got home. Yes, on the back porch, he would do that if the rain stopped. Even if it didn't stop. He deserved it.

And the world would tip right again, and rebalance, and Rosemont would return to its small-town policing and manageable problems. Mrs. Sally Mason, wherever the hell she came from, would vanish like smoke in the wind. He wished her well, and he wished he'd never heard of her and her encounter with... whatever.

CHAPTER 17

The squeaky windshield wipers frantically slapped away splotches of rain, as Kyle Fisher gripped the steering wheel with clammy hands, his eyes round and nervous. Overhead, thunder rumbled, traffic crawled, and the taillights of the car ahead were a ghostly crimson blur.

"It's really pouring out there," Sally said, peering out of the watery windshield.

"It's climate change," Kyle said with disgust. "The whole world is getting hotter, and it rains like hell now. Big government doesn't care. The rich don't care, and who gets shafted? We do, the poor bastards like me, the working nobodies. Nobody who has any power and money cares. Just like those people at the medical center. They just want money. They don't care about the patients. Believe me, I've seen it, and when I said something about it, some fat-ass nurse told me to shut my mouth. They treated me like shit, so it's time I got them back. I showed them. I'm glad I done what I done and got you out of there. They didn't have any right to keep you locked up like that. You ain't done nothing."

Sally looked at him, her face a worried frown. "Are we being followed?"

Kyle was lanky, with long sandy hair over his ears, a sulking face, and insolent brown eyes. He glanced into the rearview mirror, at the back window washed with rain. "I can't see nothing. It's getting worse out there. I may have to pull over. I can barely see the road."

"Don't pull over. They'll find us," Sally said, alarmed.

"Ain't nobody going to find us in this shit. Anyway, let them try to take you. I won't let them. Not those cheap bastards. I wish I could have seen their faces when they found you was gone from that room. I'd have paid good money. A week's salary, not that that's any money. None of them were nice to me. None of them. All looking down their noses at me and ordering me around."

He shot Sally a sneering grin. "They was going to fire me, you know? Did I tell you that?"

Sally nodded. "Yes, Kyle."

"I heard about it from one of the nurses. She's okay, I guess. I mean, at least she gave me some warning."

Sally cast her head about, squinting. "This is Route 9, isn't it?"

"Highway 9, yeah," Kyle said. "Damn. It's like a gray wall of rain out there."

Sally twisted around, fear building in her gut. "They must be out there looking for us."

"Don't worry, Sally. I said I'd get you to the truck stop, and that's what I'm going to do. Once this rain lets up, it's only about five miles. I'll get you there in no time. But I think you should just take the train."

"No… they'll find me on the train. I'll get a ride at the truck stop."

"I'd take you any place you want to go, but this is my brother's car, and he would kick my ass if..."

She interrupted. "... It's okay, Kyle. You've done enough. You got me out of that hospital room. I couldn't stand it another day," Sally said, the words giving her new strength. "I couldn't stare at those walls and listen to more questions and take more pills that make me all floaty and crazy."

"Okay, good, so you're gone now, thanks to me. I got you out of there, Sally, because you was nice to me. And you're hot looking, you know? I mean, I know you know that."

"Hot?"

"Yeah. You know you're hot. Hot body and face."

Sally turned away, uncomfortable.

"And isn't this like, awesome? It's like we're, I don't know, Bonnie and Clyde or something, and we're on the run. It's so cool."

Sally wiped her glossy forehead, facing her rain-splattered window.

A clap of thunder made her jump. "Oh, my goodness," she said, gulping down fright. "That scared the life out of me."

Kyle slapped the steering wheel with a fist and cursed. "When is this traffic gonna move? All right, move already," he shouted.

"Is there another way? A shortcut?" Sally asked.

"No, this is the best way... Well, usually it's the best way."

Kyle was struck by an idea, and he brightened, tossing Sally a hopeful glance. "Hey, you know what? Just up a-ways is the street where I live. How about we turn off this road and stop there? I've got some beer and snacks and stuff. We can hang out there, watch TV and, you know... well, we can hide there and wait the storm out. What do you say?"

Sally's lips compressed with concern. She didn't want to anger him, didn't want to go with him, and didn't trust him. There was a naughty lust in his eyes—what her mother called "a dirty, secret eye." Sally had seen that "eye" when Kyle had first entered her hospital room, as he and the nurses had helped spruce up the place. While he'd worked, he'd kept his beady eyes on her, and his leering smile.

It's not something Sally thought she'd ever do—flirt with a man to solicit his help. But she had been desperate, and that desperation had made her strong and determined to escape that hospital room, and all that was to come. So, now that they were in his foul-smelling car, what could she say to him?

"Thank you, Kyle, but I really do have to get on the road. I've got to go see my daughter in St. Louis." Sally figured that getting to St. Louis would be easier than getting to Florida, where her son was.

Kyle stared ahead, pouting. "So, maybe you should do something for a guy when he's done something for you? Ain't that how the world works?"

Sally wanted to get out of that car, but, once again, she was trapped. Her voice trembled as she talked. "I'll send you money, Kyle. I will. Once I get to my daughter's house and get settled, I'll send you the fifty you loaned me and another hundred. I promise."

He slapped the steering wheel again. "Dammit! Move it up there. Move the friggin' traffic already."

Waves of rain washed the windshield, and a gust of wind shook the car.

Kyle looked about angrily. "This is bullshit, man. There must be an accident ahead."

Then his eyes lit up—a light bulb going off in his head. "Hey, wait a minute. Maybe there's like a roadblock up there. Maybe the cops are searching for you?"

Sally froze. "Road block? No. Why?"

Kyle shot her a look. "What did you do, Sally? You said you'd tell me when we got into the car why they locked you in that room. What the hell did you do? Kill somebody?"

"No... No. Nothing. It's just that..."

He cut her off, cursing. "Ah, man, this is... I mean, I don't believe this. What kind of dumbshit am I? I should have listened. You killed somebody, right? Maybe you whacked your husband or a boyfriend? Ah, shit! You said you had a husband, right? *Had*? *Had* a husband? Did you kill him and then freak out, and like go nuts or something? Is that why you were locked up, and the cops were hanging around, and that shrink was coming and going?"

Sally fought a sudden grip of panic. "No... I didn't kill anybody."

Kyle's face darkened. "I heard them talking, but I didn't believe them."

"Believe who?"

"The nurses said you'd probably killed your husband or your boyfriend. One of them heard you screaming one night. You said, 'He's right there and he's going to kill me.'"

"I didn't," Sally shouted, about to lose her mind. "I didn't kill Ronnie. I didn't kill anybody."

Kyle's face flushed red. "Then why did they lock you up? Why the shrink?"

He turned his agitated face from her, his mind spinning like a top. "Why the hell did I do this? Am I nuts? My brother says I don't think so good sometimes. Okay, so now the cops will toss my ass in jail for busting you out of the hospital. Now, I'm going to do time for nothing. I didn't do anything, and I'm going to go to prison."

He glanced at her, giving her an ominous glare, his volatile mind made up. "Get out!"

Sally's eyes went wide. "What? It's pouring rain."

"I don't care. Get out. I'm not going to jail for this. This is bullshit. Get out before we get to that roadblock."

With a dejected frown and an aching dread, Sally found the door latch, shoved the door open, and was instantly socked by a burst of wind and pelting rain. She ducked into it, turned, and passed a final pleading look to Kyle.

His face hardened. "And give me back my fifty bucks."

"But… then I'll have nothing. No money at all. You said you'd loan it to me. I'll pay you back. I promise."

He leaned toward her, extended a hand, and jutted

out his chin. "Give it to me. If my dumb ass is going to be tossed into jail because of you, I'll need it. Give it to me."

Fighting emotion, Sally fished into the small shoulder bag Dr. Stanley had given her for lipstick, a comb, and tissues. The cops still had her own purse. She pulled out the two twenties and then the ten and dropped the bills in his hand.

He hand-fisted the bills. "Yeah... well. Good luck in prison."

Sally raised the collar on her blouse and readjusted her sweater before exiting and slamming the door.

On the muddy shoulder of the road, she trudged ahead, her head tucked, shoulders hunched, rain soaking her in minutes. Glancing up, she saw a line of cars, bumper to bumper, and a blue shaft of light sweeping through the hanging fog.

She stopped, her frantic mind racing back to that alien night, and the flashing lights on the spaceship. Strangely, it had all happened on Route 9, maybe near or on the very spot she was now standing.

A roll of thunder anchored her to the present, back to the cold, beating rain on her head and face. She raked wet strands of hair from her eyes, shivering and fighting tears, but she pushed on, her clothes sticking to her, the trees thrashing, the wind coming at her in wheezing gasps.

Startled by a car horn, she jolted, heart racing, nearly jumping from her skin. She glanced left and saw a face loom from a blue sedan's passenger window. The window slid down, and the face became clear. It was the lined face of an aged man, with thinning gray hair, horn-rimmed glasses and a Van Dyke white beard.

And then the door swung open. "Get in," he called.

Sally stood as still as time, frightened, cold, and conflicted.

"Get in before you catch pneumonia," the man demanded.

Sally glanced left and right. What should she do?

CHAPTER 18

S itting in the front seat of the blue sedan, Sally was rigid with fear, her gaze fixed ahead. The driver cranked up the heater and it roared to life, the rush of warmth helping to ease her shakes and tension.

"What were you doing out there, young woman?" the man asked, struggling out of his tan parka. He handed it to her. "Put that on. You're shivering like a leaf."

Sally didn't look at him as she accepted the coat and draped it over her shoulders.

"My name's Bert August. So, what the hell were you doing out there in the pouring rain, walking about like it's a summer day in July?"

Bert looked her over. "You don't look crazy, but then who knows these days?" he said gruffly. "Between the politics, and all the drugs, and what passes for music these days, I think most of the world is crazy. But then, look at me. I'm an old man, so what do I know about anything?"

Sally ventured a look at him, and she thought he looked like something painted. A portrait of a gruff man with a crinkly, lined face, a brusque manner, and a twinkle of mischief in his eyes. The black and green checkered flannel shirt was faded, the jeans baggy, and the red sneakers just didn't fit with his age or manner.

A country music tune played on the radio. The singer, a woman, whined about how her man was cheating on her in his mind.

Bert craned his neck, looking ahead. "You got nothing to say? Well, you young people today are something. I'll give you that. You're going to inherit the wild winds of change, and the bad air, and all that artificial intelligence, and more pandemics, so I hope you all have the energy and the problem-solving skills to survive it. But then, who knows? Maybe aliens from some damn planet will appear and zap the entire planet, and that will be that. Put us out of our misery."

Sally's startled gaze froze on him. Aliens? Had he read her mind?

"Don't look at me like that, young lady. Anything's possible in this spinning world."

Just then, the traffic crept ahead, and the rain subsided, nearly at the same moment.

"Well, will wonders never cease? Hallelujah, we're on our way."

Sally glanced back over her shoulder, but she couldn't see Kyle's car. Had he seen her get into Bert's car? Facing the windshield, she noticed the blue sweep of light just ahead. Was there a roadblock, as Kyle had said? Were they searching for her? Her hands formed tight fists, and her pulse was strong in her neck.

Bert switched the speed of the windshield wipers and eased back in his seat. "There it is," Bert said, pointing to his right. "A car accident, just as I thought. Some bonehead was driving too fast and was probably texting. Well, it doesn't look serious. They messed me up, though. It's going to be dark soon, and I missed my class."

"What class?" Sally asked meekly.

"Art class. I'm a teacher."

Sally stared at him until he stared back. That was it. With his beard, the horn-rimmed glasses, and his colorful clothes, he looked like an artist.

"Do you paint?" Bert asked.

"No."

"Ever want to?"

"I don't know. Maybe," Sally said, distracted, her eyes focused on a patrol car.

They drove past the accident, the patrol car's blue lights flashing. Two cars were parked on the shoulder of the road, one with its right tail light bashed in.

As Bert's car gathered speed, he inhaled a big breath and sighed out relief. "Okay, well, since I had to cancel my class, I'm going for an early dinner at Chili's. I'm in the mood for a fajita and a beer. Did you tell me your name? I don't think so."

"Sally."

"Sally," Bert said, testing the sound of it. "Yeah, Sally. Good. I like that name. Okay, I presume, being the perceptive geezer I am, that since you were out walking in the rain, you must be without a car or companionship… or somebody threw you out of his car?"

Sally lowered her chin. "Something like that."

"Well, Sally, how would you like to join an old man for dinner? I know a waitress at Chili's who will get you some towels so you can dry off and dry out. Once you do, I think you will return to being a pretty young woman."

Sally stared ahead, considering his offer. Could her life get any more bizarre? Her stomach shifted and groaned. She was hungry and, although she'd never heard of Chili's, getting warm and dry and eating something all sounded heavenly. If he turned out to be nuts, she could run away from him.

"So, what's it going to be, darlin'... as we country folk like to say when we want to sound all friendly and country-folk like."

She nodded.

"Good. Then you can tell me your sad story, and I'll tell you mine because all of us have a sad story to tell, Sally. That's why I love country music, and especially the old country music. I love Charlie Pride, Faron Young, and Ray Price and... Okay, what's his name? Ah, damn. Wait a minute. I'm having a senior moment here. Hang on, now, I've almost got it," Bert said, his face pinched up in thought.

Sally figured Bert was lonely, and that's why he talked so much. That was okay because she didn't want to talk. And she was lonely, too, as well as being probably the most lost person in the world.

Bert thumped the steering wheel with a hand. "I've got it. Garth Brooks. Yeah, Brooks is all right. Do you like him?"

"I don't know who he is."

Bert made a sour face. "Well, how stupid of me. I bet you listen to that rappin' and tappin' music, don't you? That scratchin' and thrashin' stuff. Well, anyway, that's what I call it."

Bert held up a hand and shook his head. "Now, don't get all upset and call me bad names, Sally. I'm not a bad guy. And don't call me politically incorrect, at least not before we've had our dinner. All I'm saying is: I like good music with a tune. Okay, Sally, Chili's is just up ahead. I've been talking like the old big-mouthed windbag I am. Once we get seated, you'll do the talking and I'll listen."

With Bert leading the way across the wide parking lot to the electrically-charged-looking restaurant, Sally stared in startled admiration. Inside, Chili's was vast, and loud, and crowded, and hot-wired with energy.

The couple moved past the heaving bar, and Sally's eyes lifted on the wide TV screens that were alive with color, and sports, and flashing statistics. Some team scored a touchdown, and there was a boozy chorus of cheers.

Waiters and waitresses in red tops hustled and seemed gassed up on high-octane fuel, hoisting trays of food with the smells of grilled steak, fish, and burgers.

Sally walked beside Bert, swerving around tables and people, staring at the spectacle in a kind of hypnotic trance.

"Look at this place," Bert said, shouting over

the noise. "Busy as can be, and on a rainy night. Everybody's making up for lost time after COVID and spending money like there's no tomorrow."

Meg had told Sally about the pandemic, but Sally had forgotten what it was called, and she hadn't wanted to hear about it. As it was, she had enough to deal with.

An attractive, thin, gum-chewing, pink-haired waitress appeared from around a booth, with a smile for Bert and two laminated menus. "Hey, there, Bert. Got a friend tonight, huh?" she said, presenting the menus with a grin, showing pearly white teeth.

"Yeah. Molly meet Sally. Sally, get a load of Molly, the best waitress in these parts, with her hair as pink and as full as cotton candy."

"Funny, Bert," Molly said. "Maybe I should join the circus?"

"You're the best waitress in these here parts, Molly," Bert said, with a Western drawl.

"Yeah, right, and I've got the psychic scars and brain damage to prove it," Molly said, pointing and chewing. "Take that booth over there, Bert. It's in my station. Do you want a beer?"

"Yeah, sure. Draft. Whatever."

Molly looked at Sally. "What can I get you, Sally?"

Sally glanced about. "I don't know."

"Bring her a draft, too, Molly, and a shot of whiskey. Sally's had a bad day. Look at her, she got drenched in that storm. Can you bring some towels or something?"

Molly jerked a nod, pivoted, and went striding off, dodging guests, head-high moving trays, and servers.

Bert indicated toward the red booth, and Sally slid in as Bert lowered himself down opposite her, wincing. "Got a bad hip, Sally. Going to have to get a replacement, but I keep putting it off. That's what happens when old age comes creeping up on you. But enough about that."

Sally was unable to relax. The energy in the room was charged and boisterous. She cast her gaze about the place, taking in the vibrant electric colors, the loud, slamming music, the revealing, casual clothes, and the animated crowd. Her distant past felt ages away and only a few days away, and the present seemed a wild, distorted dream or a frantic, futuristic movie.

Molly soon returned with two white cloth dishtowels draped over an arm and a round tray holding two foaming mugs of beer and a shot glass of whiskey. She deposited the beers and whiskey, slid the shot glass and a mug to Sally, and placed the other mug in front of Bert.

Sally accepted the towels with a smile and a "thank you", and then she asked Molly for directions to the ladies' room. She removed Bert's parka, excused herself and followed Molly across the room, weaving a path left, and right, and left again, finally spotting the ladies' room.

Inside, at the broad mirror, Sally examined herself. She made a face. Her eyes were small and tired, her face pale and thin. As she towel-dried her hair, two young girls entered, both wearing ripped jeans and quarter sleeve V-neck tops. One giggled, made a lewd comment about her boyfriend, and the other said, "Hey, I'd sleep with him. He's got a good ass."

They glanced at Sally and clammed up, each entering a stall and shutting the door.

Sally ran a comb through her hair, smoothed on some lipstick and pinched her cheeks. When she slid back into the booth, Bert looked her over and grinned. "Well, look at you. You clean up good, Sally. Pretty as a peach. Now put my coat back on. Your clothes are still damp from the rain."

Molly returned to the table in a flash, and with her e-tablet, she took their orders: Sally a Big Mouth Burger with cheddar cheese, and Bert the fajitas.

When Molly withdrew, Bert hoisted his mug. "Here's to you, Sally-from-the-storm. May you find whatever it is you want to find."

They clinked mugs and Bert took a generous swallow and stared at the mug in satisfaction. "Now, that just hits the spot, doesn't it?"

After Sally took a sip, Bert folded his hands on the table and put his eyes on her. "All right, Sally, toss back the whiskey."

Sally sat back with a nervous grin. "Bert, I've never drunk whiskey in my life."

Bert arched an eyebrow. "No? Well, this is your lucky day, Sally. Come on now. Down the hatch."

Sally hesitated.

"Go ahead. It will warm up your innards. Chug a-lug, now."

Sally reached for the shot glass, lifted it, looked at it and then brought it to her lips.

Bert narrowed his eyes on her. "Let her rip, Sally."

Sally closed her eyes, opened her mouth, and took the whiskey down in a swallow. The burning heat of it slid down her throat and her eyes popped open in shock. She gagged, coughed twice, set the glass down, and slapped her chest.

Bert leaned back and laughed. "Good, Sally. Good for you."

The booze spread warmth and eased the edges of tension. Sally's face softened and her shoulders relaxed.

"Feeling better, Sally?"

Sally's eyes were round. "I don't know. It feels warm in my stomach. My gosh, I already feel a little light-headed, like I'm high up in a Ferris wheel."

"Fantastic, Sally. Now, while we wait for our dinner, I want you to sit back and relax and tell me your story. Why were you out there walking in a rainstorm? Talk to me."

Sally slid her beer mug aside, closed her eyes and ran a hand through her still damp hair.

"Ah, come on, Sally. It can't be that bad. As the song goes, 'It's never as bad as it seems.' What is it? Man trouble? Did he toss you out on your can or something?"

Sally brought her eyes to him, the booze making her bold. "I want to go find my kids, Bert."

CHAPTER 19

"WHERE DID YOU TAKE HER?" Sheriff Connell asked, facing Kyle Fisher with a hard stare.

Kyle crossed his arms, looking sullen. "No place. I told you. I told her to get out of my car. That's all I know. I don't know what happened to her after that."

"You told her to get out of your car in the pouring rain?" Sheriff Connell asked.

Sheriff Connell sat behind a metal desk in the interrogation room. The room had no windows and was lit by a harsh overhead light. Kyle Fisher sat hunched in a hard gray metal chair against a cinderblock wall, his eyes tilted down at the gray tile floor.

"Yes..."

"You're a real romantic guy, aren't you? You really know how to show a girl a good time," Connell said with biting sarcasm. "Why? Why break her out of the hospital at all? What was the point? I don't get it."

Kyle's gaze shot up. "Because they're all assholes, okay? Everybody in that hospital has disrespected me. They look at me and treat me like I'm a piece of shit, okay? So, she asked me to get her out of there, so I did. I was doing her a favor."

"Okay, Kyle. Fine. Then why go to the trouble of springing Mrs. Mason from the hospital, and then pushing her out of your car into the middle of a rainstorm? What was that about?"

Kyle's eyes were round and defiant. "I didn't push her out, and you can't make me say I did. I want a lawyer. I don't have to answer any more questions. I know my rights. I'm not saying anything else. Nothing. Nada."

Sheriff Connell sat back, calming his voice. "No, you don't, Kyle. You're right about that. That's your right. But helping us will demonstrate your willingness to cooperate and give us a clearer understanding of the events. And it could help you down the line and maybe save Mrs. Mason's life."

Kyle hung his head. "She was okay when she left the car. I swear. She was fine, okay? And that's all I know about it."

Connell let the silence stretch out. "Did you intend to harm Mrs. Mason?"

Kyle's head came up. "Hell, no... No way, but I didn't know she'd like killed her husband. I didn't know that, or I wouldn't have busted her out of the hospital. I mean, I didn't know you cops were holding her for murder."

Connell straightened, processing Kyle's words. He almost spoke, but he waited, a sudden thought rising. Maybe it would be a good thing to let Kyle think Sally had killed her husband. After he was released, he'd blab it to anyone who'd listen, and maybe it would help dispel the gossip about Sally and a UFO.

Kara Gonne and Chief Gosser stood in an

adjoining room watching the interview behind a two-way mirror, the chief looking impatient, and Kara nibbling on a thumb nail.

Connell continued his questioning. "Did Mrs. Mason tell you she killed her husband?"

Kyle squirmed, and with wary eyes, he glanced at the mirror and pointed at it. "Is that one of those two-way mirrors? Is somebody watching us on the other side? Because if they are, it's bullshit, and I'll stop talking right now, and I mean it. I'll stop."

Connell didn't hesitate. He spread his hands, putting on an innocent face. "Kyle, this is a small police department. Do you really think we have the money to install something so sophisticated as that? It's only in the movies, Kyle. Only in the movies. No, it's just you and me here, and the recorder. Now, once again, did Mrs. Mason tell you she killed her husband?"

He sat up. "I'm not stupid, you know. I can read people and things."

Connell nodded with a confirming smile. "I'm sure you can, Kyle. I'm sure you can read people."

"I mean, what are you charging me with, anyway? You told me, but I don't remember. I was confused and freaked out, okay? Is it kidnapping or something like that?"

"Maybe you were smoking something when we found you, Kyle, and maybe that's why you don't remember? You were arrested for aiding and abetting an escape. Obstruction of justice. Accessory after the fact."

Kyle got agitated. "Oh yeah? Well, what is that? Accessory? I don't think I did that."

Sheriff Connell leaned forward. "When a person assists an escaped individual after the escape, such as providing transportation or financial support, they may be charged as an accessory after the fact."

"I made her give me back the fifty bucks, okay? So you can't charge me with that. No way I'm going to jail for that. I saw that coming, and that's why I told her to give the money back. So, I didn't do that accessory thing. That's bullshit, and I'll say so in court."

In the adjacent room, Kara turned from the two-way mirror in irritation. "We're getting nowhere here. I believe everything this kid says. He's a loser with an I.Q. of room temperature. His motives are simple: stick-it to the hospital, feel like a hero and spring the pretty, mysterious girl, and then maybe get laid."

Chief Gosser scratched his head and then reached into his pocket for a tin of Altoid peppermint mints. Opening the tin, he selected one and extended the open container toward Kara, who declined it with a shake of her head.

"I was a Certs man until they stopped making them," Gosser said, as he popped the Altoid into his mouth and then returned the tin to his pocket.

Gosser fixed her with a stare. "Don't you have people on this? I know you do because you people never work alone. But you've been close-mouthed, Kara. You're always close-mouthed, and I get that, but I'm also getting real tired of this whole business. So, just tell me, are you working with someone else?"

Kara smoothed back her hair, and sighed with resignation. "He was tailing Kyle Fisher, but lost him in the storm, in that flash flood that partially washed out the road and swept away two vehicles in front of him. My guy barely survived it. But then you know about the flash flood."

"Yeah, I do, and I need to get out there and not be here with you. What else?"

"Being the nice guy he is, he searched for survivors. Two of the survivors were kids he helped pull to safety."

"Well, good for him and the kids," Gosser said. "That's real good news."

And then Kara continued. "So, how's that for being unclose-mouthed," she said, with a nod and a grin.

Chief Gosser sucked on the Altoid. "I've got four deputies on it, and there are five cops from the next county over helping out. Bridges washed out. Property damage to hell and back. Welcome to our world of climate change, even if I'm still not sure I believe in it. Anyway, I've got to go, and so does Sheriff Connell. We've got no more time for Mrs. Sally Mason from outer space. She's not committed any crimes, and I'm not spending one more dime of the county's money on her. She's all yours, Kara, so have at it."

Kara faced him, and her hand shot out. "Thank you, Chief."

He took her hand and gave a firm shake. "You'll find her, won't you, Kara?"

Kara lowered her hand to her side and nodded. "Yeah, I'll find her, and it's for her good, and ours, that I do find her."

"Do you really think so, Kara? Does she really need the government, or whoever you people are, in on this? She might do just as well or better finding her own way out there in the big bad world of 2023. She might be a whole helluva lot better if you folks just left her alone."

"Whether you believe it or not, Chief Gosser, Sally Mason does come from 1953. I've done some additional research on her. In 1951 and 1952, Sally was admitted to what was then the Rosemont Hospital for bruises on her upper body and face. In those days, spousal abuse was seldom reported. It was a family matter, best kept behind closed doors. Her husband, Ronnie Mason, had a police record for drunk and disorderly. He once spent a week in jail for punching a woman and breaking her jaw. After a little more digging, I learned the woman's name. Linda Hughes. She also attended Rosemont High and was in the same graduating class as Ronnie and Sally. And she was featured in the yearbook as a cheerleader, standing right next to Sally Anne Davis. It was a killer smile. A sexy smile."

Chief Gosser nodded. "What's your point, Kara? Did he have a fling with this woman when he was married?"

Kara's voice was smooth with confidence. "After

Sally disappeared in 1953, Ronnie Mason married Linda Hughes."

Chief Gosser's eyes held Kara's. "Go on."

"No doubt, Sally's kids knew their parents were fighting, and that their father sometimes struck their mother. The kids may have witnessed some pretty ugly things. In those days, houses weren't as big as they are today, so you could hear people talking and shouting and fighting, even if the bedroom door was closed. Can you imagine how you'd feel if you were forced to leave your kids behind? And to a violent spouse? You're a parent, right?"

Gosser nodded. "Yep, and I love my girls more than my own life."

"Sally Mason was fragile, Chief, even before her encounter with the UAP. She needs help emotionally and psychologically. I can find the right people to help her."

Chief Gosser pulled on his nose, glancing back toward the mirror where Sheriff Connell still questioned Kyle Fisher.

"You're not really with the government, are you, Kara?"

She canted her head left and grinned. "If I tell you, I have to kill you."

"Okay... Okay. So, most of me doesn't give a damn one way or the other about men and women from Mars. But I'm a cop, and I've been a cop for a lot of years, so I keep asking myself, why? What would some alien spaceship—that can no doubt travel light years, or faster, and that possesses powers far beyond what we can imagine—what would they want with Sally Anne Mason? Why transport her from 1953 to 2023? For what reason? What purpose?"

Kara's stare was honest and sharp. "I don't know, but I'm going to find out, Chief."

Gosser bent his head, looking at her, trying to understand.

"I have a contact," she said.

"What do you mean, a contact?" Gosser asked.

She grinned and winked. "You'll never be the same if I tell you."

"So, tell me, and I'll stay up nights sipping a good Kentucky Bourbon."

"Okay, Chief, you asked for it. I have an extraterrestrial contact."

Chief Gosser's crafty eyes looked her over, searching for a joke.

Kara threw up a hand of a pledge. "Girl Scout's honor. No joke. I'm going to ask him... my alien contact. I'm going to ask him if he knows anything about Sally Anne Mason."

Chief Gosser stared with heavy astonishment.

CHAPTER 20

Sally didn't want to sound stupid, but her thoughts were rambling and disjointed. How could she tell Bert August the truth? She was time's patsy, time's plaything, time's experiment. Had she faced the truth of it? Yes and no. Dr. Stanley had helped, and she'd been kind, but Sally wasn't convinced that Meg Stanley believed the spaceship story, so how could she explain it to Bert, a man she'd just met?

"Take all the time you need, Sally," Bert said. "You tell me about your kids when you're ready. I've got a beer right here in front of me and I've got fajitas on the way. Life's good. So, tell me your story when you're ready."

Sally saw kindness in Bert's eyes. She hadn't seen it before, and it nearly brought tears to her eyes, but she stopped them. She'd cried enough in the last few days. She'd cried out all the grief, the fear and the loss that was in her. She'd cried out the regrets and the guilt, and the old bad thoughts. Thoughts about Ronnie. Dark thoughts about Ronnie. Was she being punished for those thoughts? Black and awful thoughts that pictured him dead, a mound of earth ready to be tossed down onto his casket by a tall, gaunt grave digger.

Sally prayed every prayer she'd ever learned, asking for forgiveness, and some she'd made up out of desperation. And then she thought of her kids—her precious kids—and she remembered a summer vacation when Ronnie had rented a cabin near Burnett Woods. Don and Mary had loved the place. They'd romped and run and played. In the evening when they'd tumbled into the cabin, they were like wild things from primitive woods.

Was there any God out there in space or were there just advanced aliens from other worlds flying all over the universe? Maybe those aliens were even advanced enough to create other worlds. Other planets.

But why her? Why had they bothered with her? Why had they snatched her from her children, whom she loved more than anything else? Why hadn't they taken Ronnie instead? Why?

"My name's not really August," Bert finally said. "It's Hansel. Bert Hansel, but I thought August sounded more artistic and poetic, so I use it for my in-person and online courses. During Covid, my daughter Ellen helped me set up Zoom classes, and it saved me from going house-crazy."

Sally had no idea what he was talking about, but she let it go. In the last few days, she'd taken in and digested all the information she could hold. She pushed her thoughts away and smiled. "I like the name Bert August, too. And you look like an artist with that beard."

Bert brightened. "Do you think so? Guess who came up with the name? My wife."

"Oh, how nice, Bert. What's her name? Where is

she?"

Bert shut his eyes for a moment, as if summoning her face. "Her name was Lynn, and we were teachers over in Frankfort, not so far from here."

"In Indiana or Kentucky?" Sally asked.

"Right here in Indiana. Frankfort's a bigger town than Rosemont, and the high school was a good one until a few years ago, about the time I retired. I don't know, things got lax... too lax for me. I retired at the right time, and so did Lynn."

"And you taught art?"

"In high school I taught mostly science, but they let me teach one art class. Now, before you think the two don't go together, I'm here to tell you that they go as well together as Lynn and me did. Think left brain and right brain. Lynnie taught English, and everybody loved her. Yes, everybody loved Lynnie. 'Lynnie with the laughing face' is what we called her. She didn't mind it."

Bert turned reflective. "Yeah, those were good days. Well... Lynnie passed away over three years ago... about three years. COVID took her."

"I'm so sorry, Bert."

He reached for his beer and gulped down a drink. "Do you know what, Sally? I wrote her a poem when she was in the hospital, just before she went. You should have seen her light up. 'You, Bert Hansel, wrote me a poem?' she asked. She was amazed. Well, you know, she was having trouble breathing. But anyway, I said, 'Yes, ma'am, Lynnie girl, I did.'"

"Do you remember it?" Sally asked.

Bert gave her a wispy smile. "That I do, Sally. Well, I remember a verse of it. It goes like this…"

Bert licked his lips, lifted his head, and raised his voice. "He's a dreamer, a fighter, with fire in his eyes. She's a wanderer, a poet, seeking truth in the skies. They were like ships who met in the night, destined to roam. But when the stars aligned, they found a piece of home."

Sally smiled. "That's good, Bert. I really like it."

He flicked a dismissive hand. "Nah. It's awful, but Lynnie liked it and that's all that mattered. And we did roam, you know. In the summers, we roamed all over the place. Route 66 out west, Europe, South America, the Caribbean… even Hawaii. Yeah, Lynnie and I roamed and had some great times."

Molly arrived, a tall food runner beside her holding the food tray aloft. He lowered it, and Molly seized the entrees and delivered them.

"You enjoy them now," Molly said, backing away, hands spread. "Another beer, Bert?"

"Nope, I'm driving," he said, his eyes on Sally's barely touched beer. "Drink up, Sally, *you're* not driving." Then he turned to Molly. "Bring her another, Molly. Though I might have to help her a little."

After Molly left, Sally grabbed her burger and took a bite, suddenly famished. As she savored each mouthful, she realized she felt more at peace at that moment than she had at any other time since arriving in 2023. Bert's comforting and cheerful presence relaxed her and made her hopeful. He'd been a family man, happily married. Maybe she could confide in him. Maybe he'd understand. He was educated, and he'd been a teacher, and he'd traveled.

She wished she'd gone to college and traveled. She might have been able to understand her predicament better and be a better problem solver. Could she trust Bert, even though they'd just met? She needed to trust somebody.

After Molly dropped off the second beer, Bert pointed at it. "Now, Sally, you drink some of it, so I don't drink it. If it's in front of me, I'll eat it and I'll drink it. That's what Lynnie used to say. Go ahead now and drink the fresh one. Yours has gone flat."

Sally obeyed. She wanted to please Bert. He wasn't much like her father—he was more worldly and talkative—but she'd always felt safe with her dad, and here, in this whirling, loud place, she felt safe with Bert.

"How many children do you have, Bert?"

He chewed and grinned. "Three. All girls. Ellen, Jennifer, and Allison. Ellen and Jennifer went off to college, one in California and one in Massachusetts, and they got married and never came home. Unfortunately, Allison was taken from us when she was in her twenties. She wasn't so happy in her life and in the world. God bless her. She got on drugs, and they took her."

Sally stopped eating. "Oh, my heavens, Bert. I can't imagine. It must have been so difficult for you and your wife."

"It was, Sally. It broke us both up for a long time. It's as sad as anything that can happen to a parent, to lose a daughter before her natural time. But you go on with life, Sally, and that's what we did, not that I don't think about Allison every day of my life."

"I have two kids, Bert," Sally said abruptly, without thinking. Bert's old grief had brought her fresh grief. "I've just got to go see them."

Bert put his mostly eaten fajita down, licked his fingers, then wiped his mouth with a paper napkin. He gave her a penetrating stare. "Sally, if you're not with your kids, you must be in a lot of pain. Now, tell me why you're not with them. Why are your children not with their mother?"

With a finger, Sally traced the thick rim of the beer mug. "Bert, something happened to me. Something I can't explain and something that's just crazy."

"I've heard crazy before, Sally. I've heard it from kids I taught, from colleagues over the years, and I've even heard crazy from my own kids. I can handle your crazy, Sally, so go ahead and let's talk about it. Then, who knows, maybe we can find a way for you to go get your children."

Sally slowly lifted her eyes. "I'm a long way from home, Bert."

"There are airplanes, Sally. There are cars."

Her mouth opened, but nothing came out.

Bert inclined forward. "Sally, do you have any place to go tonight? Any place to stay?"

She shook her head.

"Do you have any money?"

"No."

Bert clapped his hands, his mind made up. "All right, then. You'll come home with me and get a good night's sleep."

Sally dropped her head, staring at her plate of food.

"Don't you worry about what you're worrying about. I'm a father, Sally, and a grandpa. I don't know where your father or your husband are, but for now, we won't worry about it. I've got a four-bedroom house with two full baths. You'll have your own upstairs room and bathroom. The house was built in 1935, but Lynnie and I bought it in 1988, and it has shutters and a new roof that cost me a fortune, beautiful trees, a large living room with a fireplace and a breakfast sunroom. And the backyard has plenty of privacy, with a nice little stone path that Lynnie and I built together. Do I sound like a real estate agent?"

Sally smiled, despite her nerves.

"You've got heartache, Sally. I can see that plain as day. So, we'll go home. You can soak in the tub, and then climb into that queen-size bed, and sleep as long as you like. I won't bother you till morning. Then I'll make us both pancakes, bacon, and coffee. What do you say?"

Sally raised her head, and a quivering smile came and went. "Why are you being so kind to me, Bert?"

His eyes warmed on her. "Because we've all been in a bad way, Sally, and needed help. What good are we if we can't help someone when they need us? I can see you're not on drugs or out to rob anybody. I can see it in the way you talk."

Their eyes met.

"By the way, what's your full name?"

"Sally Mason."

"All right, Sally Mason. I'm a lonely old man whose wife is gone and whose kids have moved away. Despite being a scientist and a painter, I'm not a loner. I like people. And anyway, you need a friend right now, and I can be a good friend. It's that simple. Don't complicate what's not complicated. There are enough complications in the world."

Sally gave him a half smile. "Thank you, Bert."

"It's nothing. Now, drink your beer, and let's finish up here and go home."

When their plates were empty, and Bert asked for the check, Sally braced herself, ready to talk. "Bert, when you were teaching science, did you ever discuss spaceships and aliens?"

She stared nervously, trying to gauge his reaction.

He leaned his head back, examining her anew. "Spaceships and aliens?"

She nodded.

"Are you serious?"

She nodded, and there it was again, that cold gnawing in her stomach, making her feel vulnerable.

Bert folded his hands, carefully contemplating her. "I'll tell you what, Sally. Let's put this conversation on hold until we get home. I might need a glass of wine. I see something there in your eyes I haven't seen before, and it's curious, and it's made me curious."

CHAPTER 21

"ARE YOU DECENT?" Bert called, standing outside Sally's bedroom.

"Yes, come in," Sally said, having just slipped into one of Lynnie's nightgowns and robes. "I'm wearing one of your wife's robes. I hope that's okay."

"That's fine. As I told you, I kept some of Lynnie's things in case the kids wanted them... and for me, if truth be told. I wasn't ready to part with them," Bert said.

Sally pinched the bathrobe at the neck as Bert poked his head in, holding up a flashlight and a woman's olive-colored jacket. "I was thinking you might want to go for a walk at some point. I usually have to roam around a bit the first night I'm in a new place. It's like my mind and my body need to get familiar with the space. Anyway, this jacket is warm. I'll just put it on the chair here, along with the flashlight. You have a good sleep."

"Thanks for everything, Bert."

He stood in the doorway with a welcoming smile. "It's all my pleasure. You get some rest, and we'll talk at breakfast."

"And I'll make the pancakes and bacon," Sally said. "I'm a good cook."

Bert nodded. "I look forward to it. Goodnight, now."

Bert was right. Though she fell asleep as soon as

her head hit the soft pillow, Sally woke from a bad dream a few hours later. And then once again, she relived that terrifying night when she was ripped from one world and tossed into another.

Sally went to the bathroom, drank some water, and then paced the room, finally opening the curtains and staring out through the closed window. The sky reminded her of the sky on that night when her whole life changed.

Suddenly hungry to be in fresh air, she pulled on her shirt and slacks and shrugged into the jacket Bert had placed on the chair. She left the bedroom and descended the stairs with the help of the flashlight beam, creeping through the living and dining rooms and then into the kitchen. The digital clock on the stove read 3:05. She quietly unlocked and opened the back kitchen door and stepped out into the cold night.

The storm was gone, leaving behind clear skies, a glowing three-quarter moon, glittering stars, and a cool stillness that relaxed her. She'd been cooped up inside for too long, and even this small freedom felt wonderful. Taking deep breaths of the bracing, fresh night air was exactly what she craved.

But when she started to step off the small back patio, an unexpected anxiety stilled her. She hadn't been outside in darkness since that night. If only she'd had the nerve to ask Bert to buy her a pack of cigarettes.

Nearly every night, after Ronnie and the kids were in bed, she'd go outside to smoke a cigarette and think her own thoughts. She could almost taste the filter and hear the click of the lighter; could almost feel the smoke filling her lungs as she inhaled the first puff. It always helped her to relax as she tilted her head and slowly exhaled the smoke, watching it fill the air above her. It helped ease the rough edges of the day.

She lowered the flashlight and let her eyes adjust. *Okay, no cigarette, but I can still take a deep breath*, she thought. She took one, exhaling slowly, as if she were smoking. Then she took another, and then another.

Gradually, her fear subsided.

Sally stepped off the patio and explored the backyard of Bert's house, ambling past a birdhouse, a birdbath, a couple of white wrought-iron chairs, and a flowerbed that had seen better days, surrounded by a cute Victorian-style plastic fence.

She shoved her hands into the jacket pockets, tilted her head back, inhaled, and once again blew her breath back into the vast vault of sky and stars. The moon hung like a magical thing and gave off a magical light; its glow glazed the grass and the changing autumn leaves.

In that peaceful and entrancing moment, Sally allowed her imagination to run free, and she dreamed of distant galaxies, and other worlds and other people. These thoughts were new to her. She'd never put her mind on such things before. Her life had been a set thing, a predictable experience, one of school, marriage, and family.

Standing in the center of the lawn, gazing out over the trees and up into the dazzling mass of stars and constellations, it came to her that her encounter with the spaceship and the alien had shattered her small view of life and the world. Her mind had been pulled and stretched. Her little dollhouse of a world had been swept away and replaced by... what?

She hadn't told Bert what had happened. They'd driven through Rosemont, a town that looked both familiar and at the same time so different, and by the time her memories had crashed in, she was mentally and physically exhausted.

To her, Rosemont was a small town, but now it was expanded and modernized. Keith's theater, where she used to sell movie tickets at seventeen, had turned into an Apple Store. She didn't know what that meant until Bert explained it to her. She'd noticed his initial surprise when she'd asked, but he was too much of a gentleman to ask his own questions.

Memories resurfaced of people streaming out of the theater after a movie, men dressed in suits, ties and hats, couples on dates holding hands, heading to the ice cream parlor nearby.

In 1953, the movie theater was the center of town, and the weekends were always bright and cheerful, with action and celebration. As Bert's car crept along Main Street, Sally sadly recalled Woolworths, Van's Grocery, the pool hall, and the bookstore—all gone. The narrow two-story brick building which housed *The Rosemont Chronicle* was also gone, replaced by a new fire station.

During high school, and especially after reading the article about her being chosen as the Miss Rosemont Queen of 1944, she'd held the dream of writing for *The Rosemont Chronicle*. It was the reason she'd began studying shorthand—to work as a secretary and then, after a few months, submit some human-interest stories, hoping they'd be accepted.

It was an impossible dream to think she could be a reporter, when only two men worked there: the editor, Art Wright, and the reporter, Jimmy Long. They were tense, clever men. Sally had often sat near them in the Town Diner, listening to their banter. Art, the older of the two, had a gruff voice with a feverish sulking look, and Jimmy was an Army veteran who smoked, cursed, and ran with women, or so Sally's mother had said with frowning disapproval.

But to Sally, that newspaper building had sat on hallowed ground, and whenever she'd passed it, admiration and longing had bloomed in her chest. She'd view the black-and-white sign that hung on hinges over the front door...

THE ROSEMONT CHRONICAL

News Worth the Ink

... and she'd imagine herself working there.

After they'd turned into Bert's driveway and braked to a stop, Sally had no voice and no words.

She felt beaten and depressed, and she'd followed Bert into the house, with her head down and her hands pushed into her pockets. He seemed to understand her state of mind, without knowing the thrashing storm that raged inside her. He'd taken her immediately up to her room.

Still outside, Sally ambled through the Indiana night in a mood of reflection and contemplation. Her thoughts reran the events at the hospital the evening before she'd escaped with Kyle Fisher. Dr. Stanley had come into Sally's room and shown her a laptop computer, setting it on a table and inviting Sally to sit behind it.

It was a miracle—a thing unimaginable, with its glowing window that looked out on a world of places, movies, people, and ideas.

"I've found additional information about your children, Sally," Dr. Stanley said in a quiet voice.

Sally braced herself, and then Meg informed her about her son, Don Mason. "He lives in Fort Pierce, Florida, and he's seventy-seven. He's retired now, but he owned two hardware stores and, by all accounts, he was very successful. He was married three times, lives with his third wife, and he's the father of two sons and a granddaughter."

While Sally closed her eyes, digesting the information, Dr. Stanley continued. "Your daughter, Mary Mason Donovan lived in St. Louis, worked as a nurse, and married a plumber."

Sally's eyes opened. "Is Mary dead?"

"No, she's not dead. Her husband died in 2018,

and they had two children and three grandchildren. Mary is not well, Sally. She's living in a nursing home, and she has Alzheimer's."

"I don't know what that is," Sally said.

"Alzheimer's disease is a progressive and irreversible neurological disorder that affects the brain. You might know it as a form of dementia. Mary's daughter is looking after her. Even if you went to see Mary, she probably wouldn't know you, and it might be too much for her. And how would you explain your difficult situation with her daughter?"

Sally closed her eyes, and her quivering chin lowered to her chest. "God forgive me..."

"It wasn't your fault, Sally. You had nothing to do with what happened to you."

Sally blinked tears. "My poor, beautiful baby..."

Gathering courage, Sally faced Dr. Stanley and asked about her husband, Ronnie.

Dr. Stanley turned the laptop toward Sally so she could read what was on the screen. "Take a few deep breaths, Sally, before you read this."

As Sally's eyes moved across the screen, she didn't emotionally connect with the words. They swam in and out of her consciousness, like water flowing through fingers. It was a generic obituary written for any man at any time. But when she saw *her* name, it seemed to rise large and bold from the thicket of all the other words. A hand moved to cover her heart as she choked back emotion.

CHAPTER 22

Sally read her husband's obituary from 2002, her lips moving as she followed the words.

In Loving Memory of Ronald David Mason (1926-2002)

Ronald David Mason, affectionately known as "Ronnie," passed away peacefully on July 19, 2002, at the age of seventy-six. He was a devoted husband, father, friend to many, and a respected Rosemont businessman who owned and operated Mason's Construction Company. His life was marked by both love and loss, and left a lasting impact on those who knew him.

Ronnie's life took an unexpected turn in 1953 when tragedy struck his family. His beloved wife, Sally Anne Davis Mason, vanished without a trace, and despite extensive efforts, her body was never found. It was a heart-wrenching event that left a void in Ronnie's heart for the rest of his life.

Despite the profound loss he experienced, Ronnie found the strength to move forward, and in 1955, he married Linda Hughes, also from Rosemont. Together, they built a loving home and were blessed with two wonderful children, Mrs. Peggy Lewis of Camden, Maine, and Mr. Lawrence Mason of Indianapolis. Ronnie cherished his second family and devoted himself wholeheartedly to their happiness and well-being.

Ronnie's capacity for love knew no bounds, and he remained a dedicated father to his children from his first marriage, both of whom survive him. His daughter, Mrs. Mary Donovan, resides in St. Louis, Missouri, and his son, Mr. Donald Mason, resides in Fort Pierce, Florida. Both of them carry their father's legacy in their hearts.

Throughout his life, Ronnie embraced the joys and challenges that came his way, and he was known for his warm smile, kind demeanor, and unwavering support for those he cared about. His presence will be sorely missed, but his memory will be cherished by all who had the privilege of knowing him.

As Sally gazed into the laptop screen, a sense of darkness enveloped her, pulling her into a void of memories. The scent of Ronnie's Aqua Velva aftershave filled her senses, and she vividly recalled the taste of his mouth and the sound of his commanding voice. The weight of the moment was suffocating, and when she remembered one of his fiery slaps across her cheek, she grew nauseated.

Gritting her teeth, Sally turned her head from the screen. The words chilled her, and it was as if Ronnie's presence were still there, reaching out across time and death.

In Bert's backyard, under the vast night sky, the house loomed, a big shadow. Sally shook the painful memories away and went wandering, her mind restless. She'd lost her life, both the worst and the best of it. She'd lost all that time, all the happy moments and all the sorrows. Her children had grown up without her, not knowing what had happened to their mother, and now, maybe she was even losing her mind.

The distant moan of a train whistle brought Sally back to the present, and as she paced and pondered, she vowed again she would find Don and Mary, and she would tell them she hadn't abandoned them. She'd tell them the truth if it was the last thing she ever did.

A flash of light to her left drew her eyes. Was it a flash, or did she imagine it?

There it was again, this time to her right, and her head jerked around. Fear drummed. The night sky seemed close, the moon staring back at her, the stars swirling patterns. She searched the sky, the trees, circling the space, looking for it. The spaceship.

Something in the trees seized her attention, and she whirled about, vigilant. A torch of light flared up, illuminating the night like a bonfire. A blue flame expanded, danced, and rippled into the shape of an iridescent man. Sally breathed hard as he locked his eyes on her, only forty feet away.

Sally didn't move, her heart pounding, but she was determined to hold her ground. This time, she wouldn't run or faint. This time she'd stand firm, wait, and watch.

Minutes passed—or was it hours? The tall man kept his glowing eyes on her, the color of sparkling rubies. Was it the same man she'd seen before on Route 9? She wasn't certain, but there was the same short, snow-white hair, and the same splendid countenance.

"What do you want?" she said, at a whisper, the fright growing in her. "Why are you here?"

He didn't answer, and he didn't move, so Sally didn't either.

The moment expanded into an eerie, silent solitude, a private, intimate moment. He didn't approach, and so she waited, pondering her choices. Stay or run?

Suddenly, a peculiar thing happened. Within her mind, echoes of a past conversation resounded, and a vivid scene unfolded before her, as though it were being projected onto a cinematic screen.

Sally watched, transfixed, as she and Linda Hughes, the woman Ronnie married after Sally had vanished, were standing together on the sidelines of the Rosemont High School football field, dressed in their cheerleading outfits.

It was a cool and golden autumn afternoon, just before a home game. Ronnie, the quarterback, was throwing the football to a teammate, warming up his arm. Even during practice, Ronnie was all power and skill. All shouting, and pointing, and condemning the slightest mistake, and he dominated the field.

Linda Hughes edged in close to Sally, her eyes fixed on Ronnie, with a gleaming adoration. "You're so lucky, Sally. Ronnie is the neatest guy in school. A real dream."

The players darted about the field, sliding, pivoting, falling back, blocking. Ronnie snapped the ball, and a wide receiver broke away, sprinted, and reached. The spiraling football struck the tips of his straining fingers, bounced from them, and went sailing to the ground, wobbling away.

Angry, Ronnie threw his hands to his hips. "Mike! You dumbshit, you should have caught that. A fat grizzly bear could have caught that ball. Get the hell away from me. I'll never throw you the ball again, you pimpled-face cripple."

Linda had swooned at Ronnie's swaggering performance. "Gee whiz, Sally. If you ever get over him, let me know, and I'll move in."

As the vision continued, Sally watched Ronnie parade across the field as if he owned it. She didn't like his ugly words. Mike was skinny, with a flame of acne on his face, but he was a nice boy, kind and respectful, and shy.

She saw the embarrassed despair on Mike's face as he tugged off his helmet and then went shambling off to the bench, sitting, head down.

Ronnie approached Sally with a sneering grin. "I'm going to tell Coach to kick Mike off the team. He's no good. He's a clumsy, deaf-and-dumb idiot who has no business on the football field."

Sally defended Mike. "Mike is not deaf and dumb, Ronnie. He's one of the smartest students in school, and he's nice to people."

Ronnie turned to her, his face pinched in anger.

He slapped her, hard, and then he went storming off to the bench. Sally had felt the sting of that slap for an hour.

As her memories and the vision melted away into the sounds of the night—the chirp of a cricket, the murmur of a truck on the highway—Sally staggered, regaining her balance.

The voices in her head were gone, and the blue shimmering man, who had stood among the dark trees, was also gone. It had all happened in a flash.

She cast her anxious gaze about, searching for him, searching the sky, the shadowy corners near the house, and the dimly lighted stone walkway that led to the birdbath.

He was gone, and in the stillness, her mind sharpened and questions arose. Why had she married Ronnie when she knew he could be violent? Had she been sleepwalking in high school? Had she really loved him?

As Sally started for the house, she glanced back over her shoulder to the spot where the extraterrestrial had appeared. Would he have transported her back to 1953 if she'd had the presence of mind to ask?

CHAPTER 23

K ara Gonne and Morgan Compton strolled under sunny October skies in Washington's Lafayette Square, an historic public park located directly north of the White House. They didn't speak for a time as they wandered the paved pathways, passing trees, benches, and the imposing statue of Marquis Gilbert de Lafayette, a young French nobleman who had fought for American Independence, despite a degree prohibiting Frenchmen from joining the Continental Army.

Tall trees, blazing with fall colors, provided shade and also created a sense of privacy and seclusion amidst the bustling city. Because of its proximity to the White House and its historic significance, Lafayette Square Park was often monitored by law enforcement and security personnel, and it was an ideal location for covert meetings. Frequently, agents strolled, mixing with tourists and students, watching as they took photos of the White House, the statue, and the fall magic.

Kara and Morgan found a secluded spot near the edge of the park, away from any major pedestrian traffic, and sat on a bench, Morgan crossing his long legs and Kara sitting rigid.

She looked at Morgan, a middle-aged man with curly, carelessly combed graying hair at his temples and over his ears. He had an indifferent expression, languid gray eyes, and a prominent nose passed down from his old-monied Massachusetts family.

Morgan had pursued a double major in International Relations and Computer Science at Harvard, where he'd graduated with honors. His exceptional academic performance caught the attention of the CIA's recruitment program, and he was approached during his senior year.

After joining the CIA, Morgan's analytical skills and technological abilities quickly set him apart from his peers. He was initially assigned to the agency's Cyber Division, where he excelled in identifying and countering cyber threats posed by hostile foreign actors. His ability to navigate complex computer networks and uncover hidden information was invaluable.

As he gained experience and proved his capabilities, Morgan's responsibilities expanded beyond cyber operations. He underwent rigorous training at "The Farm," as the CIA's training facility was dubbed, where he honed his skills in intelligence collection, surveillance, and counterintelligence, skills that later helped him to identify and neutralize moles and double agents.

When Morgan was forty one years old, senior officials within the CIA recognized his skills and talents and moved him to a top-secret team that investigated UAPs (Unidentified Aerial Phenomena, formerly known as UFO sightings). He underwent specialized training, focusing on the history of UFO investigations, advanced data analysis techniques, and protocols for handling sensitive information related to UAP sightings.

He became part of a select team of experts, which consisted of other top intelligence agents, scientists, engineers, and analysts. The team worked collaboratively to investigate and interpret UAP data, analyze patterns, and attempt to understand the nature of mysterious aerial phenomena.

Morgan was divorced and had a son, Justin Morgan, who was a junior at Columbia University, majoring in business administration.

"You're sitting at attention and you're staring at me," Morgan said, not looking at Kara.

"Yep, I am. I hear your mind working," Kara responded.

"Not working. I love the fall. I love the cool air and the changing leaves. Last night I listened to Sinatra's *September of My Years* album."

"Never been much of a fan."

That turned Morgan's head, and he stared, incredulous. "No way. Not a fan of Frank Sinatra? Why, Kara?" he asked, with an over-exaggerated lift of his eyebrows. "Say it ain't so, Joe."

"Now, what's that expression a reference to?" Kara asked.

Morgan sat up. "Come on, Kara. You, Kara Gonne, the woman with the I.Q. as high as the Eiffel Tower, and you don't know about the 1919 World Series Black Sox Scandal? I don't believe it."

Kara held up a hand. "Okay, I think I saw the movie. Somebody on some baseball team plotted with gamblers to lose The World Series, right?"

"Yes. The two teams were the Chicago White Sox and the Cincinnati Reds. Eight players from the Chicago White Sox were accused of accepting bribes from gamblers to lose the series intentionally."

"And did they throw the game, pardon my pun?" Kara asked.

"Well, as I recall, the players were acquitted on insufficient evidence—because the evidence had disappeared from the grand jury files—but the players were banned from playing professional baseball for life."

"So, where did the quote come from?" Kara asked.

Morgan kept his eyes ahead. "After the allegations surfaced and during the trial, a boy reportedly approached Joe Jackson, who was an outstanding outfielder and hitter for the White Sox, and one of the kid's baseball idols. The boy looked at Jackson with pleading eyes and he said, 'Say it ain't so, Joe.'"

Kara crossed her arms. "Poor kid. I like stories like that."

"Like? What's to like? It's a sad story," Morgan said. "Old Shoeless Joe ended up running a liquor store and operating a barbecue stand. He's still not officially recognized in the Baseball Hall of Fame."

"Yeah, I guess it is sad, but it brings me back to Earth. It keeps the world local, and not out there in the universe of aliens and UAPs, and Mrs. Sally Anne Mason from 1953, who's out in this world somewhere."

"Is Mark Ravic still searching in Rosemont?"

Morgan asked.

"No, he left for St. Louis. I'm thinking that Sally will turn up there first. It's closer than Florida, where her son is, and I think most mothers would want to see their daughter first."

"Maybe. But you said the daughter has Alzheimer's?"

"Yes, and I think that will be more of an impetus for Sally to see her first. Of course, I could be completely wrong."

"Aren't we wrong most of the time?" Morgan said, with a lopsided grin. "Isn't that what makes us humble?"

Kara ignored the comment. "I'll go to Fort Pierce myself. I know we don't want anyone else on this right now."

Morgan uncrossed his legs, leaned back, closed his eyes, and massaged them. "It's curious that Sally slipped away from you. Are you sure she wasn't washed away in one of those gushing, overflowing creeks during that storm?"

"I checked with the police. No."

"Do you like her? Sally Mason, I mean? You haven't said."

"I told you I haven't met her. Dr. Stanley was a stiff-back general, and wouldn't let me interview her, and the Chief of Police agreed with her. I could have forced it, but I didn't think it was for the best. The chief said two reporters were hanging around the hospital. He thought the fewer people who came and went from Sally's room, the better, and he was right. I was going to meet her when Mark picked her up. But... Well..." and Kara left the answer in the air.

"On paper, then," Morgan said, his eyes still closed. "Do you like Sally Mason on paper? Do you like her photographs?"

"Morgan, now we're back to 'Do I like her?' Who cares if I like her?"

Morgan's eyes opened, and he twisted around to face Kara. "Maybe I do. I'm a sensitive guy at heart, whether you believe it or not. She's a housewife from 1953 with an abusive husband and two young kids, for crying out loud. That's one sympathetic story, no? I liked her high school photo. Her smile was genuine. Natural. And I liked her cheerleader outfit with the pom-poms. Hey, and I'd love to talk to her about her memories of World War II, and the Truman and Eisenhower days."

"Eisenhower had been president for less than a year when she vanished," Kara said.

"Nonetheless. I'm a retro guy, Kara. I'm fascinated by the 1940s and 1950s."

Kara glanced away and Morgan turned serious. "Sally must be going through hell right now. And who knows who's feeding her or helping her? I hope it's someone kind."

"I want to help her, and I know I can help her."

Morgan's eyes fully opened on Kara. "Have you spoken with your alien contact?"

"Do you mean have I spoken to StrallVoss?"

Morgan nodded. "Yes, our friend, the enigmatic extraterrestrial."

CHAPTER 24

Kara rose. "Can we walk, Morgan? I think better when I walk."

They stood and wandered off down the path. Morgan strolled with his hands behind his back, and Kara's head was down, as it often was when she was deep in thought.

"About StrallVoss, no, I haven't spoken to him yet. I want to interview Sally first. Dr. Stanley shared little about her sessions with Sally, but she told me that when Sally was under mild hypnosis, she said she saw an alien on the road, while the UAP hovered."

"Description?" Morgan asked.

"Not a Grey or a Reptilian. Sounded like a Pleiades or a Nordic. Resembled a human man, tall, short white hair, not blond, but it was probably the light that made his hair appear white, and Sally said the alien had an otherworldly beauty."

"Any theories?" Morgan asked. "Why would a Nordic ship hurl her into the future? It's not like them. They're hands off."

"Don't know. A mistake? An abduction gone wrong? A joke?"

"A joke? Do you really think so?"

"No."

Morgan pondered for a moment. "I thought it might be an experiment. Maybe they have new equipment, and they wanted to try it out."

Kara glanced down at her newly manicured white fingernails. "I don't think so."

"We don't want to lose her, Kara," Morgan said, with gravity.

"Of course we're not going to lose her."

"I was thinking this morning..." Morgan said, as he ran a hand through his tousled hair. And then he held his thought as they ambled past a family of four, the father snapping a family selfie, struggling to capture the White House in the background.

Morgan paused and offered to take their family photo, to which they eagerly agreed. He captured three shots while Kara stood back, smiling.

After they moved on, Morgan glanced back over his shoulder and waved at the young red-headed girl, who grinned back, displaying a gap between her front teeth.

"I wanted to have a daughter," Morgan said, as they continued along the curving path.

"There's still time," Kara responded.

"No... Too old, and too much the bachelor now."

"Earlier, you said you were thinking?" Kara asked.

"Yeah, I was thinking that maybe you should make contact first. It might help us when we speak to Sally."

"I don't know, maybe. I wish I knew what her thoughts were. Dr. Stanley said that Sally was still struggling with the truth of it all."

"Remember your first time?" Morgan asked.

"By my first time, I'm assuming you mean the first

time I met the Grey extraterrestrial?"

"Yeah, and don't look at me. I'm blushing."

"He didn't like me," Kara said.

"He didn't like any of us. Didn't trust us. And I didn't trust him or the other two Greys that hung back in the shadows, waiting by their shiny grey spaceship."

"I've never forgotten what he said to us," Kara said.

"What, specifically?" Morgan asked.

"The bit about how he said we're a planet of babies who are destroying the planet. I thought it cliché, if perhaps correct."

Morgan looked skyward. "Personally, I thought he was an arrogant alien."

"He thought the same about us," Kara said.

"You mean, when he said we're arrogant beings who think the Earth is ours and ours alone?"

"Yes. And then he got all dramatic," Kara added. "He said they've been visiting Earth long before the human race came along, and they'd be visiting it long after we're gone. That put a chill in me."

Morgan chuckled. "Yeah. A real funny alien he was. I'm sure he's a great stand-up comic back on his planet."

"Comic? He scared me," Kara said. "No humor at all in that little shit, with his big vacant eyes."

"*You* scared? I don't believe it," Morgan said, with a cheeky grin.

Morgan lowered his gaze and slid his hands into his trouser pockets. "I'm glad StrallVoss is a Nordic. I trust them, and I trust him."

Kara viewed the White House. "So, the House Oversight and Accountability Committee will hold a hearing next week on unidentified aerial phenomena?"

"Yes, I told you, didn't I?" Morgan asked.

"I read your memo. I read all your memos."

Morgan stared off into the distance. "The hearing will be led by Representative Tim Burnett. He's earnest and ambitious, and he loves to get clicks on social media."

"All because of Dexter Ratchen, the whistleblower?" Kara asked.

"Yeah. Ratchen's an Air Force veteran, and a former member of the National Geospatial-Intelligence Agency. We've met and talked."

"He'll spout the usual, I suppose," Kara said, presenting her face to the sun. "The government is withholding UFO information."

"Yes."

"And they'll talk to the Navy Commander who shot the leaked video of the UAP flying off the coast of San Diego, then disappearing into the water?"

"Oh, yeah."

"Who else knows about Sally Mason, Morgan?" Kara asked abruptly.

Morgan's voice was calm. "Earl Hickman, the Senator from Indiana, called me yesterday evening. He heard some rumors."

Kara glanced at Morgan. "What did you tell him?"

"The usual. That we're looking into it. He wanted

more, but I said we didn't have more."

Morgan adjusted his tie and squinted into the sunlight. "Do you think StrallVoss will help us, Kara?"

"The last time, he said not to contact him unless it's an emergency."

Morgan said, "He must know what happened to Sally Mason, and he must know we want to know, right? If we talk nice to StrallVoss, and if they were behind the whole thing, maybe he'll agree to send Sally Mason back, if they can."

They stopped and faced each other, staring eye-to-eye.

Kara glanced at her watch and said, "I've contacted Ayita Wells and asked her to remote view Sally's encounter back in 1953. After she and I talk later this afternoon, I'll ask her to contact StrallVoss."

"She's good," Morgan said. "One of the best, if not the best. And then what?"

"I'm off to Florida to hang out near Sally's son, Don, and wait for Sally. If she shows up in St. Louis first, I'll hop a plane."

Morgan pursed his lips and nodded. "Would you want to be shot back into the past or ahead into the future, Kara?"

She shook her head. "Neither... The past is over, and the future scares me."

Morgan looked skyward. "I'd go either way, Kara, past or future, in a heartbeat. I envy Sally Mason, and I'm looking forward to meeting her."

CHAPTER 25

"WELL, YOU'RE UP AWFULLY EARLY," Bert said, putting a hand to a yawn as he stood at the entrance to his spacious, modern kitchen. He shouldered into his black suspenders, hooking them over a blue and white flannel shirt, and smiled at Sally, who was leaning against the stainless-steel stove.

"Good morning, Bert," she said, brightly.

"And a good morning to you, Sally. I hope you slept all right."

"Fine, thank you."

"I heard someone open the kitchen door last night. I guess you needed to get the lay of the land."

"I'm sorry if I woke you."

"Not at all. I was already awake. I've always been a light sleeper. So, did you manage to get any sleep?"

Sally smiled timidly. "A little, but I've always been an early riser." She moved toward the large kitchen island. "I hope you don't mind that I invaded your kitchen. And what a kitchen." She ran her hands over the granite countertop. "I've never seen a kitchen like it. You don't mind that I started breakfast, do you?"

"Of course not. I'm glad you're making yourself at home. And I love that ponytail," Bert said, stepping fully into the room. "It looks cute on you. Makes you look like a high school girl from the 1950s."

Sally laughed. "Thank you, Bert. What a sweet

thing to say."

"Now, that's the first time I've seen you laugh. You must have had a little sleep."

Sally turned toward the counter and the yellow pancake bowl, and stirred the batter with a sauce spoon. "Yes, I slept fine. I found the pancake mix in that cabinet, and the eggs, and milk, and bacon. That is one big refrigerator."

"Lynnie loved the thing."

"Should I start the pancakes? Are you hungry?"

Bert gave a shake of his head. "Well, aren't you something, Sally? So efficient. And, yes, I'm hungry. Why don't I make the coffee?"

"Good. I didn't know how to use that coffee machine. I'm used to a percolator."

Bert moved to the Cuisinart coffee maker. "My mother had one of those old percolators, and she swore by it even after I bought her a Joe DiMaggio Coffee Maker. This thing takes some getting used to, but it makes good coffee."

"It has so many buttons," Sally said. "I was afraid I'd push the wrong one and blow something up."

Bert laughed. "Yeah, you have to be an engineer to figure it out."

Bert went to work, filling the carafe with water and measuring four teaspoons of coffee.

"Do you like big pancakes or small ones?" Sally asked.

"Chef's choice," Bert said, putting on his glasses, squinting, and pressing the BREW button.

When the skillet was hot, Sally poured batter into

three circles. "I like medium size," she said. "My husband, Ronnie, always liked big round ones. Had to have them that way."

Bert gave her a curious glance, and once the coffee maker was going, he leaned back against the counter, crossing his arms. "And where is your husband, Sally? If you don't mind me asking?"

She lowered her head and nudged the pancakes with a spatula, watching the batter form bubbles. The bacon sizzled in the frying pan, and the silence grew.

Sally said, "I didn't mean to talk about him."

"It's okay. Talk about him or don't talk about him."

"I guess I don't want to talk about him, Bert, if that's okay? Not right now."

"Fine, then let's talk about the weather. That's always a safe subject. I just checked my weather app, and it's not supposed to rain today. Partly cloudy and cool. Perfect fall weather."

They didn't speak again until the coffee was ready, and Sally had scooped three golden pancakes onto a warmed serving dish before pouring three more onto the skillet. When the bacon was crisp, Bert went over and forked them, piece by piece, laying them out onto a separate plate covered by a paper towel.

"The bacon's perfect, Sally. Just the way I like it. I think we should eat in the dining room instead of at the counter. I get tired of sitting on a stool."

A few minutes later, Bert was seated at the round mahogany dining table, with its ornate white-candle centerpiece. Built-in cabinets held china plates and cups, elegant wine glasses, and tchotchkes from Hawaii, France, and the Caribbean. The walls, painted white with blue trim, displayed lovely watercolors of shimmering lakes, leafy trees, snow-covered pine trees on winter hills, and sailboats shining under a yellow sun.

Through the skylight, dim gray light streamed in.

Out of habit, Sally entered the dining room with Bert's plate of pancakes and bacon. She placed his plate before him and stepped back, glancing out the large dining-room window, which offered a view of the backyard and surrounding trees, near where she'd seen the alien the night before. She shivered a little at the memory, remembering that silent moment when, it seemed to her, the other worldly being was trying to communicate something. But what? And why had it returned?

Sally left for the kitchen, soon returning with the coffee pot, filling Bert's cup. She was about to butter his stack of pancakes when Bert gently rested his hand on her wrist to stop her.

"Thank you, Sally, but you don't have to wait on me. You're my guest."

"But guests must always help and not be a nuisance. That's what my mother used to say. Besides, you've been so nice to me."

"Sit down now, Sally, and have your breakfast. Relax."

Sally returned a minute later with her own full plate, sitting down opposite him. Bert rose, reached for the coffee pot, and poured her a cup.

"Milk and sugar?" Bert asked.

"Just milk," Sally said, and Bert scooted the quart of milk toward her. She smiled up at him. "You're a real gentleman, Bert. No man has ever waited on me before."

Sally went to work on her pancakes, light on the butter, but heavy on the golden-brown maple syrup.

As they ate, Bert observed her studying the watercolors, her gaze briefly lingering on each piece.

"These pancakes are delicious, Sally. Best I've had in years."

She smiled her thanks and nodded to the paintings. "Did you paint those, Bert?"

"Yes. Do you like them?"

"I do like them. I like them very much, especially the one with the sailboats. I've always wanted to go sailing."

"I painted that about fifteen years ago, when Lynnie and I were in the Caribbean."

"I don't know that much about art, but I really like them, especially the colors and the skies."

"Thank you, Sally. Skies are hard to do with watercolors. Much easier with acrylic and oil."

Sally reached for her coffee cup and stared at the paintings longingly, as if she wanted to climb inside and experience them in person. "There were so many things I wanted to do, Bert. Places I wanted to see and things I wanted to learn."

"Come on, Sally... You're still so young, a young woman with your whole life ahead of you. You have plenty of time to do whatever you want to do."

Gazing into the distance with a trance-like intensity, Sally reflected on her life in 1953— her roles as a wife and mother, and the dreams and aspirations of the woman she had yearned to become. The desire to break free from her confined existence, to experience the life of a journalist, had always burned within her; to travel and engage in stimulating conversations about meaningful topics beyond the confines of small-town chitchat and idle gossip.

And, in a perfect world, she could have managed it, and been a better wife and mother because of it.

Strangely enough, and in a peculiar way, her prayers had been answered. She'd escaped her small world, but she was utterly lost, confused and alone, and she couldn't explain any of it.

"You seem a million miles away, Sally."

Sally shook away her thoughts. "Oh... I'm sorry, Bert. Maybe I didn't sleep enough."

Bert leaned back all smiles. "Well, I'm happy you're here, Sally. Do you know how quiet this house gets with just me and the old ghosts and the old memories?"

Sally swept the room with her eyes. "It's a beautiful house, Bert. Maybe you should get a dog."

Speaking in a small voice, Bert said, "I had one. He up and died on me a year ago. I can't go through that again, at least not yet."

Bert looked about wistfully. "Can you believe it, Sally? This house was once filled with people, and laughter, and arguments. My girls used to camp out in the bathrooms, putting on their makeup, and trying out new hairdos. I yelled at them to get out, but that didn't work, so I finally gave up and built a half bath downstairs. And Lynnie and I used to argue over every damn thing under the sun: money, teaching, how to raise the girls and what color we should paint our bedroom."

With a nostalgic gaze, Bert smiled. "But our Christmases, Sally. Yessiree, our Christmases were just magical, with heavenly baking smells, and lights strung outside in the eves and in the hedges, and we'd have a seven-foot Christmas tree, and the house was loud with singing. Neighbors from all along the street would come, and they'd say, 'Hey Bert, it's not Christmas without one of yours and Lynn's parties."

Bert looked around at the empty rooms and his smile faded. "Now, I can stand in the middle of that living room and hear my own heartbeat in my ears."

A long moment later, Sally said, "Bert, you'll meet somebody else. I know it. You're a really special man. Maybe she'll come to one of your painting classes."

Bert appeared sad and solitary as he reached for his empty coffee cup. "Thanks, Sally. You may be right about that. You never know who you might meet, just driving around the next corner, do you?"

Sally thought, *You have no idea.*

CHAPTER 26

T hirty-two-year-old Ayita Wells was born in the small, quaint town of Serendipity Springs, nestled amidst the lush forests and rolling hills of the Pacific Northwest. She grew up in a close-knit and spiritually inclined family, feeling a unique connection to the mystical and unexplained. Her parents, both deeply interested in metaphysics, nurtured her unusual interests, and supported her journey into the realm of the unknown.

During her formative years, Ayita discovered her innate psychic gifts. As a child, she began experiencing vivid dreams and intuitive flashes that often turned out to be premonitions of future events. Fascinated by her ability to perceive information beyond the ordinary senses, Ayita delved deeper into the world of psychic phenomena.

As she grew older, her fascination led her to join various online forums and discussion groups dedicated to metaphysical topics, where she could share experiences and learn from like-minded individuals.

After high school, Ayita's desire to understand and hone her psychic abilities drove her to enroll in a renowned parapsychology program at Heyer College in Northern California. During her college years, she explored various psychic practices, from tarot card reading to meditation and energy healing. It was during that time that her talent for remote viewing and telepathic communication truly flourished.

Ayita was barely five-feet tall, with short black hair, soft feminine features, and sea-blue, mesmerizing eyes, the first thing most people noticed. Her voice was a rich contralto, her manner quiet, her style of dress casual: jeans, sneakers, and a plain blue or brown top, never with patterns. She wore rings on several fingers of both hands, and they all had symbolic meanings, which she never discussed.

As Ayita progressed in her studies, her abilities caught the attention of a top-secret division within the CIA. They had been investigating mysterious sightings of unidentified aerial phenomena and needed someone with her unique psychic talents to aid in their research.

Ayita's first encounter with the CIA's team was both thrilling and daunting. They had data on various UAP sightings but lacked insight into the origins of these enigmatic crafts and the intentions of their occupants. Harnessing her telepathic abilities and remote viewing skills, Ayita embarked on a journey of interstellar communication.

Through telepathy, she attempted to establish contact with the beings piloting the UAPs, and her experiences were both awe-inspiring and occasionally unsettling. Once, an alien being told her, in telepathic images, "Do not contact us. You are not ready. You are too primitive for us. We come and go on your planet, and we have done so for centuries.

No further communication will be granted."

From another UAP contact came a friendlier tone. "We explore many other planets than Earth. We conduct experiments and take samples. We are not interested in harming anyone. Sometimes our spacecraft can be seen with your eyes. Sometimes not. When you see us, it is because we want you to see us. It is part of Earth's learning, or evolution, if that word is clearer for you. You are not the only ones in the universe. Little by little, you will understand this. It will take more time. We, and others like us, are patient."

Ayita became an indispensable asset to the CIA's UAP research efforts, as they worked to understand the mysterious extraterrestrial intelligence. She walked the thin line between the Earth's reality and the realms of psychic exploration, as she developed interstellar contacts and encounters.

Ayita had worked with Kara Gonne on three occasions, the first when a crashed alien craft was found in Southern New Mexico, the two pilots dead, the craft damaged. Ayita's job was to contact the pilots' superiors and thereby learn the source of the craft.

For two days, she'd been unsuccessful. On the third day, she received a telepathic message.

"We are, what you would call us, Zeta Reticulian, or Greys."

Ayita had studied all known extraterrestrials, and Greys were the most frequent subjects of close encounters and alien abduction. They were human-like, with smooth, gray-colored skin, small bodies, enlarged heads, small noses, and prominent black eyes.

Ayita responded telepathically. "Are you aware that one of your spacecraft crashed and both pilots are dead?"

"Yes, we know that. You can think of it as occurring because of a computer malfunction."

"What was their purpose?"

"To gather samples. To observe."

"Have you sent others like them to observe?"

"Yes."

"What do they observe?"

"They are what you would call scientists."

"Do those scientists sometimes abduct humans?"

"We will not discuss this."

"Why?"

"It is not useful."

"It might be useful for us."

"We will not discuss it. You will not understand."

"Do your scientists want to harm us?" Ayita asked.

"No. There is no reason for that. All things are connected. We explore. We observe."

"I would like to understand you and your race better. Where do you come from?"

"We will not discuss this. We will go now."

Ayita's second encounter was with an extraterrestrial who didn't identify his race or where he was from. Ayita had been working with a secret branch of the CIA, and she and the other psychics were conducting communication experiments. They were "pointing their intentions toward the heavens" in search of aliens who might be somewhere within the Earth's atmosphere. Ayita was the only psychic who had contacted an alien whose craft was under the Atlantic Ocean.

"So, you are currently hundreds of feet below the ocean?" Ayita asked.

"Yes."

"Where are you from?"

"You would not understand where we come from. Your race believes in a thing, and then your race cannot conceive that an alien thing can be true. Or, in your imaginations, you make it into a scary monster or a threat. Your minds are small. They won't always be small, but now, in your evolution, you have too much fear and too much belief in old things."

"Will you help me understand so that my mind is not so small?" Ayita asked.

"When you are not afraid, we will meet. It is the way of this universe. Big and small are connected."

Ayita's third communication was with an extraterrestrial named StrallVoss, who was a Nordic. After a series of sightings were reported over Southern California, Kara Gonne had called Ayita and asked her to try to contact the aliens involved. Ayita did so, communicating telepathically with StrallVoss, a commander, a master communicator, and a kind of ambassador.

"Thank you for communicating with me,

StrallVoss," Ayita had said.

StrallVoss had answered, "I am here for those who can connect to me with their minds, and who are not afraid."

"Why are your spacecraft exploring our world?"

"All races, as you call them, explore and probe. It is how we grow and learn. It is how we... that is, how our people connect to other worlds and races, whenever it is possible."

"Will you harm us?"

"There is no reason to harm anything. Your race is unique and interesting to us. We learn from you. Why would we harm? It is not helpful to the universe."

"Are you trying to connect with us?"

"We do, from time to time, but only to beings like yourself, who have the mental skill... the ability to connect. Your species, for the most part, lacks clear thinking. There is too much static and chatter in your minds. Very cluttered. You are an exception. Your mind is calm, and we can communicate. But most of your kind are too afraid, too quick to fight. Unity is discarded. Tribal power is sought. Your planet is evolving."

"Have you visited Earth many times?" Ayita asked.

"Yes, for many long times. Since ancient times, and before."

"Why are your flying crafts visible to us?"

"Sometimes it is for—as you would think of it —technical reasons. Other times, it is to let your species know that you are not alone in this universe. I must end now."

"Can I contact you again?"

"If there is a need, but only if there is a need. Otherwise, I will not respond. Your race and ours are not yet destined to meet. Therefore, we have little to say to you that will be helpful."

Ayita was working in her garden in the backyard of her Northern California two-bedroom house when she received a secure call from Kara Gonne.

Ayita rose and pulled her cellphone from her back jeans pocket. "How are you, Kara?"

"Having a vodka martini at a Florida patio bar, which means I'm doing better. What are you doing?"

"Gardening."

"I can't download that picture of you in my head. I always picture your head in the stars."

"It helps me stay grounded," Ayita said. "Besides, I like it. It's a beautiful and chilly fall day with not a cloud in the sky."

"What kind of gardening does one do in Northern California in October?" Kara asked.

"Sow wildflower seeds. Pull the weeds and grasses, scatter the seeds as evenly as possible, and then rake the soil gently. No fertilizers, only a thin layer of compost. You should join me sometime."

"Can I bring a martini?"

"Sure. I have olives."

"I like a twist."

"I've got lemons."

Kara's voice lowered. "Ayita, can you meet me at the New Mexico hangar in, say, a week? Could be less. I'll be in touch."

"Yes. I can."

"I need you to contact StrallVoss."

There was a pause before Ayita spoke. "He may not want to talk."

"I think he will. I've forwarded you the file for a woman named Sally Mason. It's... well, shall I say ... very unusual. It's priority on steroids."

"Our team?" Ayita asked.

"Limited for now. Only Morgan and three others. No one political, which I know you'll be glad to hear."

"Anything more?"

"Not now. Once you've read the file, you'll understand."

After Ayita had finished the call and shoved her phone into her back pocket, she lifted her head skyward and let her eyes peer deeply into the infinite blue sky. In a flashing second, she sensed danger, but she couldn't mentally grasp it. Kara's voice held not only concern and secrets, but also a feeling of danger.

Ayita lowered to her knees and went back to work, pulling weeds, preparing the soil, and wondering if it was time to cease her work with the CIA. Perhaps she could put her skills and talents to better use? She thought so. But she was intrigued by Kara's call.

Fifteen minutes later, she left her garden, went inside the house, peeled off her garden gloves and went to her laptop. Sally Mason's file had arrived.

CHAPTER 27

S ally and Bert had finished their breakfasts, the pancakes gone, the bacon gone, some lukewarm coffee still in their cups.

Bert noticed Sally was fidgety, her eyes reflecting inner turmoil. "Do you feel like talking now, Sally?"

She looked at Bert, conflicted. Could she trust him? There was no one else, and she had no place else to go.

When she looked into Bert's eyes, she saw a worldly wisdom, similar to what she'd seen in her Grandpa Fred's eyes. He'd fought in a war, lost a business, and lost a child in a drowning accident. Despite it all, he'd laughed easily, and he'd been one of the most generous people Sally had ever known.

There was a similar lifetime of joys and sorrows in Bert's eyes, and a warm patience.

"Bert…" Sally said, and then she stopped and tried again. "Bert, you've been so kind to me, and you don't even know me."

Bert rested his soft eyes on her. "I know you're in trouble, Sally, probably running away from your husband. I don't know why, and I don't need to know, but if I can help you in any way, I'd like to, if you let me."

She looked at him for a long minute. She took a drink of her coffee, replaced the cup into the saucer, blotted her mouth with the napkin, and then turned to stare out the glass doors.

"Bert... It was my son, Don, who first mentioned the lights in the sky. He said, 'Mommy, last night, I saw lights outside my window, and they moved around in the sky.'"

Bert folded his hands on the table, listening closely.

"I said, 'They're shooting stars, Don,' and then I pointed at the sky. 'You should make a wish when you see them. Make one special wish, and it will come true.'"

"'But Mommy, they move over the trees,' Don said. 'Sometimes they light up my window.'"

Sally lifted a hand, trying to explain. "I didn't think anything of it. I mussed Don's hair and told him to go to sleep. I told him that shooting stars don't fly around the woods at night. I told them they flash across the sky like magic.

"Don said, 'They don't fly in the woods, Mommy, they fly over them.'"

Sally stared in front of her for a long time. "For a week or so, strange lights were seen over Rosemont. We lived not too far from here, Bert, on North Maple, but the street's not there anymore. When we drove by there last night, it was all changed. But I remember this neighborhood. I loved the houses in this neighborhood, and the quiet streets."

Bert leaned forward slightly, absorbed.

Sally picked up her fork and then laid it down again. "Anyway, several people in town said they saw those lights. I'd read about it in the newspaper, and people talked about it on one of the local radio stations, WQMI. It was one of those call-in shows. And I heard a woman talk about seeing lights in the night sky when I was shopping in Carl's Grocery Store, and another woman, at the beauty salon, said she saw lights, too. There was a lot of gossip about it, and I didn't know what to think."

Bert reached for his coffee, keeping his eyes on her, concerned. Her voice was low and shaky with emotion.

Sally's eyes connected with Bert's. "Even Deputies Carter and Wysong said they saw something in the night sky they couldn't identify. In the newspaper, the sheriff said, 'I'm not saying it was one of those flying saucers. I'm just saying I don't know what it was, but whatever it was, it shined, or sparkled, and it hovered for a time out over Ned Parker's field, not far from his barn. Then, just like that, it just went—zoom—flew away like a flash, and then it was gone. That's all I'm saying.'"

Sally put a hand to her throat as the memories returned. Now that she had started, the words came easier, and the story began to tell itself.

The sun broke free from the clouds, filling the dining room with morning light. It seemed an omen, a reassuring sign that Sally should continue.

With her face bathed in sunlight, Sally's hands crafted gestures in the air while she recounted the journey through the night, the bursts of lights in the sky, and the hovering spaceship. She searched for words to capture the exquisite, luminous extraterrestrial being and to express the terror that had left her completely frozen on her car seat.

While she continued, there was birdsong outside, and the drone of a commercial jet, and the gleeful shouts of children hurrying off to school.

Bert listened to Sally with patient respect, his face impassive. When she had finished, her head lowered to her chest, her shoulders sagging. After a moment's silence, Bert turned from her and stared at a shaft of sunlight that painted a rectangular plank on the silvery gray dining room carpet.

Pulsing with anxiety, and drained from recounting her story, Sally waited, her hands busy with the napkin. Would Bert think she was crazy? Would he ridicule her? Would he call the police? His face told her nothing.

Time seemed to taunt her as the living room mantle clock ticked, loud, in the infinite silence.

Finally, Bert looked at her and his eyes wouldn't let her go.

"Do you believe me, Bert?" she said, aware it was a plea for help. "I feel like a drunken woman, and everything is spinning around. I keep thinking that maybe I'm crazy, but if that's true, can insanity explain all of it? I just don't think so."

Breathing softly, Bert finally spoke. "And you said your doctor, a psychiatrist, told you that a CIA agent wanted to speak to you?"

Sally nodded.

Bert shook his head in disgust. "So that's why you were out in the storm. That knucklehead from the hospital tossed you out of his car."

Sally's eyes misted. "I don't understand it, Bert. Why me?"

"And you saw the same alien from 1953 outside the house last night?"

She nodded again. "I think so. I don't know for sure."

Sally leaned forward. "Bert, you don't think I'm crazy, do you?"

His gaze dropped, then came back up. "No, Sally, I don't think you're crazy. I'm going to be honest with you and say, I don't know what the hell happened to you, but you're not crazy. I've heard about people being abducted by aliens. Some years ago, a student of mine told me he'd been abducted. Maybe I should have believed him, but I didn't."

Sally looked down and away. "I just want to see my kids... My grown kids. I want to tell them what happened, and that I didn't abandon them, and that I still love them."

Bert stood up, giving a tug to his suspenders. "Sally... Have you thought what it might do to them, when they see you like you were seventy years ago? You haven't changed, but they have. They're about my age. It will be quite a shock. It would be one helluva shock to me if my young mother knocked on my door and told me she had time traveled seventy years into the future. It's a real risky thing, Sally."

"I know, but I've just got to see them, Bert. I've just got to."

He thought about it, turning his head to look

outside. "Well, I suppose I could use an adventure. I haven't had one in years. You said you want to see your son first, in Florida?"

"Yes. He will remember the lights. I know it. My daughter, Mary, has Alzheimer's. Do you know what that is?"

Bert looked at her soberly. "Yes, Sally, I do. She probably won't remember you, young or old."

Sally breathed in and let it out in a rush. "Yes, that's what the doctor said."

Sunlight fled the room as dark clouds appeared.

"Okay, then. Let's pack a bag. I'll book us a flight to the nearest airport to Fort Pierce, and then we'll see what happens. Oh, wait a minute. Do you have any ID, Sally?"

She shook her head. "No. The police took my purse."

Bert pocketed his hands and sighed. "Okay... Well, I guess we'll have to drive it, then. But that's okay. It will be a good old-fashioned road trip."

Sally shot to her feet, her face coming alive. "Oh, my heavens, Bert. Will you? Will you take me?"

The joy in her face cheered him. "Yes, Sally, I will. I haven't had a good jolt like this since I won the lottery eight years ago."

"You won a lottery?"

He winked at her. "Oh, yeah. Twenty bucks."

CHAPTER 28

That afternoon, Bert insisted they drive to the mall so Sally could purchase toiletries and clothing.

"You can't wear that same outfit every day, Sally. I'll get tired of looking at you," he said with a grin.

"But I have no money, Bert, and I can't ask you to pay for everything."

"Don't worry about it. Someday, maybe you'll buy me a new fishing rod and a bucket of worms. Anyway, you've got to look pretty when you meet your son, don't you?"

At the mall, Sally bought underwear, capris, jeans, shorts, a sweatshirt, a jacket, three t-shirts, two blouses, a pair of sandals, and some makeup. It took her a while to figure out the sizes, but Bert waited patiently after he'd bought himself a pair of Bermuda shorts, two polo shirts and a pair of white sneakers.

Sally and Bert set off for Fort Pierce, Florida, early the next morning, Sally nervous, Bert as excited as a kid heading for a circus. As they hit the open road on I-65, Sally was astonished by the vast super highways with their twisting ramps and bridges, and how well-maintained they were. The racing speeds frightened her, the endless car models baffled her, and the extravagant rest areas made her laugh.

"I could have never imagined this, Bert," Sally

said. "None of it. None of those telephones you carry with you, and the computers and those huge jet airplanes."

"Do you know what, Sally? You're making me see the world in new ways; I'm seeing things I took for granted and never really noticed. I feel like a kid again."

"I was thinking," Sally said. "What about your art students? You'll be missing your art classes."

"It's okay. I don't ask them for a set fee or anything. We meet at the Senior Citizens Center, and they pay what they want. So, I emailed them and said I needed a vacation, and I'd be in touch. No big deal, Sally."

Weather on the first day was perfect—clear skies and a cool, gentle breeze. Bert played country music from his playlist and sang along as they drove past scenic meadows and rolling hills.

Outside Nashville, Tennessee, they checked into a quaint motel called Melody Inn, which had a live country band playing in the courtyard. While they ate dinner on the patio, Sally and Bert tapped their feet to the music and, after dessert, they crowded onto the floor and danced to the song *Cowboy Casanova*.

They retired to separate rooms and were up at dawn, ready to go. After breakfast, they drove off into a light rain, rolling through the lush landscapes of Tennessee and Georgia. Sally's nerves eased as she became acclimated to freeway driving and listened to Bert's stories of his "young and wild" days. Once he nearly burned the house down while conducting a science experiment in the basement of his parents' house.

Sally admitted that she'd wanted to go to college but had become a wife and a mother instead.

"What did you want to study, Sally? What did you truly want to do after college?" Bert asked.

Sally looked at him with a wistful smile. "I wanted to be a journalist."

"Really? A journalist?"

"Yes... Of course, I never told anybody, but I wanted to be like Anne O'Hare McCormick or Lee Miller. Have you heard of them?"

"No, I haven't."

"I read about them in *Life* magazine. I was so amazed by their courage. Anne McCormick interviewed everybody: Hitler and Stalin and Churchill and Roosevelt. She wrote for *The New York Times* and was the first woman to win a Pulitzer Prize for journalism. I'm surprised you've never heard of her."

"So tell me more, Sally. Enlighten me."

"You must have heard of Lee Miller?"

"No, Sally. I don't know her either."

Sally glowed with enthusiasm. "Her real name was Elizabeth. She had a wild life. She started out as a model, but she became a photographer and a war correspondent during World War II for *Vogue* Magazine. She photographed nurses all over Europe, but also went to liberated concentration camps... and there's even a picture of her in Hitler's bathtub, in his apartment in Munich. He wasn't there, of course. He was in some bunker with Eva Braun, committing suicide."

Bert kept his hands on top of the steering wheel, driving in the right lane, a light mist making the world blurry. He glanced at her with admiration. "Well, I'll *Google* them both, Sally. See, you're a good influence on an old guy who thought he knew everything there was to know," he said, flashing his signature lopsided grin.

Sally eased back in her seat. "I was living in such a small world, Bert, and now, this world seems so big and mysterious."

"Well, do you know what, Sally? Once you've seen your son, you have some big decisions to make. You'll have to make your way in this new world and you're going to need help to do it. With the right help, you just might be able to go to college and become that journalist you wanted to be."

"I don't know what I'm going to do, Bert, but I'm smart enough to know that there are people out there, people who work for the government, and they believe my story—that I came from 1953. They'll be waiting for us in Fort Pierce."

"Then don't go. Let's go somewhere else. Fool them."

"I've got to see my son, Bert."

Bert tapped off the music, his expression earnest. "Sally... I don't know if what happened to you has ever happened before. Maybe it has—it probably has —but who's going to know, except maybe some covert CIA agency? And if they do take you away, who in this world is going to know what happened to you?"

CHAPTER 29

"ARE YOU TRYING TO SCARE ME, BERT?" Sally asked.

"No. I'm just thinking out loud. I had a physics professor in college who told us to always keep an open mind about science and life. So that's what I'm doing. The bigger part of me doesn't believe your story of alien transport and time travel, but another part of me is open to it. Now, let's say I believe you, even eighty percent. Okay, fine. I know you want to see your son, but let's think about this thing another way. Why should you let yourself be taken by the CIA, or whomever, and then be questioned and pushed and pulled and controlled, when you could simply fade into the background, set up roots in some small town somewhere and start a new life?"

Sally gazed out her window at a distant row of condos that all looked the same. "I want to go back home, Bert. That's what I really want. I want to go back to my kids when they were children, and I want to raise them and be a part of their lives."

"And go back to your husband?"

"I don't know," Sally said. "I just don't know what I should do."

For lunch they stopped in Georgia at a family-run roadside barbecue joint called Southern Smokes. Sitting outside at a picnic table, they shared finger-licking ribs, brisket, and golden fries. Sally commented on the two energetic waitresses with tattoos and heavy Southern accents, and the loud clashing rock music.

"This world is so different from the one I left, Bert. I don't know if I'll ever get used to it."

Bert sat across from her, licking barbecue sauce from his fingers. And then he surprised her with a suggestion. "Sally, my younger brother has a beach house in Ormond Beach, not so far away. I could call him, and you could stay there for a while. He and his wife won't come to Florida until after Thanksgiving, so the house is free. His son, my nephew Terry, is one of the owners of a very successful tech company. I won't go into what that means, since you probably wouldn't understand it, but he's a whizz kid, as they say, and by kid, I should clarify that he's thirty-nine years old. I bet Terry could help you build a new identity, with a new name, a passport, a driver's license, and a Social Security number. There's no guarantee, of course, I'd have to ask him, but we always got along, and he's recently divorced, which means he might jump at the distraction. If I explained all or part of your situation, I think he would help."

Tipping the soda can, Sally poured the last of her *Coca-Cola* and watched it fizz over the ice. "Why? Why would he help me?"

"Because I would ask him, as I said, and because I think he would find your situation more than just interesting. And, anyway, it would give you another choice."

"And what would I do for money?"

"I'll loan you some until you can pay me back."

"And what if I can never pay you back?"

Bert shrugged. "Then, so far, I've had one helluva good time, and spending the money is well worth it."

Sally reached for a French fry and paused before putting it into her mouth. "I don't know."

"Sally, when we get to your son's house in Fort Pierce, if what you say is true, and if the CIA is waiting for you there, you will be picked up and you'll never be permitted to speak to your son. They can't allow it. Surely, you understand that. They can't let this—your situation—your very strange situation—leak out into the world."

Sally propped her elbow on the table and placed her chin in a palm, looking sullen and discouraged.

"You're a beautiful young woman, Sally. You'll have unlimited possibilities. You can go to college and have the career you never had. In 2023, women have career options that were unthinkable in 1953. You'll find a good man, fall in love, and have another family."

He leaned toward her. "Sally... I think it's best if you face reality. Your life in the past is over. It's sad, yes, but it's gone. For whatever the reason, you're now living in 2023, and you have your whole life in front of you."

As they approached the Florida state line, the weather cleared, and they were greeted with sunshine and blue skies. Sally had not spoken for miles, aware that time was running out, and she'd soon have to make a decision that would radically change her life, no matter what she chose.

Sally and Bert stopped for the night at the small coastal town of Seaside Serenity, near St. Augustine. At a rambling motel with an electric, green-and-yellow sign that read *Ocean Breeze Lodge*, they checked into separate rooms.

At sunset, Sally left her motel room and took a leisurely stroll across the sand, wading into the foaming ocean surf for the first time in her life. She inhaled the salty air and gazed out at the horizon, crimson and golden. The vast, rolling ocean was as much a mystery as her own life, and her mind was rolling and pitching like the sea.

When night descended and stars twinkled, and the ocean tide rolled in, Sally sat on the beach, pulled her knees to her chest, and wrapped them with her arms. Would Don believe her, or would he think she was some crazy woman? Mary had already left the world, her mind and surely most of her memories gone.

Bert was right, of course. Her past was over. Ronnie had been dead for over twenty years and her children had moved on with their lives long ago. She had vanished in 1953, and she was a nobody in 2023, but a curiosity, a freak to be captured, locked up and studied like some laboratory creature.

As her thoughts rambled, she felt the rise of warm possibility and muted excitement when she considered the new world. Could she go to college? Could she become a journalist? Could she meet a man and fall in love, truly fall in love this time?

She leaned back, stared up into the sky and saw a big, glittering star. *Make a wish, Sally. Make a wish with all your heart, and pray it comes true.*

A moment later, the wind blew as if from out of the past, and with a cold feeling, Sally pushed up and returned to her room.

CHAPTER 30

The New Mexico night was cold, the stars close, the full moon white on the horizon.

Standing outside a gray airplane hangar in a top-secret area, Kara Gonne and Ayita wore winter coats, hats, and gloves. Ayita gazed up into the wide expanse of sky and smiled. "So many stars. So many galaxies, and so many mysteries."

"How was your trip?" Kara asked.

"Smooth skies. Didn't see any UAPs," Ayita said, joking.

Kara glanced over. "Funny."

"So, Sally Mason is MIA," Ayita said. "A no-show at Fort Pierce and St. Louis?"

"I waited four days in Florida. We still have personnel at both locations."

"Maybe she's sick or waiting you out. She knows you're searching for her."

"She's had help," Kara said, tugging gently on her right hooped earring.

Ayita locked her hands behind her back. "Any theories who it might be?"

"Random. Has to be. She had nothing when she left. Just the clothes on her back. No money or ID when that idiot hospital orderly kicked her out of his car. Has to be random. And I think Sally Mason is smarter than I thought she was."

"And are you sure she's alive?"

"You're the psychic, Ayita. You tell me."

"Not my specialty. Do you want to hear my remote view report, or should we wait for Morgan?" Ayita asked.

"We should wait, but I'm anxious," Kara said, turning to face her.

Ayita smiled. "I finally had a conversation with my grandfather and told him what remote viewing is."

"Why?"

"He asked me. He's a retired engineer... very left brain, a non-believer in anything he can't touch, tinker with, or see, and he's not well. My mother told him about it, and he said he wanted to talk to me. So, before I left, I went to see him."

Kara glanced over to see three F-35 fighter jets parked side by side near the hangar. They were single-engine stealth fighter aircraft with an angular design, sharp edges, and smooth surfaces. In the dim light spilling out from inside the hangar, they appeared ominous, futuristic, and lethal.

"And how did you tell him about remote viewing?" Kara asked. "Even my ex-CIA husband was wary of it, calling it pseudoscientific and paranormal."

"Well, I kept it simple, and I gave him the textbook explanation, that it's the paranormal ability to perceive a remote or hidden subject without the support of the senses. I said, some people can perceive information about a location, a person, or an event without using their regular physical senses; they can get impressions about a distant or unseen subject simply by sensing it with their mind."

"And did he toss you out of his house?" Kara asked, amused.

"No, but his eyes glazed over. We sat in wicker chairs on his porch, and I held his hand."

"Are you close to him?"

"We care for each other, but he doesn't like to show his feelings. He didn't pull his hand away, though."

"So tell me what you told him, Ayita. My right brain could use some exercise."

"I told him that a person or a team, known as the 'sender,' selects a 'target,' which could be a specific location, object, or event, even an event that happened in the past. The target is kept hidden from the remote viewer. Then, the viewer attempts to describe the target, based on the impressions, thoughts, or mental images they perceive. They can draw sketches or use other means to record their impressions."

Kara's eyebrows raised in query. "Did he make any comments?"

"Oh, yes. He asked if I made any money from it."

"Does he know you often work for the CIA?"

"No. Only Mom and Dad know about that."

Kara stared into the star-filled night. "Look at all those glimmering stars, Ayita. Some of them are hundreds of thousands of light years away. And that's just in our galaxy. It makes one feel small, doesn't it?"

Ayita's serene eyes took in the magical night sky. "And yet, we can see the endless sky and all those stars, and, with our minds, we can embrace them and we can breathe into the space. So maybe we're not so small after all."

Kara looked at Ayita, her warm human magic in the air. "You're much too New Age and poetic for me, Ayita, but then, I can't talk to extraterrestrials, can I?"

"Who knows, maybe StrallVoss will talk to you, too."

"So, tell me, Ayita. The target was Sally Mason's 1951 Chevy Belair on a dark and quiet Indiana road on October 5, 1953. What did you experience?"

"I saw light and I felt fear. Not my fear. I saw the shapes of things. A car. A hovering thing. It was large. Quite large. I had the impression of a Being standing close by. It wasn't human, at least not the way we think of human, but it also wasn't so different from, well, a human being. It's difficult to explain. I probed the Being's mind. It was a clear and intelligent mind, but I sensed conflict, as if it had done something... something it shouldn't have done."

"What about Sally Mason?"

Ayita shut her eyes for a moment as if to bring back the memory. "I had the impression that someone was in a car, but that... How do I say this? That the car was blinking in and out, or off and on, like flipping a light switch. When I put my focus on the car, it was gone. There was nothing there but the hovering craft and the Being. On reflection, and in my debriefing, I described the extraterrestrial as being a Nordic. Tall, radiant, and highly intelligent."

Kara nodded. "Anything more on Sally?"

Ayita opened her eyes. "One thing. As I was coming out, gently bringing my focus back to this world and time, I saw a woman slumped in her car, the same car I'd seen with the alien and the hovering craft. I saw a patrol car, with its blue sweeping light. I saw traffic passing, and I zoomed in on one of the car's license plates as it passed. It was a 2023 plate."

Kara's cellphone vibrated, and she glanced at it. "Morgan's here, waiting for us in the conference room."

Dressed in his customary dark suit and tie, Morgan Compton sat behind a round conference room table under artificial lights, his hands chattering across a laptop keyboard. He glanced up when Kara and Ayita entered the room, nodded, and continued to type. They joined him at the table, sitting in high-quality, ergonomic chairs, both women placing their cellphones before them on the table.

Neatly tucked away in a corner, a small refreshment station offered water, coffee, and tea, and a side table held stationery, notepads, pens, and markers. The walls were bare, the carpet was a bluish gray, and there were no windows.

A minute later, Morgan removed his glasses, set

them aside and pushed the laptop forward, his gaze shifting from Ayita to Kara, and them back to Ayita.

"I made coffee, so it's fresh."

Both women shook their heads.

Morgan said, "I read your remote view report, Ayita. Thank you. Impressive as usual."

He looked at Kara. "Anything new on Sally Mason?"

Kara shook her head.

Morgan reached for his white mug of coffee. "I was just emailing General Felson, and I attached your report, Ayita."

"When did he get involved?" Kara asked, her eyes showing displeasure.

"Since somebody leaked. He called me. He asked me. I told him."

"Who leaked?" Kara asked.

"He said Dr. Megan Stanley made some enquiries. She demanded to know how Mrs. Sally Anne Mason was being treated. The doctor said more than she should have, and I'm sure you can imagine the rest. She demanded to see Mrs. Mason and threatened to go to the police and the press if she was not granted her request. She mentioned your name, Kara."

Kara stared down at the table, and then shook her head and crossed her arms. "I thought she was smarter than that."

"We need to find Mrs. Mason, Kara," Morgan stressed.

Kara kinked her neck. "Dr. Stanley can go to the cops, but they won't know anything more than she does. She was in the room when we all heard about the orderly sneaking Sally out of the hospital. The Rosemont police will brush her off. Chief Kennie Gosser is done with Sally Mason. And I can't believe she'd really go to the press because she knows what will happen if she does, and she cares about Sally too much to put her through it."

"So, what do we know right now?" Morgan asked.

"Sally Mason is long gone from that town."

"How do you know, Kara?"

"Because she wants to see her kids."

Morgan rubbed his chin with the back of his hand. "I don't care about Dr. Stanley, but I don't want General Felson sticking his nose in this. He'll go to his congressional friends. They have big mouths and want more clicks on social media so they can raise money. Long story short, I don't want to be called to testify behind closed doors before some ridiculous subcommittee."

Kara lifted a helpless hand. "Sally Mason is off the grid, Morgan. I mean, she was never on the grid, was she? She has no cellphone, no ID, no credit cards, and no Social Security number. Years ago, it was flagged as 'deceased' and has been purged."

They fell into silence. Morgan sipped his coffee and tapped his fingers on the table. "Somebody in that town knows where Sally is. When she left that hospital orderly's car, someone must have picked her up and helped her, and they're probably still helping her."

Kara gave Morgan a focused stare. "I have a photo

of Sally when she was in the hospital. Chief Gosser sent it to me, and we have two agents, one male, one female, passing it around to restaurants and businesses in Rosemont."

Morgan smiled with pleased satisfaction. "Why didn't you tell me?"

Kara shrugged. "I was about to."

"I like it, Kara. Old school."

"It's the only school we've got, Morgan."

"Obviously, no luck so far?" Morgan asked.

"It's slow work."

"Put another agent on it."

"Happy to."

Morgan turned his full attention to Ayita. "Any communication with StrallVoss?"

"Yes."

Morgan and Kara sat up and put their full attention on her.

"Why didn't you tell me?" Kara asked.

Ayita excused herself, went to the refreshment station, reached for a bottle of water, screwed off the cap and took a swallow. She replaced the cap and turned to them.

"Pardon the pause, but my throat was dry, and what I'm about to say is somewhat… well, let me say it this way. It was something I didn't expect." She turned to Kara. "That's why I waited to tell you until I could include Morgan."

Morgan and Kara remained still and waiting.

"I contacted StrallVoss last night. It took several attempts. He was, as he put it, 'far from you, and very much occupied.'"

Morgan slid the laptop to his right side, leaned back in his chair, and laced his hands behind his head. "Please do tell, Ayita. I've never seen you be so dramatic."

Again, Ayita removed the bottle cap and took a drink. Her energetic, adventurous eyes blinked twice. "StrallVoss wants to meet face to face. He said it is important that we meet, and he has proposed tomorrow night, here inside the hangar."

Morgan gave her a concentrated stare.

Kara's face was eager with the unasked question. "Did you mention Sally Mason?"

"No… StrallVoss did. That is, he didn't mention her by name. He called her 'the female traveler,' but he knew what had happened—that she had been, as he put it, 'moved in time.'"

Morgan pursed his lips as he gazed up at the ceiling. A moment later, he lowered his eyes on Ayita. "Well, well. What have we here?"

Ayita continued. "He knows about Sally Mason, which probably means it was one of his own spacecraft that transported her ahead in time."

"Did he say why?" Kara asked.

"No. He just stressed that it was important we talk."

Kara's eyes seemed to go inward as she imagined herself at the meeting. It would be her first encounter with StrallVoss. "Did he say who could be present at the meeting?"

"Yes. Only you and me, Kara. No one else."

Kara smiled. Morgan inclined forward, his forehead wrinkled in disappointment. "Did you mention me to him, Ayita?"

"I didn't mention anyone. He spoke the names twice: Ayita Wells and Kara Gonne."

Morgan spread his hands with finality. "Well, all right, then, ladies. I guess StrallVoss is a ladies' man, so you will meet the enigmatic alien, and I will sit here, waiting with bated breath for your full report."

CHAPTER 31

The lone airplane hangar stood in the heart of a secluded desert facility, its metallic walls reflecting the moon's soft glow. One single runway stretched out into the fading night, where all seemed dead and quiet.

Inside the expansive hangar, Kara's restless footsteps echoed against the cold concrete floor as she anxiously awaited StrallVoss. Ayita remained composed near the open front doors, peering out into the moonlit night, her eyes gleaming with a mix of curiosity and anticipation.

At the rear of the hangar loomed a solitary B-21 Raider, a formidable long-range stealth bomber capable of delivering devastating payloads. It was nuclear-capable and designed to accommodate manned or unmanned operations. Its dark silhouette gave it a mythical quality, as if it were a slumbering beast awaiting the moment to unleash its power upon the world. Kara had not wanted it there, but Morgan couldn't do anything about it. Making any request would have involved more brass and explanations than he was willing to reveal.

Kara approached Ayita and glanced at her watch. "Five minutes, if he's on time."

"He'll be on time," Ayita said. "He said he might be early."

"Are you nervous?" Kara asked. "You look so

damned calm. Let's face it, one doesn't get to meet an extraterrestrial every day."

"No, I'm not nervous. StrallVoss is powerful, I feel that, but he also has a humility about him."

Kara looked at her warily. "Ayita, do you consider yourself in any way naïve?"

"It's possible."

"Evil does exist, Ayita. I have seen it and I have had to deal with it. And we all have a bit of badness in us, don't you think?"

Ayita smiled.

"What's that smile for?" Kara asked, crossing her arms.

"I often find that when most people are confronted with death, either their own or that of someone they love, they get philosophical. I have never known you to be philosophical, Kara. For some reason, now that you are about to meet StrallVoss, you have become philosophical."

Kara screwed up her lips. "I would say I'm being cautious and skeptical. We know nothing about StrallVoss, where he comes from or what he wants. I want to know what he wants. Fear and desire are powerful motivators. What does he fear, and what does he want? And what does he need to get what he wants?"

Ayita turned back to the night, and a dry desert breeze washed across her face. "He'll be here soon, and you can ask him."

As soon as Ayita's words died away in the breeze, the air hummed with electricity. Kara's eyes darted to her wristwatch. Both women heard a crackling sound behind them, and they whirled about. They saw a subtle blue ripple dance through the air. The atmosphere shifted, as if time and space were bending around a glowing celestial presence.

Ayita's gaze locked onto the foggy radiance. Kara held her breath, her instincts on high alert.

A figure began to materialize, flickering into form before their eyes. StrallVoss stood tall, straight, and luminous, his shimmering essence casting a gentle blue and golden glow around him. His alien form seemed ethereal, translucent, lit from within. The intelligence in his soft, ruby-red eyes sparkled, and when he looked at the women, his gaze sent shivers rippling up Kara's spine to the crown of her head.

StrallVoss inclined his head in a bow of courtesy, his presence exuding a blend of profound serenity and vibrant energy that filled the hangar with a blue, misty aura.

"I am here, and I am happy to see you two are also present. I am StrallVoss."

Remarkably, Kara heard his voice in her head, a rich mechanical voice that held warmth. His thin line of lips didn't move. His eyes did not blink. And then Kara also heard Ayita's voice in her head, and she shot her a startled glance. Her lips also didn't move. It was obvious that Ayita and StrallVoss were speaking to each other telepathically, and Kara could hear what she would describe as "digital sound packets." And she saw "images of words" that were as clear as any 3D movie.

"StrallVoss, welcome. I am Ayita Wells and this is Kara Gonne. Thank you for agreeing to meet us."

"The request was mine, and your agreement is appreciated."

Kara swallowed, opened her mouth to speak, then she stopped. Her voice got swallowed in her breath and she could only make a raspy wheezing sound. She tried to speak again, but the words froze on her lips.

"Kara Gonne," StrallVoss said, again the words sounding in Kara's head, "you can speak without sound, and you can hear without ears. It is natural, and how the true meaning of communication is not misinterpreted. Words can be lies, or they can be truth. Thoughts reveal intention. Please think your thoughts to me. I will hear them, and I will see them, just as you will hear and see mine."

Kara struggled to form a thought. One single thought, but her brain locked up.

Kara heard Ayita break through the static of her brain as she spoke.

"StrallVoss, why did you want to meet us? Are you truly here or are you projecting an image of yourself? It seems to me that you shimmer, and although your image is clear, it does not appear to be solidly formed."

For a moment, StrallVoss's form became wavy, then steady. "Part of me is here, and part of me is projected. I will try to be clear to you. Think of me as one of your movie actors who is currently being interviewed on a TV or an internet program.

During the interview, behind me are two separate TV screens where I am also being projected. I can be in more than one place. Is that clear for you both?"

Ayita nodded. "Somewhat. So, you are here at the same time you can appear in other worlds?"

"Think of me as an avatar, who can take form in three separate video games simultaneously. I'll conclude by saying we are all entities of many parts. You will know this truth from your dreams, which is a separate world from your so-called 'waking' world. But that dream world is real to you at the time you are dreaming. Is this not so? If you are consciously aware in those dreams—something you call lucid dreaming—then you can be actively aware in those two worlds at once. Is that clear?"

"Where are you from?" Kara blurted out in her mind, her voice quiet, her lips not moving.

"Your thought question is clear, Kara Gonne. For our purpose here, it is not important for you to know where I am from."

"Was it one of your spacecraft who captured Sally Mason and sent her into the future?" Kara asked, mentally.

Ayita had wanted to lead the conversation and not ask direct questions, but somehow StrallVoss allowed Kara's mind to communicate telepathically.

StrallVoss's aura shifted from blue to a mint green. "Your question will be answered."

CHAPTER 32

K ara lacked the experience to control her swirling thoughts, so words and images burst out of her head with no finesse. "StrallVoss, if part of you is projected, then why do you need a spacecraft? And how do those spacecraft travel such long distances?"

Ayita broke in. "StrallVoss, please pardon us for asking so many questions at once."

"I will answer Kara Gonne," StrallVoss said calmly. "And then I will speak about why I have come and why we are here. First, Kara Gonne, we, my 'species,' do not limit ourselves. We are an exploring race. We have spacecraft, as you call them, but some of us can also project. Our race does not exist all at the same level, just as your species does not. Not all 'people,' as you might say, are as advanced as others. Just as on your planet, in our world, there are also levels of skill, education, and knowledge. We explore in whatever mode, and at whatever level, we can explore. Some use craft, some do not. As to your second question, at your current level of knowledge, you will not understand the mechanics of our interstellar flight. Simply put, our flightcraft use contraction and expansion to travel the vast distances of what you call the universe."

"StrallVoss, why was Sally Mason transported from 1953 to 2023?" Kara asked.

Ayita said, "Was it one of your craft that sent Sally Mason into the future?"

With a graceful motion of his ethereal hand, StrallVoss indicated toward the ceiling of the hangar, and it suddenly melted away and, in its place, was the sky, glittering with billions of stars.

"In your year 1953, we had three flightcraft exploring your world for over a five-month period. Our craft have been to Earth many times, spanning thousands of years. Ayita Wells, you are not the first of your kind we have communicated with. We made friends thousands of years ago and have lived among tribes on two separate continents. In the past, we have offered advice to your kind, and your kind has offered advice to us. It is the best way to live, that is, to live in cooperation. It is evolution."

StrallVoss seemed to float closer to them, but his energy was calm and non-threatening. Kara took an instinctive step back, but Ayita held her ground, her hands at her sides.

"In 1953, one of our pilots observed the one you call Sally Mason. I will use words to describe him, although they are not entirely the way we think of these things. This pilot was a being of great strength and ability, and a being of compassion. We have the ability to view the future, but only the immediate future, because the future is not set. It is not deterministic or materialistic. It is based on choice and intention and focus. This pilot felt a pull toward Sally Mason. He had observed her for many days. It is not usual for us to feel this kind of pull."

Kara jumped in. "By pull, do you mean he was romantically attracted to her?"

"Those words are not words we use. We do not carry emotions like your people do. Is that clear? By pull, I mean, he could see her life played out before him on a viewer screen inside the craft. He saw her partner, who was often violent to her. He observed it was a life she believed had trapped her. She was living her life in sacrifice for her children. In our world and culture, sacrifice is highly prized, admired, and sought. That is, to surrender oneself for the sake of a higher purpose, for the good of another or for a group. This was one more reason our pilot felt a pull toward Sally Mason. When she was driving on that night road, our pilot saw her immediate future. Ahead, on that road, was a driver who was drunk. He was driving fast, and he was weaving over the center line of that road. Sally Mason was about to collide head-on with this drunken driver. Our pilot saw that Sally Mason would survive the accident, but she would never walk again, and her mind would be seriously impaired."

Ayita and Kara exchanged a glance of wonder.

StrallVoss continued. "Our pilot had but seconds to decide and act. At random, he engaged a time device that we developed only for emergencies, for training of our minds and our characters, and for what you would call religious and philosophical purposes. This time device is sacred, and it is never to be employed on any other being or race without the consent of our most esteemed and wise commanders. Without consent, our pilot activated the device. As I stated, no precise time was set, so the device was engaged at random, and Sally Mason was transported seventy years into your future."

Ayita shut her eyes, and Kara felt the hair on the back of her neck rise.

A long hanging moment later, StrallVoss said, "Our pilot was removed from his command, but because his intention was positive, he was deployed back to our world, where he has done penance for his choice. He is getting long on years now, and he will transition soon. I have spoken with him, and he is sincere in wishing Sally Mason a good new life."

Ayita opened her eyes and narrowed them on StrallVoss. "StrallVoss, if we tell Sally Mason the truth, and if she says she wants to return to 1953, do you have the ability to send her back? That is, with your device, can you set it for a minute or two before the accident occurs, so that when Sally returns, she can pull her car to the side of the road and wait for the drunk driver to pass?"

"It is forbidden, Ayita Wells, as you heard me state."

Kara said, "But surely, StrallVoss, you could correct the mistake, if that's what you want to call it. Do you understand that? If a mistake was made, then can't it be corrected?"

StrallVoss radiated a vibrant rippling orange, as if his energy had shifted. "Kara Gonne, time is, let us say, plastic. It is malleable, not so precise. A clock truly measures nothing, but only what is agreed upon by those watching it. Time shifts, and flows, according to person, event, and perception. Even if we could send Sally Mason back to 1953, and even if she knows the drunk driver is racing toward her, minutes could actually be seconds, or seconds could shift into minutes. And, in your world, time does not like to be manipulated. We have learned this after many years, and after many experiments. It is entirely possible that if we took Sally Mason back to 1953, the accident would occur nonetheless, and it is also possible that Sally Mason could be killed. Do you understand StrallVoss?"

Kara said, "But StrallVoss, if Sally knows what's going to happen to her, then she won't leave the house that night, and go to that night school course. She can stay home."

StrallVoss's aura transformed from orange to a royal purple. "Sally Mason must be sent back to the approximate time from whence she time traveled, and not earlier or later. Also, Sally will be confused, just as she was confused when she arrived in 2023. And if she is sent back in time, she will have only seconds to respond, and with a confused mind. As I have stated, time is not fixed. It is not predictable. Time is a play of seconds and minutes and years. And time can be long or it can be short, depending on one's choice, perception, or experience. Despite Sally Mason's having knowledge of the past, as I have said, she will be sent back to within seconds of the accident, with only seconds to respond."

Ayita looked at StrallVoss with deep meaning. "If Sally Mason agrees to the risk, would your commanders consider sending her back to 1953?"

StrallVoss's aura turned a lovely golden red. "It has not been done in my time, but this has happened before on your Earth, hundreds of years ago. But since that time, your world and its cultures have changed greatly. Many aspects of this issue must be considered."

"But it could be done?"

"Perhaps. For your information, I visited Sally Mason one night soon after her time travel journey. She did not seem as frightened, and I could feel her emotion, but we did not successfully communicate. Sally Mason is confused and predictably distraught. So I do understand your concern for her."

Kara said, "We may choose against Sally returning, StrallVoss, but it would be useful to know your decision, so that we have the option."

Ayita's gaze was troubled. She didn't like Kara's choice of words, that they might choose against Sally returning.

StrallVoss's color faded into vibrant yellow and then into a shimmering white.

"I will propose this issue to my superiors. But first, I must meet Sally Mason and receive her consent to this time travel reversal."

A shadow crossed Ayita's face.

StrallVoss continued. "She must be made aware that by returning to 1953, she might avoid the accident, or she might not avoid it, and she could become tragically infirmed. Her choice might even result in her death. Before I bring this issue to my superiors, I must speak to Sally Mason and gain her consent. Do you understand?"

CHAPTER 33

The two-story Florida beach house owned by Bert's brother was the color of sunbaked sand, and trimmed with sea-foam green and light blue accents. The front lawn had a green shine. Red hibiscus plants covered the front windows, and swaying palm trees were languid under the warm afternoon sun.

At the rear of the house, rugged wooden stairs led up to a deck, which offered grand views of a wide beach and infinite blue ocean. Sally Mason was reclined on a chaise under the baking sun, sunglasses glinting, her hair damp from a recent swim. Bert and she had gone to a nearby surf shop to buy her a one-piece aqua swimsuit, a floral pattern cover-up and some sunscreen.

Bert, dressed in his new Bermuda shorts, a straw hat and yellow t-shirt, exited the downstairs sliding doors, carrying two glasses of iced tea. He mounted the stairs and joined Sally on the upper deck, offering her a glass.

"You're an angel, Bert," she said, sitting up, accepting it. "I was just dreaming about a glass of iced tea. You must be a mind reader."

Bert stepped to a patio chair and eased down with a sigh, squinting up into the sun. "Well, who doesn't want a glass of iced tea on a hot Florida afternoon? But this coconut-smelling sunscreen makes me want a Piña Colada."

Sally took a long drink and gazed out at the sea, at the deep warm blue. "How is the painting going?"

"I've painted two watercolors, both sunsets. I can sell sunset paintings. Who doesn't love a good Florida sunset? How was your swim?"

"It was wonderful. It's so beautiful here. It's only been a little over a week, but it seems like months, and I'm feeling so relaxed."

"Good. Yes, it has been a wonderful little vacation. I haven't been here for five years, and Lynnie was with me the last time. It was sort of a winter family reunion."

Sally looked at him warmly. "You miss her every day, don't you?"

"Yes, I do. I hope I'm not boring you to death. I know I talk about her too much."

"You don't bore me at all. I wish I could say I missed my husband, but I don't. My kids, yes. I ache for them every day—for the kids they were— but I don't miss Ronnie. I feel guilty about it. A wife should miss her husband, shouldn't she, Bert?"

"I don't like the word 'should,' Sally. We are who we are. It's best to be authentic. I think you get more that way as you get older. You don't care what people think so much. So, Sally Mason, if you don't think of your husband, and if you don't miss him, then so be it. You'll get no judgement from me. From what you've said about him, he didn't sound so likeable, anyway."

Sally stared down at her glass. "I'm nervous. I

mean, I'm nervous about meeting your nephew."

"Nervous about Terry? Nah. Don't be. He's a nice guy. Always did live in his head too much, and work too much, but he's okay."

"Why did his wife divorce him?"

Bert glanced away. "Oh, I don't know. She was a pretty gal, all right, and smart. She's a lawyer and works for a good law firm, but I think Terry was always working, or thinking about work, or always talking about his work, and maybe she wanted more than that."

"Do they have kids?"

"A boy, Lance, and he's a fireplug of a kid. Rough and tumble and always on the go. Loves sports. He lives with his mother and his grandparents, and Terry sees him most weekends."

Bert checked his watch. "He'll be here any time now."

"And you didn't tell him everything?" Sally asked, gently wiping the perspiration from her upper lip.

"No, not everything. As I told you this morning, I said you were a friend, and you needed help that only his expertise could provide. I also told him you were pretty, and you have a good head on your thin shoulders. Now don't look at me like that. There's nothing wrong with telling a man he's going to meet a pretty, intelligent woman. It speeds things up and moves things along."

Sally set her glass of tea down on a plastic patio table. "Do you think they're still looking for me? The CIA, or whoever?"

Bert slapped away an insect. "Yes, I'm sure they are, but if we work fast enough, and if Terry is as smart as I think he is, in no time at all you'll slip away from them, begin your new life and that will be the end of it."

Sally's smile didn't reach her eyes. "I can't imagine what my life will be. I wake up every day, and I look around and I don't know where I am or who I am."

"You will. You've had a shock. You've had a shock that no one else on this Earth, as far as we know, has ever had. So, be patient with yourself, and we'll get it all worked out."

When the sun drifted behind a cloud, Sally watched blue shadows shimmer across the sea and a flock of pelicans wing across the tideline.

"I thank God for you, Bert. Who knows where I'd be if you hadn't come along?"

"Yeah, well, where would *I* be? Back home alone in Indiana, painting some boring vase of autumn flowers and munching on a Pop Tart, wishing I was in Florida with a pretty girl like you."

Sally laughed. "You always make me laugh."

They heard a voice calling from the lower patio. Bert set his glass down on the wooden deck, pushed up, and called out, "Terry! Is that you?"

Sally swallowed away nerves and stood up, hearing footsteps on the stairs.

Bert met Terry as he stepped onto the deck, and they gave each other a man hug. Terry wore brown khakis, a blue-and-white striped polo shirt, deck shoes, and aviator sunglasses.

The men turned to face Sally. She stood awkwardly, with a shy smile and damp brushed back hair. Her tanned pretty face and stunning figure took Terry by surprise, and he removed his sunglasses, his eyes taking her in fully.

Bert gestured toward her. "Terry Hansel, Sally Mason. Sally Mason, Terry Hansel, my favorite nephew."

Sally's eyes stuck to the man. Terry didn't fit the type she'd imagined—a skinny, serious egghead, with thinning hair. This man was tall, dark, and very good looking. In the jargon of her 1950s high school days, she would have called him "a dream."

Terry approached her, all smiles, and stretched out a hand. "Hello, Sally. It's a pleasure to meet you."

Sally took his big hand and smiled into his eyes, feeling a hot spasm of attraction shoot through her. "It's nice to meet you, Terry. Thank you for coming all the way from Chicago."

They didn't release their hands, and Bert noticed.

"I have some business in Miami, anyway, so it's sort of on the way."

"Sit down, Terry," Bert said, indicating to the chair next to his. "Right here under the umbrella, so that Chicago white skin of yours doesn't burn."

Terry released Sally's hand and joined Bert, sitting in a deck chair, while Sally eased back down on the chaise.

Terry kept his pleasing smile on Sally. "Wouldn't you like an umbrella to shield you from the sun, Sally?"

"No, thank you, Terry. I love the sun, and I tan easily."

"So, I see," Terry said. "You should do a commercial for Coppertone."

The compliment thrilled and embarrassed her, and she turned her face toward the sea. "Thank you... that's nice of you to say."

Bert rose and put his hands together. "All right, then. I'm going to leave the two of you to chat for a bit while I get back to my painting. Terry, can I get you a beer or iced tea or something?"

"No thanks, Bert. I had a late lunch. You go ahead."

When Bert was gone, Sally watched the waves climb the beach, and the afternoon sun warm the clouds with color. She was aware that her pulse was high from the sun, from the sparkling sea, and from Terry, the attraction between them heating her skin.

Sally couldn't recall the last time she'd felt the rushing, eager rhythms of desire. Her attraction to Ronnie, her sexual desire for him, had ceased soon after their marriage. That's when he'd begun to curse her and call her names; when he'd slapped her or slugged her for "mouthing back", and when he'd forced her to have sex after she'd tried to refuse. "It's a husband's right," he'd said.

Here and now, so far away from her 1953 life, so far away from Ronnie, who was dead, and so far away from the reality she'd known, she looked out at the sea and then back at Terry, and a strange hunger arose. For a few seconds, she allowed herself to slip away into a dreamscape of romantic haziness, her body suddenly ripe for the tender touch of a man, and for the soft kiss of a man.

Terry brought her out of her daydream. "Sally, Bert tells me you need a new identity, but he didn't say why. As I'm sure you know, it's very unusual that you don't have a digital footprint anywhere. I did a name search, and you didn't appear on any database I have access to, governmental or otherwise. I admit, I'm baffled. Have you been involved in some underworld activities? Do you have a Mafia boyfriend out looking for you?"

"Oh, my heavens, no, nothing like that."

Terry's eyes showed relief. "Cool. Very cool." He squinted at the sun. "It's a little hot out here. Do you mind if we go inside to have our chat? I think I might have that beer after all."

Fifteen minutes later, Sally and Terry were in the living room, with expansive windows offering views of the sea, and comfortable contemporary sofas and chairs that encircled a sleek fireplace. A portable bar with four barstools occupied a corner, under a large flat-screen TV, and the gentle hum of an air-conditioner kept the room cool and comfortable.

Sally had changed into capris and a pink top, and was barefoot, sitting on one of the sofas. Terry stood near the dormant fireplace, holding a bottle of beer by the neck.

"Bert said you were married," Terry said.

"I was… Not now."

"I suppose he told you I'm divorced?"

"Yes."

Terry looked out the windows, but his gaze kept straying back to Sally, and the slightest indication of a smile passed over his face. "You're not what I expected."

Sally shifted her legs and folded her knees beneath her, surprised by how comfortable she felt with Terry. "I hope you're not disappointed."

"No, I'm not. Not at all. You are a mystery, though. Why is it that you don't seem to exist, at least in the digital identity world?"

Sally had decided to be blunt, but she was changing her mind. What if her truth drove Terry away? Did she care? Yes, she did. Terry Hansel attracted her physically, and, after all, she was only twenty-seven-years old, and she had the wants and the needs of a woman her age. And she was single, wasn't she?

Bert entered the room quietly, neither Terry nor Sally noticing his entry. He said, "Sally is from another time, Terry."

Terry shot him a look, annoyed by the interruption. "What did you say?"

Sally grabbed a bracing breath. "Bert's right, Terry. I'm from 1953. A spaceship abducted me in my car and transported me seventy years into the future. That's why I don't exist on any of your databases."

Terry stared at Sally, and then his gaze shifted to Bert, then back to Sally. He searched for a joke. He waited for one or both to laugh. They didn't.

Sally shrugged. "I'm sorry, Terry, but there's no other way to say it. I don't know why it happened, but it did. I time traveled."

CHAPTER 34

T erry sat slumped in a chair, staring down at the hardwood floor, his beer bottle empty, his eyes empty. Sally was standing at the window, gazing out at the sea, and Bert sat in a chair opposite Terry.

It had taken nearly a half hour for Sally to tell her story, including her hospital stay, her sessions with Dr. Meg Stanley, and her escape with the orderly.

"Terry," Bert said, "can you help Sally? Can you integrate her identity into 2023?"

Terry slowly lifted his head, staring at Sally's back with a perplexed curiosity. "I don't know if I believe all this or not. It's the craziest thing I've ever heard and I've heard some pretty crazy stuff."

Sally didn't turn to him. "If I wasn't here, I wouldn't believe it either."

Bert spoke up, waving his hand dismissively. "Well, I believe her. What else explains why she doesn't exist on any database, and what does Sally have to gain by making up the story? Nothing. She's not looking for money or notoriety. So, can you help her, Terry?"

Terry heaved out a sigh. "She'd have to take a new name, and we'd have to come up with a fake birth certificate. I don't know, maybe we can pay off some doctor who'll say he delivered her at home. And then we'll have to apply for a Social

Security number or use Sally's old one. I'm certain her own Social Security number was purged from the system long ago, and we'll have to hope it hasn't been assigned to anyone else. We'll also have to create an online history, including social media profiles, email accounts, and any other digital traces that would support Sally's new identity. And then I'll have to put together a convincing backstory, including a family history, educational background, work experience and social interactions consistent with Sally's age."

Sally turned, her expression hopeful. "Can you do all that, Terry?"

Bert leaned forward, eager for Terry's answer.

Terry rose, his hard eyes boring into her. "You've told me the truth? All the truth? I mean, this isn't some kind of hallucination or mental illness, or drug-induced belief?"

Bert said, "No, Terry. I've just told you..."

Terry threw up a hand to stop him. "... Let Sally speak, Bert. I want her to swear to me. I want to see the truth of it in her eyes, because this will not be easy, not to mention illegal. I could get into a lot of trouble, especially if the CIA is after you. And after I've managed the initial input, I would need to monitor your new identity over time, making adjustments and adding new information to maintain a realistic and consistent portrayal. I'd have to stay alert against potential detection by people who might question Sally's identity. Any discrepancies would have to be promptly addressed and rectified. So, Sally, are you telling me the truth?"

Sally kept her gaze steady on him. "Yes, it's true, Terry. Everything I said is true. I swear it."

A moment later, Sally saw him change. There was a dark delight in his eyes, and the wary concern was gone.

"Okay, then. I can help you, Sally, and I will help you."

Bert noticed Terry seemed excited by the sudden challenge. He stood. "So Terry, now you're completely convinced? I mean, just like that? Not the least bit skeptical or concerned about the legal consequences?"

Terry scratched his cheek, a sudden enlightening thought passing across his face. "The CIA will find you, Sally, no matter what we do."

Sally's face fell. Bert took a step forward.

"They will. No doubt. Your ordeal, or whatever you want to call it, is too extraordinary for them not to find you."

Bert pinched the bridge of his nose. "Then what is the point of giving Sally a new identity? I don't get it."

Sally waited, the moment unstable and scary.

Terry took a few steps toward Sally. "Your story is crazy, Sally. I mean, it is really batshit crazy, so I'm going to propose something just as batshit crazy that may save you when the CIA finally catches up to you."

Bert and Sally traded a glance.

"Are you ready? Here goes. Marry me."

Bert's eyes went wide. Sally blinked slowly, twice.

"Now, before you both freak out on me, hear me out. If we're married, Sally, it's going to make everything easier. Your identity will be easier to build, and I will make sure that all my friends, employees and colleagues know that you and I have had a secret relationship for some time, and we finally decided to make it legal. It's modern, it's sexy and, more important, I will splash it all over social media, along with your new history. If any government agency comes for you, I'll have my lawyers go after them, threatening to expose anything and everything."

Bert collapsed into the nearest chair, unable to speak.

Sally knew she should be stunned, and part of her *was* stunned, but oddly, Terry's idea didn't frighten her. It soothed the horror that had bloomed in her chest.

Terry continued. "Once we're married, we can take our time. That is, I wouldn't expect anything of you sexually unless the relationship naturally moved in that direction. In all honesty, I hope it *will* move in that direction, but we've only just met, and we know nothing about each other. Let me also add that I'm a wealthy man, and you'll not want for anything, Sally. I have three homes and, if you wish, you can choose to live in one of the homes without me... until we decide we want our marriage to become an intimate marriage."

Bert frowned fiercely. "I don't know about this,

Terry. I don't. I just don't know. It just seems so…"

"Implausible and crazy?" Terry said. "Yes, but isn't Sally's entire situation, let's say, out of this world?"

Bert and Terry looked at Sally. She was still, her head down, her hands at her sides. There was something about the idea that ignited Sally's imagination. She would have money. She would be able to go to college. She might even fall in love with Terry. Why shouldn't she fall in love with him? He was rich, smart, and good looking. It seemed like a possible solution, but only if he was as kind as he seemed.

Bert spoke softly. "Well, Sally? What are your thoughts?"

"I don't know. My head's spinning and it's been spinning for days. I need time. I need time to think and try to figure things out."

Terry's voice was mild. "I understand, Sally, but, unfortunately, there isn't much time, 'time' being the word of the hour. Once the CIA finds you, I don't know what they'll do, but I don't think you'll have much choice about whatever it is they decide. To put this in practical terms, you are a much-wanted commodity."

Sally moved to the sofa and sat, pensive. A minute later, she said, "With all your computer machines, Terry, can you find out what happened to my kids? I mean, can you find out if they had happy or sad lives? Can you tell me if, when I vanished in 1953, their lives were negatively affected, I mean in the long term?"

Terry trained his eyes on her. "I don't know, Sally, but I can try. I'll call some people who work for me, people I trust, and I'll see what I can do."

Sally smiled with gratitude. "Thank you, Terry. Thank you for everything. You may have just given me a new life."

Terry responded with a nod and a charming smile.

Bert pushed himself to his feet. "For fear of sounding like an old matchmaker, Terry, why don't you take Sally out to a nice restaurant so you can get to know each other a little better?"

Terry held his smile. "I'd love to. Sally?"

She smiled her answer. "I'd like that."

Later, after Terry and Sally had dressed and left for dinner, Bert paced the living room, eventually ending up in the kitchen. He microwaved a macaroni and cheese frozen dinner, grinning with boyish pleasure. From the fridge, he pulled a couple of leaves from a head of romaine lettuce, rinsed and tossed them onto a salad plate, along with some bottled vinaigrette, sat at the wooden table in one of the six chairs and set his plate of food before him, feeling like an old king. He ate pensively—and then he began to worry.

Had he done the right thing in sharing Sally's predicament with Terry? He loved his nephew, but Terry had not been faithful to his wife, and that had been the primary reason for the divorce. Bert hadn't shared that detail with Sally.

In college, Terry had been a playboy, and he'd

been proud of it. Bert wondered how many women employees or women clients he was dating, and if he'd broken off the relationship that had ended his marriage. Bert licked his lower lip. He should have told Sally that, but then he didn't think the two of them would take to each other so fast.

And then there was the issue of the CIA. Bert had never been a conspiracy theorist or revolutionary, but he had his opinions and beliefs about secret government agencies. He'd been a teacher for many years, and he had first-hand experience of an administrative bureaucracy and the secrets within it. He'd been a part of it. He'd had to be in order to keep his job and his pension. And within that small-town public-school bureaucracy, the left hand seldom, if ever, knew what the right hand was doing.

And then there were loose lips and gossip, and someone always wanted all the control and power, and they'd fight to get it. Surely, secret government agencies were no different. Human beings were human beings.

So, where did that leave Sally? As Bert nibbled on his lettuce, reminding himself of a big rabbit, he considered piling Sally back into his car and making a run for it. Terry might help her, but then, when another woman caught his fancy—if he followed his predictable pattern—he might leave Sally to fend for herself.

If the CIA grabbed her, Bert knew he'd never see Sally again, and he'd never know what happened to her. Could he abide that? No. He cared for Sally, and he needed and wanted someone to care for. He'd protect her and treat her as if she were his own daughter. She needed him. She trusted him. She liked him. Sally had told him so, and it felt so good to be needed again. He was sick and tired of living alone. He wasn't built for it.

Bert finished his dinner, got up, opened the fridge, and grabbed a can of ginger ale. He popped the tab and swallowed a drink. A decision was hanging in the air, and he'd have to make a choice, and he'd have to do it soon.

CHAPTER 35

J on Tanner, at the young age of thirty, was a gifted intelligence prodigy serving as a CIA agent. From an early age, his sharp mind and keen curiosity had set him apart from his two brothers and his classmates. He attended Vanderbilt University, where he majored in computer science, sharpening his technical skills and problem-solving abilities.

During his college years, Jon's exceptional talents were noticed by the CIA, and they approached him with an offer he couldn't resist. Fascinated by the prospect of working on classified missions and having a real impact on national security, Jon accepted the offer, and, after graduation, he embarked on a clandestine career.

Jon's journey within the CIA had been striking, due to his natural ability to decipher complex patterns and connect disparate data points. His easy and bright personality earned him accolades among his colleagues, and despite being relatively new to the agency, his track record was impressive.

Seated behind his desk at the Central Intelligence Agency in Langley, Virginia, Jon sat bolt upright when a call popped up on his secure cellphone. It was from the one-and-only Kara Gonne, a superstar within the agency. With a curt introduction, she told him what she wanted.

"It's old gumshoe work in a small Indiana town, hitting the pavement and flashing a photo of a woman to businesses, restaurants, and other targets we've identified. Two agents have already searched, and they've found nothing. There's no glamour. There's no computer analysis. There's no excitement. It will be a down-and-dirty Philip Marlowe kind of job. You do know who Philip Marlowe was, don't you, Jon?"

"Yes, ma'am. I was reading Raymond Chandler and Dashiell Hammett when I was ten years old, and breaking into houses when I was twelve, pretending to be Sam Spade."

Jon heard Kara chuckle. "Then I've got the right man, don't I, Agent Tanner?"

"Yes, ma'am. I'm a down-and-dirty kind of guy."

"You'll be the only one on the job, Jon. The other agents have been pulled."

"That's okay with me. I'll get new insoles for my best shoes and have them resoled. Should I start smoking, to be authentic?"

"Get some Tootsie Roll Pops. I used to love them."

"Okay, ma'am. I'll be looking for the file."

"You're a champ, Jon. And expense yourself a trench coat and fedora. I'll okay it."

Jon Tanner drove his rental car from Indianapolis to Rosemont, Indiana on November 2, and booked a room at the Holiday Inn Express. Snow flurries drifted, an icy wind cut like a knife, and Jon thought the town looked gloomy, the perfect atmosphere for his retro detective role.

The mission's top-secret nature intrigued him, and he couldn't shake the feeling that there was more to the story than the usual covert action and counterintelligence. And what was Sally's story? Why was she so special? Didn't the agency perform open-source intelligence—gather information on her from publicly available sources, such as newspapers, websites, and social media?

The lack of concrete information available on Sally Mason only fueled Jon's growing curiosity. Despite what Kara Gonne had said, he was going to find his assignment exciting. He felt a sense of pride in being chosen for the job, and he was determined to prove himself worthy. He would tirelessly chase down leads and follow any hint, no matter how small. If Kara Gonne had chosen him, then this was an opportunity to showcase his brilliance and find Sally Mason.

Jon began his quest by dressing in casual jeans, a sweatshirt, sneakers, and a faded brown parka. He was on the short side, with a square face, dark hair and brown eyes. He wore a navy blue ski cap, practiced a stoop and a boyish grin, hoping to look disarming and yet not stupid.

He went to a couple of bars and talked to the bartenders, one male and one female. Sitting hunched on a barstool, looking unassuming and shy, he started a conversation about the holidays and his family. Then he brought out his cellphone and tapped the photo of Sally. "She's my sister, and she's missing. I've got to find her before the family meets for Thanksgiving. Have you seen her?"

No luck. No one had seen her.

Jon visited two hair salons, a pharmacy, a pizza shop, and a diner, holding up Sally's photo to store clerks, waiters, hostesses, and hairdressers. He got the same response from all—a head-shake, or a "Sorry," or "I've never seen her. Hope you find her."

At night in his hotel room, Jon soaked in the tub, his body tired, his feet aching. How could a small town seem like such a large one? He ordered room service and was asleep by ten o'clock.

On the fifth day, in the evening, Kara called Jon when he was sprawled on his bed, watching TV. He grabbed his phone on the second ring.

"Agent Gonne," Jon said.

"Agent Tanner, I got your report a couple of hours ago."

Jon sat up, grabbed the remote, and shut off the TV. "I'm still at it."

"I was intrigued by the nurse you met in Starbucks."

"Yeah, well, we were just standing there waiting to order, and she dropped her cellphone. I picked it up and handed it to her. She says to me, 'Thank you,' and then she says, 'You look a little like an old boyfriend.'"

"Was she attractive?" Kara asked.

"Well, yes, she was."

"Did you get her number?" Kara asked, lightly.

"No, but I got her name. Nurse Tiffany Hill. I told

her my sad story about Thanksgiving Day coming, and then I jumped into my spiel about how I was looking for my lost sister."

"Dedicated you are, Agent Tanner. Surely, you got her phone number."

"Is that why you called?" Jon asked, with a small laugh.

"It helps break the monotony, doesn't it? Anyway, keep me posted, Agent Tanner. I called because it's good news that the nurse recognized Sally from the hospital. That's progress, and I wanted to congratulate you. I also called to tell you to stay away from the hospital."

"I will. Nurse Hill suggested I go to the police. I told her I would, then I got my coffee and fled like a thief."

"One more comment," Kara said. "The fact that you haven't been successful could mean Sally is long gone. We've still got people in Fort Pierce and St. Louis, but it's curious Sally hasn't turned up in either place, given her determination to do so."

"Do you think she might be dead?"

"It's possible, but I don't think so. More likely, someone is advising her not to show herself. Give it two more days and then return. Interestingly, we recently ran a facial recognition search on Sally and found a match. We're tracing the source and, whoever it is, they are pros. Someone is in the process of building Sally Mason a new identity."

Jon blurted it out. "Who is Sally Mason? I mean, truly?"

Kara deflected the question. "Have you been wearing that trench coat?"

"Too cold here for that."

"I'll be in touch, Agent Tanner. Goodnight."

CHAPTER 36

The following evening, Jon was cold, discouraged, and hungry. He turned into a mall and parked in the crowded lot near Chili's. He pushed through the front door and entered, moving beyond the loud bar to a side table set for two. Shaking off the frosty night, he removed his hat and parka, placed them on the chair opposite and sat.

An energetic, pink-haired female server appeared, pumped up on adrenaline and three cups of coffee.

"Hey, I'm Molly. How are you? Something to drink?"

"Yeah, sure," Jon said, studying the little curling snake tattoo on the side of her neck. "Any IPA on draft?"

"Got three."

"You choose."

"What if you don't like it? Then you'll hate me and give me a bad review on *Yelp*."

"I won't. Promise."

"Flying Solo?"

"Yep. Nobody likes me. Even in school. Nobody ever liked me or wanted to play with me."

Molly narrowed her amused eyes on him. "No, I mean the IPA. It's called Flying Solo."

"Oh... Well. Okay. I'll take it."

Molly's smile and twinkling eyes held flirtation. "I'll be back with your beer."

Jon studied the menu, thinking that Molly was quite attractive. She had a smart, sassy quality he liked.

Minutes later, Molly seemed to slide back to Jon's table, a frosty mug of beer on a tray. She set it down before him on the tabletop and then stepped back. "Okay. Go ahead. Try it. See if you like it."

Jon did so. He swallowed dramatically, then made a sour face. "That's awful. The worst beer I've ever tasted."

Molly made a face, swung out a hip and placed a hand on it. "You're a real funny guy, aren't you?"

"I'm crazy about that tattoo," Jon said, pointing.

"I got it because some guy dared me. He said he'd give me two hundred bucks, and he'd pay for the tattoo."

"Obviously you did. Did he?"

"Yep."

"Good for you."

Molly turned, and patted her butt. "Then I got another one just like it on my ass."

"Right or left cheek?"

"Right. I'm left-handed."

"I guess I don't know what that means."

"It means I made four hundred bucks, and it paid most of my rent. So, what can I get you? And don't ask me to choose."

Jon looked up from his menu. He liked Molly. She wasn't a beauty, but she was feisty, direct, and attractive. "Hey, what if I ask you out after your shift?"

"You said nobody likes you," Molly said. "Maybe I don't like you."

Jon offered an exaggerated smile. "I've got good teeth," he said, talking through his teeth. "Had braces for two years. Surely that gives me some points."

Molly crossed her arms and grinned, entertained and interested. "Yeah, okay, I'll go out with you. I like your eyes and your teeth. Maybe I like your smart-ass face. What do you do?"

"You won't believe me."

"You're right, I won't."

"I'm a private detective."

Molly lowered her arms, considering him anew. "Actually, I do believe you."

"Really?" Jon asked, surprised. "You believe me?"

"Sure. Why not? I bet you're looking for somebody, aren't you? Who is it?"

That set Jon back, and his eyes widened on her. "Actually, I *am* looking for someone."

She snapped a finger. "I knew it. I've got a feel for this kind of thing. Got a picture? Hurry, I've got three tables, and they're all giving me vicious looks."

Jon yanked his phone from his pocket, found Sally's photo, tapped it, and held it up. "Have you ever seen her?"

Molly took the phone, studied the photo, expanded it with two fingers, nosed in for a closer look, and jerked a nod. She handed the phone back to Jon, and with a confident stare she said, "Yeah, I've seen her. Here."

Jon blinked and gulped in a breath, as if he'd been under water and had just come up for air. "Are you kidding me? You've seen her? Here?"

"Yeah. I've seen her. Look, I've gotta go…"

"No wait. Please wait. What's her name?" Jon asked. "Do you know her name?"

"No idea. She came in with a regular, an older dude named Bert August. He's an artist. Gives classes somewhere in town and online."

Jon shot to his feet, and Molly stepped back, startled. "What the hell?"

"Do you know where Bert August lives?"

"No."

Jon fished for his wallet, found a twenty, and slapped it down onto the table. Without another word, he grabbed his coat and hat and dashed off, Molly watching him go.

She crossed her arms and shook her head. "A nut job."

She shouted after him, "Come on back, nut job. I'll be waiting."

Outside, Jon made a secure call to Kara Gonne. When she answered, he steadied his voice and went into his professional mode. "Agent Gonne, a waitress recognized Sally Mason. She came into Chili's Restaurant with a local man who teaches art. His name is Bert August."

Kara's voice rose with delight. "Agent Tanner, I knew you were the right man for the job. I'll be in touch."

CHAPTER 37

Bert reversed the car out of the driveway of his brother's Florida residence. On the lawn, Terry Hansel, hands on hips and with frosty eyes, didn't offer a wave. As Sally sat slumped in despair, Bert swung the car around and drove off down the quiet suburban street.

"I just couldn't do it, Bert. I'm so sorry," Sally said, for what seemed like the hundredth time.

"I said it's all right, Sally," Bert said, relieved. "So, you couldn't go through with it. Good. It's okay. Now you're moving on to something else."

Both were silent until Bert turned onto I-95 South, heading for Fort Pierce, under a bright morning sun. Neither was aware that they were being followed by a blue and white SUV.

Sally lifted her head, still sitting low in the seat. "It's just that I still feel married to Ronnie, as silly as that sounds, and everything was way too hurried. Once I really thought about it, it seemed silly to get married so fast like that. I don't know Terry, and he doesn't know me. And what if everything didn't work out? I wouldn't know what to do."

"And you're right, Sally. Absolutely right. I didn't like it from the beginning. In his own way, Terry is a very aggressive guy, Sally. That's what's made him successful and rich, and he's used to getting his own way. So, he got upset, but he had no reason to shout at you like he did. That was uncalled for, and I told him so in his face."

"I tried to explain it to him."

"And you did explain it to him. I love the guy, but he was always stubborn and not so easy to get along with. Maybe that's good for running a company, but not so good with personal relationships. He shouldn't have called you a silly airhead. That wasn't nice or respectful."

Sally looked at Bert. "Do you think he'll call the police... the CIA?"

"I don't think so, but frankly, I don't know. Hindsight is always pointless, but I shouldn't have called him. I just thought he'd help us, and it was the only thing I could think of at the time."

Sally moved her hand up to her cheek. "Well, I guess it doesn't matter anymore, since I'm going to see Don. They'll pick me up, won't they?"

Bert glanced at her. "Yes, Sally, but we talked about this at breakfast."

"I know, Bert. I'm sorry I keep jabbering on about it, but I've got to see Don. I have to see my son, no matter what happens to me."

"I understand, Sally, but I wish you'd wait a little longer. Maybe in time those CIA people will give up and think you're dead, or maybe I can come up with a plan. I had a thought that maybe I can contact Don and tell him to meet you somewhere."

"They'd just follow him, wouldn't they?" Sally asked.

Bert nodded in resigned agreement. "Yeah, you're

right, of course. They surely would. For all we know, they're already following us," Bert said, glancing into his rearview mirror. "And I'm not so good at sneaking around and being devious. I wish Lynnie was here. She could be devious *and* secretive... well, you know, in a good sort of way."

Sally stared in doleful meditation for long minutes. "It was that report, Bert, that changed my mind. That report that Terry gave me about my kids."

"I know, Sally. I saw your expression while you read it. Can you talk about it now, or would you rather not?"

"It hurts, that's all. It just makes me want to scream at something. I don't know what."

"So scream away. Nobody will hear you but me, and I can take it."

Sally shook her head. "I keep seeing them as kids. And then to think that after I vanished, Don turned angry, and Mary wouldn't talk. When Don grew older, he blamed Ronnie for what had happened to me. In the court record, he even accused Ronnie of killing me and hiding my body. He didn't do well in high school, and he was expelled a couple of times. As soon as he graduated, he joined the Marines."

Bert glanced at his phone's GPS app and then back at the road, waiting for Sally to continue. "How long did your son serve?"

"He was in Vietnam for nine months, was wounded in the arm and leg, and spent two months in a V.A. hospital. I don't remember how long he served, but he got a medical discharge and moved to Maine and eventually opened a hardware store. He married and divorced twice. One of those court documents said he was volatile and had anger issues. Can you believe it? Don was such a sweet kid, Bert. And now he lives in Fort Pierce with his third wife."

Bert glanced over and saw the tender sadness in Sally's eyes. "And what about your daughter?"

"She saw a child psychologist until she was a teenager. I suspect that wasn't Ronnie's idea, but probably his mother's. When Mary was twenty, she tried to commit suicide. She took pills, but I don't remember what they were. Her roommate in college found her and saved her life. According to the marriage license, she married when she was thirty-one, to a plumber, and they had two kids, and they stayed married until he died in 2018. From the report, I couldn't tell whether she was happy. I think I told you she has Alzheimer's."

Bert made an empty gesture with a hand. "Yes, and I'm so sorry."

Sally turned to face Bert, her eyes damp with tears. "I could have made a difference in their lives, Bert. We were so close, and I loved them so much."

"Well, whatever happens in Fort Pierce, I'm here for you, Sally, and I'll help you any way I can."

"Thank you. You're the only friend I have in the world, and that's the truth, isn't it?"

Bert's gaze stayed on the road. "Sally, I keep wondering why it happened. Why did that alien spaceship send you into the future? Do you have any idea?"

"No, I don't, but after I see Don, I don't care what happens to me. If they want to lock me up because I'm some kind of threat to the country, then so be it. I won't run anymore, and I'm so nervous about seeing Don that my stomach feels like it's filled with a hundred fluttering butterflies. I can't think straight about anything."

"We'll be there soon. About another thirty miles."

Thirty minutes later, Bert arrived at the entrance of Ocean Haven, a retirement complex that offered one-level condos surrounded by palm trees, magnolias, bougainvillea, and hibiscus. Bert turned the car into an entry driveway, and stopped at the white barrier gate, where a burly security guard emerged from a security booth. "Can I help you?"

Bert said, "We're here to see Donald Mason at 325 Sunrise Lane."

"Is he expecting you?"

Bert hesitated. "No... But we're family."

"I'll have to call him. What's the name?"

"Tell him it's Bert August."

Sally began to sweat.

A minute later, the security guard reappeared. "Mr. Mason said he doesn't know you."

Frustrated, Sally leaned toward Bert's window and said, "Tell him I knew his father, Ronnie."

"What's your name?"

"Sally."

Endless minutes later, the security guard stepped

out of the booth and pointed to the main road. "Turn left at the second street. It's four doors down."

Bert thanked him. The security gate rose, and the car moved past a manmade pond, which featured a gushing fountain in the center and a solitary gliding swan. Following the guard's instructions, Bert parked the car curbside at Don Mason's condominium.

Sally stared at her son's condo with momentary uncertainty. "What's he going to say, Bert... when he sees me?"

"Only one way to find out, kid. Do you want me to go with you?"

"No."

Bert glanced into his rearview mirror, then cast his eyes about. "I don't see anything suspicious. Could it be Don's condo isn't being watched?"

Sally finger-combed her hair and straightened her sky-blue blouse. "How do I look?"

"Beautiful. Casual, but stylish. Those jeans look terrific on you."

Sally heaved in a big breath and blew it out the open window. "Okay, here I go."

She pushed open the door and climbed out, feeling the warm sun on her face. She closed the door, and it sounded loud in her ears, like the end of something; like the beginning of something.

Her stomach growled, and she realized she hadn't eaten since breakfast, when she'd only had toast and coffee.

Feeling fragile and hopeful, she moved up the

walkway, stepped up to the white door, and hesitated before pressing the doorbell. She heard a faint "ding dong," and her chest tightened in anticipation.

The door opened and a round-shouldered man, with thinning gray hair, a wrinkled sunburned face, and wary eyes, looked back at her.

Sally's heart stopped. She stopped breathing. She stopped thinking.

"Yes?" he asked with contemptuous indifference.

It was the eyes that she recognized. Not the face. Not the posture. Not the expression.

Sally swallowed and tried to speak. She couldn't. The startling moment was strangling her.

"Who is it, Don?" a woman called from inside.

Don's voice rose. "Who are you? What do you want? You told the gate guard that you knew my father."

Sally stared into his hard, empty face, the face of a bitter old man. "Don't you recognize me, Don?"

He narrowed his eyes on her. "Recognize you? No, I don't recognize you. What do you want?"

Sally stammered out the only words that would come. "I'm... I'm...your..." and then her words fell away into a warm breeze.

Don broke in. "Look, I'm watching a football game, okay? Tell me what you want or I'm closing the door on you."

Sally straightened her back and stammered out the words. "I'm... I'm your mother, Don. I'm your mother, Sally Anne Mason."

Don's eyes flashed sudden anger, and when he spoke, his voice was harsh with a threat. "Look, young woman. I don't know what your scam is, but if you don't get out of here right now, I'm calling the cops on you. I've already been scammed twice this year, but you take the cake. You make yourself up to look like my mother? What the hell's the matter with you sick young people? My mother? YOU, my mother? She's been dead for seventy years. Now, get the hell out of here!"

The door slammed shut.

Sally stood in a kind of trance, feeling the life force drain from her. It took all her strength to walk back to the car. She sat, closed the door, and shut her eyes.

Bert looked at her, worried. "... Sally, are you all right? What happened?"

Sally spoke in a near whisper. "He didn't believe me."

Bert sighed and stared ahead, hearing the tears in her voice. "Yeah, well... who would?"

"Let's go, Bert. Let's go somewhere, anywhere. I don't care."

Bert started the car and drove away. He left the condo complex driving north, searching for signs to I-95 North. "We'll go back to Indiana, Sally. I have a little cabin near a lake. Lynnie and I used to go there in the summer and at Christmas. It's not so big, but it's comfortable, has a big stone fireplace, and you can rest and gather yourself until you decide what you want to do next. How does that sound?"

Sally didn't respond. Her eyes stayed closed, tears leaking, her shoulders trembling.

"You'll be okay," Bert said, in a gentle consoling voice. "You'll make it, kid."

She shook her head. "I just want to die, Bert. I'm so sorry, but I just want to die."

"You just need more time, that's all. You'll be fine. You'll be better than fine. I know you will."

Bert's attention was grabbed by the flashing blue lights of a police vehicle. He checked his right and left mirrors, and then his rearview mirror. "What the hell is this? Was I speeding?"

Sally's eyes opened in terror, and Bert pulled the car to the curb.

CHAPTER 38

"WAS I SPEEDING, OFFICER?" Bert asked, removing his glasses, and looking up at the cop, who had a lantern jaw and stern eyes.

"Seven miles over the speed limit, sir."

"Really?"

"Could you please show me your driver's license and registration?" the officer asked.

Bert opened the glove compartment to get the car registration and then handed it and his driver's license to the waiting policeman. As he did so, a dark SUV with tinted windows passed Bert's car and swerved to the curb in front of him.

Bert and Sally watched anxiously as the SUV passenger door opened and a tall man emerged, wearing sunglasses and casual clothes. He closed his door and waited until the police officer returned Bert's registration and driver's license.

The officer said, "Just a warning, sir. Please watch your speed when driving in Fort Pierce."

He returned to his patrol car as the 40s-something man from the SUV, with short, cropped hair, a hard, bony face, and an erect military bearing, approached Bert's open window.

"Good afternoon, sir. Good afternoon, ma'am. Can I please ask you both to step out of the car?"

"Why?" Bert asked, with some defiance.

From his pocket, the man produced an identity

badge displaying his badge number, photograph, and title: Detective Sheriff Alex Gilbert, City of Vero Beach.

"Are you arresting me?"

"No, sir. It's a request."

"What if I say no?

"Then I'll ask you again, respectfully."

"What's this about?"

"I'm not at liberty to say, sir."

"Then I'm not at liberty to get out of the car. And how do I know you are who you say you are, and that your ID is not a fake?"

Sally spoke up. "I'll get out of the car, sir."

Bert shot her a glance, grabbing her arm. "No. Don't."

Sally smiled sweetly at him. "It's time, Bert. It's okay. I'm ready."

She gently removed Bert's hand, opened the door, and stepped out, closing the door behind her. Bert shoved his door open and got out.

"Sally, wait."

Just then, a dark sedan drew up, veered right, and braked to a stop in front of the SUV. The passenger door swung open, and a trim woman appeared, wearing a blue business suit, with slicked-back dark hair and a determined expression. She started for Sally. When Bert moved to intervene, Detective Gilbert stepped in front of him, shaking his head. Gilbert was four inches taller than Bert, and fifty pounds heavier. Intimidated, Bert stepped back.

The woman came up to Sally with a smile and

an outstretched hand. "Hello, Mrs. Mason. I'm Kara Gonne, from the CIA. Perhaps Dr. Stanley mentioned me to you. I'm sorry for all this drama, but at least I can finally meet you."

The police car's sweeping blue light slowed traffic, and the chopping blades were loud as a helicopter swept over.

Kara looked at Detective Gilbert and gave him a nod. When he stepped to the side, Bert circled the front of his car and marched up to Kara. "What the hell's going on here?"

Kara held her smile. "Hello, Mr. August, or is it Mr. Hansel?"

Bert's eyes hardened as he looked at Sally. "You don't have to go with these people, Sally."

Kara said, "No, she doesn't."

That disarmed Bert. "She doesn't?"

"No," Kara said, looking at Sally. "But Sally, I can help you."

"How can you help me?" Sally asked. "I'm living in a nightmare."

Kara looked about. "I'd rather not discuss it here. Too much traffic, and too many people. What I have to say to you is complex and personal. But if you hear me out, I think you'll agree that you'll have more options to choose from than you do now. We can talk while we travel."

"Travel to where?" Bert asked.

Kara looked at him. "Mr. Hansel, obviously you care for Sally, but can you really help her? Can you offer her any kind of future?"

"Sally can choose that for herself."

Sally's eyes lowered. "I'm tired. I'm just so tired."

Kara said, "I understand, Sally. I can offer you help, rest, and protection, and, as I said, I can offer you options you may not have believed were possible."

Bert shook his head. "Don't do it, Sally."

Sally looked at him tenderly. "Bert, you've been so good to me, but I can't keep this up, and I can't keep leaning on you."

"You *can* lean on me. You can start a new life. I'll help you. You know that. I will."

"Time's running out, Sally," Kara said. "You have to decide."

Overhead, storm clouds were gathering for a sudden and fierce Florida rain storm. Thunder rumbled.

Sally took three steps to Bert and embraced him, and he folded her into his arms.

"Okay, Sally Mason," Bert said, his eyes misting up. "All right. You go ahead, if that's what you want to do, but know that if things don't work out, you have an old codger of a friend and a home to come back to."

Sally drew back and kissed him on both cheeks. "I love you, Bert, and I'll never forget you."

Bert's mouth trembled. "Okay, kid. Please let me know how you are and what you decide."

Sally nodded, and then she reached into her purse, drew out an envelope and handed it to him.

"What's this?" Bert asked, accepting it.

"Just a little thank you note, Bert."

Sally turned, followed Kara to the sedan and climbed inside, as a burst of wind brought the first drops of rain.

Bert sat in his car, with his windshield wipers swiping the glass clear, watching with blurry damp eyes as the dark sedan's red taillights faded into the falling silver rain.

He said to himself, "Well, Sally, this is how we first met, wasn't it? In a rainstorm."

Bert looked down at the envelope in his hand, his name written on it in beautiful script. With his thumb, he slid open the sealed flap, removed the handwritten page and read.

Dear Bert,

When I was a girl, I wasn't very close to my father or my grandfather. They were not unloving men, but back then, men weren't so open about their feelings. I had a high school teacher who used to say that "all things happen for a reason," and "there's good and bad in everything," and "we should always try to look on the bright side of things."

I have tried to do that during the last few weeks. I just want you to know, Bert, that you have been the kindest man I have ever met, and I will never forget that kindness, humor, and generosity. You were the good amidst the bad, and you were like a bright sun shining when darkness surrounded me. I don't know what the future holds, but I'm pretty sure that we will soon be separated forever.

Please know that I love you with all my heart, and I will think of you fondly whenever I look up into the night sky and see all those twinkling stars. I'll think of you, Bert, and remember you. I'll think, "Bert August, the artist, came from one of those stars." And then, I'll thank God for sending you to me when I was lost and cold and wet, walking in a rainstorm. As my mother used to say whenever she met a good person, "They have angels whispering in their ears." Yes, Bert, you are my guardian angel.

Sending all my love to you,
Sally Anne Mason

CHAPTER 39

Sally was seated on the edge of a queen-sized bed in the spacious bedroom of a 3-room suite. Besides the comfortable living room, there was a kitchen/dining area stocked with breakfast food and snacks. Kara Gonne had told her she was living in a highly classified area somewhere in New Mexico. She'd also assured Sally that once the doctors had completed their physical and psychological examinations, she and Sally would convene with others to discuss Sally's options for the future.

Dressed in black slacks, a light green and white striped blouse, and low-heeled black pumps, Sally tied her hair back into a ponytail with a green scrunchie. The hairstyle made her feel young and confident, evoking memories of her high school days when she was a popular, exuberant cheerleader, and lots of boys asked her out—before she went steady with Ronnie.

As they had driven away from Bert and headed to the airport, Kara had tried to reassure her. "There's nothing to worry about, Sally. Please relax. Once we get to New Mexico, you'll have your own VIP suite, so you can rest. Clothes, makeup, and toiletries have been provided for you. Anything else you want or need, just let me know."

"And then what?" Sally asked.

"We'll conduct some tests and ask you some questions, and then we'll have a meeting to go over your options."

"Am I a prisoner?" Sally asked.

"No, you are definitely not a prisoner. We only want to protect you and gather information about what happened to you. You are very valuable to us."

"You mentioned something about options," Sally said.

"Yes, and we'll discuss those during our meeting."

Sally and Kara had flown on a private jet from a small airport in Florida to somewhere in New Mexico, and during the flight, Kara had said little. That was fine with Sally, who'd slept through most of the flight. It was dark when they arrived, and so Sally wasn't able to study the surrounding area.

Sitting on the bed, Sally reflected on her life in 1953. She couldn't shake the feeling that those times had been simpler and more relaxed compared to the fast-paced reality of 2023, with everyone constantly being pulled away from conversations by TV and cellphones and breaking news stories.

It seemed to Sally that modern technology distracted people, heightened their feelings of isolation, and hindered social interaction.

The advertising was aggressive and invasive, and it was everywhere, not just on TV, but also on cellphones and computers and blinking billboards. It was disruptive, loud, and relentless, like children shouting for attention.

Throughout her short journey from Indiana to

Florida, and during her time with Bert and Terry, she'd been unable to watch TV for more than thirty minutes at a time. All the noise and fast images gave her a headache.

Sally had also come to realize that virtually anything could be bought with a plastic card or, incredibly, with a cellphone. This scared her. Few people, if any, paid for anything with cash, and she couldn't imagine how anyone could keep track of it all.

And what had happened to the open fields? They had been overrun with big houses, sprawling condos, and tall, glass office buildings. The charming family-owned shops, the grocery stores, the shoe boutiques, the appliance stores, and the cozy restaurants had vanished, leaving behind chain store restaurants with cookie-cutter facades and bright plastic interiors. They reminded her of the artificially colored candy her mother put in holiday fruit cakes. Every car was a big block of a thing, one nearly indistinguishable from the other, and they went speeding along as if they were powered by rockets.

The trendy fashions showcased on internet sites seemed juvenile, and the hyped-up talk shows she'd watched on TV were shockingly vulgar. Her parents would have been horrified.

Sally concluded, with sadness and nostalgia, that her world back in 1953 was a kinder, simpler place, without super highways, super computers, and super heroes exploding across the super huge TV screens. Everything was called super in 2023, but she wasn't so sure.

Sally was certain that in 1953, the skies were bluer, the water and the food tasted better, and, with the ending of the Korean War in July 1953, the wars were mostly over. Despite the looming shadow of the atomic bomb, President Eisenhower assured the American people that the bomb would never be used again, and there was a rising optimism about the future of America and the world.

The modern world baffled and frightened her. She didn't feel emotionally, physically, or mentally attuned to it, and she was homesick for her time, her life and her kids in 1953. In an ironic twist, she felt like an extraterrestrial herself, as alien to this world as was the extraterrestrial who had propelled her into the future. Sally stood up from the bed and began to pace.

Over the past four days, she had undergone numerous physical examinations and psychological assessments, both written and verbal. Her interactions had been limited to female doctors, who were cordial but reserved.

Nearly every afternoon, Kara joined Sally for a short walk outside in a small, enclosed garden with high walls, and then they shared dinner in Sally's suite. Their conversations had remained superficial, with Kara inquiring about Sally's parents, friends, and education. Kara had never disclosed facts about herself, nor hinted about what was to come for Sally.

A knock on Sally's door turned her head toward it.

"Yes?"

"It's Kara."

Moments later, the two women strolled down a brightly illuminated, lengthy corridor. They descended a flight of steel grated stairs to a lower level, took a right turn towards a pair of gray doors, and proceeded down another hallway until they reached an additional unmarked gray door. A hidden security camera, equipped with face recognition technology, scanned Kara's face, and emitted a bleeping sound. The door eased open and, with a hand, Kara indicated inside. Sally entered first, and Kara followed.

The top-secret chamber lacked windows and wall decorations, and it held the scent of some lemon disinfectant. Sally's attention was drawn to a desk, a refreshment area, and a circular conference table.

Kara ushered Sally across the blue and gray tile floor, toward the table where Morgan Compton and Ayita Wells stood, waiting. After introductions, they all sat down, Sally squeezing her hands on her lap, Kara settling back into her chair, and Morgan sitting forward, intrigued and curious. Ayita's welcoming smile and calm demeanor helped to ease Sally's tension as the room settled into a cordial yet serious atmosphere.

Morgan straightened his blue and gold tie, adjusted his dark suit coat, and then folded his hands on the tabletop. "At long last, I am delighted to meet you, Mrs. Sally Mason."

CHAPTER 40

S ally sat stiffly as if she were in a court room, waiting to be sentenced for a crime.

Morgan chose his words carefully. "I hope you feel at ease, Mrs. Mason. You must know by now that none of us have any intention of harming you in any way. You've been through quite an ordeal and, I'm sure, there have been times when you have felt like the loneliest person in the world."

Sally remained silent, but she thought, *I wish Bert was here.*

Morgan let his words settle before moving on. "Mrs. Mason, we want to help you, share with you our knowledge and our thoughts, and offer you our guidance. Are you comfortable with that?"

Sally nodded. "Yes."

"Would you like some bottled water or coffee? A soda, perhaps?"

"No, thank you."

Morgan leaned forward with a smile. "Was your chicken dinner good?"

"Yes, but not as good as my own roasted chicken. I miss my own cooking," Sally said, realizing that she meant it.

Morgan held his smile. "I bet your baked chicken is delicious. I would have loved to sample it."

Morgan glanced at Kara. "Kara thought the chicken was overcooked. Ayita is a strict vegetarian, so she obviously stays away from chicken. I ordered baked salmon and it came, as always, with limp asparagus. I'm sorry to say that the asparagus is always overcooked here, but, undaunted, I continue to order it, ever-optimistic that one day the chef just might not steam it to death."

"Have you asked the chef to cook it less?" Sally asked.

Morgan shook his head. "No." He lifted an eyebrow, confidentially. "You know how temperamental chefs can be. I'm afraid he might poison it or something."

Sally looked at him doubtfully.

Kara gave Morgan a side-eye grin, aware that Morgan was trying to put Sally at ease. "So, Sally," Kara said, "aren't we just the most fascinating people you've ever met, talking about limp asparagus?"

Sally smiled, feeling her shoulders relax. She pegged Morgan to be a quiet intellectual, an introverted man with a weird sense of humor and a frank manner.

"Maybe I should talk to your chef," Sally said. "Maybe he'd let me share my chicken recipe with him. I promise I won't say anything about the overcooked asparagus."

"I'll make a note of that, Sally," Morgan said, grinning. "It might do us all good to have a change around here."

Kara spoke up. "Sally, you've been patient with us, and we thank you for that."

"Have I passed all my examinations?" Sally asked.

"Yes, you have," Morgan answered. "But we're going to ask your indulgence one more time as we pose some additional questions to you. Will that be all right?"

Sally nodded wearily. "Yes, but gosh, haven't I answered every possible question there is? What more can I say that I haven't already said?"

"I know you're sick of all this, Sally," Morgan said. "But we have learned that when a person experiences a dramatic or traumatic event, their first impression sometimes differs from their second, or fifth, or even their sixth, impression."

Kara added, "When the mind is relaxed and when one is able to stand back from the event and watch it unfold from different perspectives, often something is seen or felt that wasn't seen or felt before."

"But you do know that Dr. Stanley put me under hypnosis or, at least, a kind of hypnosis?"

"Yes," Kara said. "But she hasn't shared that information with us."

Sally nodded, as impatience flashed across her face. "All right, then I'll tell you everything I remember about that night. But I hope this will be the last time."

Sally took them all in, her expression determined. "When I finish, will you then tell me what my options are, as you called them? Will you tell me what kind of future I can expect?"

Morgan said, "Yes, Sally. Absolutely."

Sally nodded. "Okay, then let's get this over with."

"Are you comfortable with us taping the session?" Kara asked.

Sally agreed.

Kara found the recorder button beneath the table and switched it on. She named everyone present, stated the date and time, and then looked at Sally and began the questioning.

Sally adjusted herself in her chair, and then proceeded to answer every question. She recounted the events, beginning with a concise description of her departure from Rosemont High School after her shorthand class. She mentioned the name of the last person she'd spoken to in the parking lot before climbing into her car and driving away.

Ayita closed her eyes, tapping into her inner senses to merge with Sally's state of mind, thoughts, and emotions.

Morgan leaned back in his chair, fully attentive, while Kara diligently recorded notes on her laptop.

When Sally described the spaceship, she closed her eyes, as if she were visualizing it. "It's there. It's over the road. It's just hovering there."

Ayita saw it, too, within Sally's mind. It was an iridescent, disc-shaped, pulsing space craft, descending from dark skies, hovering over the road. Ayita felt Sally's sudden hot terror, and she grabbed either side of her chair, gripping it so hard her hands turned white.

Sally's eyes squeezed shut and her lips trembled. "Oh, my heavens, I didn't hear that. I've never heard that before."

"What?" Kara asked. "What are you hearing, Sally?"

Sally stammered out. "… The being—that radiant being—said something that I heard in my head. It said, 'Be at peace. Time will save you.'"

CHAPTER 41

Outside the airport hangar, Kara, Ayita, and Sally sauntered along a paved pathway, bundled in winter hats and coats. Kara held a flashlight, its beam directed forward. Above them, the dark New Mexico sky swirled and shimmered with stars, creating a tranquil atmosphere. The world and all its problems, and the future with all its possibilities, seemed light years away.

They had spent the last hour in the conference room, engaged in conversation about Sally's potential future. One option under consideration involved Sally starting anew in the Northwestern United States, assuming a new identity. This plan included providing her with a car, a two-bedroom house, sufficient funds for her to pursue a training program or a college education, and a monthly stipend until she could support herself.

Feeling overwhelmed, Sally said she needed air and a walk, so Morgan stayed behind while the ladies went for a night stroll.

As they moved along the path, Ayita looked to Kara to raise the subject of Sally's second option.

Sally stopped, stuffed her hands into her coat pockets, and gazed up into the sky with an absent, dreary smile. "It's cold. I didn't know the desert got so cold. And the sky is so clear and beautiful. There are so many things to learn and experience in this world. I'd love to write about it; to write a story or an article about this night and everything I've experienced."

Ayita and Kara remained silent.

Sally turned to them. "If I accept your offer to relocate, I won't know anyone. I won't have a past or any family or friends."

"But you'll meet new people and develop friendships," Ayita said. "And I live in Northern California. I'll come for visits until you get adjusted."

"And you'll meet some handsome man and fall in love," Kara said. "You'll be married in no time. You're a beautiful young woman, Sally."

Sally kept her attention on the twinkling stars. "And what would I tell this man about myself? I don't know, it seems like such a lonely choice. And I'd never be able to tell anyone the truth about me."

They walked on for a time before Sally stopped again, crossed her arms, and stared out into the vast, shadowy desert. "I haven't asked about the other options because I'm frightened. I know Morgan wanted to tell me, but I cut him off, didn't I?"

"I know you're scared," Kara said. "But it's time you know everything we know, so you can make your decision."

Sally tugged her ski cap down over her ears. "It's so quiet here, so very quiet. I can hear my breath. And you know what else I've been thinking? What happens to uncried tears? I can't seem to cry anymore."

Neither Kara nor Ayita responded.

Sally drew in a breath, blew it out and turned to them, holding her arms tightly at her sides. "Okay... I've been thinking about this for a long time, and maybe I have some idea about what you're going to say. So, go ahead."

The trio stood close, staring eye to eye.

Kara spoke. "Sally, we have learned that the extraterrestrial who transported you to 2023 did so in order to save you from a potentially debilitating or fatal accident. You were about to be struck by a drunk driver."

Sally nodded. "Okay... go on."

"We know this because we have an alien contact named StrallVoss. We recently met StrallVoss, and he explained that you were being watched by this extraterrestrial, who intervened, something he should not have done. And now, because it was his mistake, StrallVoss has suggested that there is the possibility you could be returned to 1953."

Ayita broke in. "However, this option comes with its own set of dangers... Sally, it appears that time is not as precise as we thought, according to StrallVoss. It seems to have its own unpredictable nature. So, you might return at the perfect moment and avoid the drunk driver and the accident, or you might not, and so you could be physically and mentally debilitated, or even killed."

In the soft beam of the flashlight, Sally's eyes shifted nervously. "All right, so I guess that's not what I thought you'd say. I thought maybe they wanted to take me... you know, take me to their planet."

Sally laughed, but there was no pleasure in it. "Gosh... that's so crazy, isn't it? I had dreams about it. Big towers for cities, dazzling lights and tall, beautiful people."

They fell into silence.

Sally lowered her gaze. "So, you actually talked to this alien person... This being? What did you say his name was?"

"It's StrallVoss," Kara said. "And yes, Ayita and I saw him here inside that hangar, and we spoke with him."

Sally mentally processed Kara's words, a trembling hand covering her mouth. When she lowered her hand, her eyes met Kara's. "Okay... And this alien is not the same alien who sent me here into the future?"

"No, but StrallVoss may have the power to send you back," Ayita said. "Now, Sally, here's the other part of this that we must share with you. StrallVoss wants to meet you. If you choose to return to 1953, he requires your personal consent before he confers with his superiors to request your return."

Sally stared with round, disbelieving eyes. "Me? This alien... This extraterrestrial wants to meet me?"

"Yes, Sally," Kara said. "But it's entirely up to you. If you would rather not, that's fine. We'll tell StrallVoss you wish to stay here in 2023 and that will be the end of it."

Sally turned away, ran a hand across her

forehead and walked off, pondering. Her emotions were bursting inside her: excitement and anxiety. The possibility of seeing her kids thrilled her. The possibility of seeing Ronnie scared her.

Despite everything that had happened, being separated from him and his volatile moods, from his criticism of her and his physical abuse, she'd learned something: if she ever had the chance to go back, she'd leave him. Divorce him, no matter the financial and mental cost, or what people thought of her.

But if she was physically and mentally incapacitated, what kind of life would that be? If she was killed, she would never see her children again. It was a terrible and unfair choice, a choice that tore at her heart. It was a lousy, twisted thing that no one should have to confront or endure.

"Maybe you need time to think this through, Sally," Ayita said. "If you need someone to talk to, I'm here, day or night. Anytime."

Kara lowered her head. "Unfortunately, though, StrallVoss has not given us much time."

Sally turned, meeting their gazes, and she walked back to them. "How much time?"

"Two days from now. Ayita will have to contact him and give him your answer in two days."

Sally was staring, thinking, hurting. "Do either of you have children?"

They shook their heads.

"Then you don't know. How can you know? You can't know how it feels to sleep and ache for your children, and to wake up and ache for your children, and with every breath and every thought, you ache for your children. Every hope you've ever had is to protect your children, and share their lives, and watch them grow."

Kara and Ayita held their compassionate eyes on Sally.

Sally smiled, and it was a beautiful, agonizing smile. "I don't have a choice, do I? No, not really. Even the possibility... the slightest possibility that I could see Don and Mary as children again makes me so happy, and it fills me with life and hope... Hope I haven't felt since I woke up in this time."

Sally maintained her smile. "I'll meet this... being. This alien. I'll meet him as soon as possible, and even if there are potential negative outcomes, if he can send me back to 1953, I don't care. I'll do it. I'll go right now."

CHAPTER 42

"SO DO YOU BELIEVE IT?" Molly asked.

"What do I know?" Jon Tanner said.

"Well, I mean, aren't you a detective or something?"

"Yeah, or something."

"Okay, so tell me something, then," Molly said. "You must have an opinion."

They strolled the Rosemont Village Green, passing the courthouse and the courthouse glowing clock tower that said it was 8:45 p.m. And then they ambled past the police station, where a patrol car sat parked at the curb, two cops standing beside it, chatting.

They'd just had dinner at The Heavenly Onion, a local burger and beer joint, and both wanted to walk off the heavy meal. The burgers were gigantic, the French fries were crisp and fat, and the beers had been served in frosted pint glasses.

"Do I think UFOs exist?" Jon asked.

"Yeah… you kept putting me off that subject at dinner. You're a very evasive and secretive guy, you know?"

"Really?" Jon asked, innocently.

"Yeah, really. So, do you think UFOs exist?"

"What do I know, Molly? Yes. Maybe. Could be. I mean, there are a lot of stars up there and lots of galaxies and planets. Why not?"

The night grew chilly. Molly pulled on a red ski cap and then buttoned the top two buttons of her long woolen coat.

She gave Jon a side glance. "Haven't you been watching that whistleblower who testified before a closed-door meeting of the House Oversight subcommittee? It's been all over the internet. I'm really into that kind of thing."

"Yeah, I heard about him."

"He's a former military intelligence officer, and he told the subcommittee that all those stories you've read on the internet are true. He said the government has debris collected from crashed alien spacecraft. I know you've read about it."

"Yeah, I think I saw him talk on CNN," Jon said.

Molly grew excited. She stepped in front of Jon, stopping him. "So this guy says that federal retrieval teams have collected biological remains from alien bodies. And why aren't you wearing a hat? It's November."

Jon hunched his shoulders against the cold. "I forgot. I always forget."

Molly yanked off her ski cap and handed it to him. "Here, take this."

"I'm not taking your hat."

"Go on, take it. I've got earmuffs in my coat pocket," she said, tugging them out and clamping them over her ears. "Take the damn hat, Jon. Your ears are turning red."

Reluctantly, he did.

They sauntered along Main Street, window

shopping at an AT&T Store, a closed bakery shop, a hair salon, and a drugstore.

"Do you know what else that guy said?" Molly asked. "He said he has interviewed a bunch of people, and several of them claim to have been injured by UFOs, or UAPs. He said that the Pentagon has been working for years to collect and study crashed UAPs."

Jon shook his head. "Okay, fine. But I say what I and others have been saying for years: where's the evidence? As far as I know, neither this whistleblower nor anyone else who claims to have knowledge of some secret government UAP program has ever been able to produce convincing photos that show crashed alien hardware. And, Molly, we're not talking about a private single-engine airplane that crashed into some cornfield somewhere. We are talking about an alien interstellar space craft that is capable of bridging millions of miles of space, with technology that is so far ahead of us, we probably wouldn't even know what it is. In other words, it would be alien."

Molly stiffened her back. "Oh, yeah, big shot? Well, I have *seen* UFO photos and videos. They're all over *YouTube*."

"Any and all of those photos and videos could be faked. I'll say it again. Where are the crashed spaceships and the dead aliens who crashed in them?" Jon asked.

"They're classified," Molly said.

"Yeah, right. So, this whistleblower's seen all the

evidence, but he can't produce it? So I say, be skeptical. Have aliens landed on Earth? From the standpoint of science, there's still no good evidence that they have, so either this whistleblower can't prove it, or he won't. Until he, or somebody else, does, I think we should consider his stories to be dreamed up."

Molly stopped short and looked Jon straight in the eye. "Well, *I* believe aliens have been here, are here, and have been coming here for a long time."

"Well, good for you, Molly Hutton," Jon said, rocking on his heels. "That's certainly good enough for me."

She slapped him playfully on the shoulder, and Jon lurched back, grimacing, pretending pain. "Hey, that hurt."

"Good! That's for being a smartass," Molly said, throwing her hands to her hips.

Their eyes met and held. Jon gave her a long look of pleasure, and she gave him a sexy grin.

"Hey, Molly, I like you."

She went to him, reached a gloved hand, and touched his lips with a finger. "Hey, you know what, nut case? I like you, too."

Jon's eyes explored her lips, her face, and her hair. "How long has your hair been pink?"

"Two months."

"What was it before that?"

"Who remembers? Blue, I think."

"Black nail polish, blood red lipstick, snake tattoos and pink hair. Yeah, Molly, you're my kind of girl.

Hey, maybe after we get some ice cream, you'll show me that other tattoo?"

"It's just like the one on my neck, but lower. It's not so different. Maybe it's not as good."

"Maybe I should be the judge of that. I mean, since I'm a detective?"

She tilted her head with a soft exhale of laughter. "How long are you going to be in town?"

"Leaving tomorrow."

"Can I go with you?"

"No."

Molly frowned.

"But I'll be back."

"Going for work?" Molly asked.

"Yes... I have to help send an antique car to a secret designated spot somewhere out in the Western United States. Now, how's that for divulging top-secret information?"

"Sounds boring," Molly said.

"Maybe."

"You'll come back? Promise?"

"Oh, yeah. I've got to see what color you've dyed your hair, and maybe I'll want to charm that snake on your neck."

Molly moved a shoulder into him, speaking in a low, caressing voice. "Oh, baby doll, it's me who's the snake charmer. I'll have you all charmed up in no time."

He reached for her, pulling her into a kiss. They held it for a long time, and it was surprisingly warm, surprisingly sweet, and surprisingly exciting.

She drew back from him, dead serious. "The hell with the ice cream. Let's go to your room. I have a roommate."

Early the next morning, Jon awoke to see Molly asleep on her side, beside him, her hair tangled, the sheet twisted around her. He hoisted himself up on an elbow, leaned over, and kissed her. Molly's eyes fluttered open.

"Good morning," Jon said, smiling.

Molly stared at him, blinked twice, and spoke in a sleepy, blurred voice. "What do you really do for a living? And don't bullshit me."

"I will come back, you know."

"You say you will, but I'm not a stupid chick, even if I do have pink hair."

"Give me a couple of weeks. Have your bags packed."

"Why?" Molly asked, sitting up.

"I'm a hero, and I'm going to take you away from here, all the way to Virginia," Jon said.

"What's in Virginia?"

"A condo. Two bedrooms. It's mine, and it has lots of room."

Molly didn't bother covering herself with a sheet, and Jon stared at her, distracted. She put a fist to a yawn and then bored into him with her sleepy eyes. "What do you do, Jon Tanner? Really?"

"Don't laugh."

"I make no promises," Molly said.

"CIA. I work for the CIA."

Molly leaned back against the headboard, staring at him as if she'd never seen him before. "Are you serious?"

"Serious as... Well, let's launch this relationship and see if it makes it into space. We hit it off right from the first, Molly, you know we did, and we did pretty good last night, too. Don't you think?"

Molly turned her face from him. "Okay... So, I'm like a little freaked out."

"Why?"

"I don't know. I have to think about all this. CIA? I mean that sounds awesome in one way and yet, in another way it sounds scary or something. And then, you want me to move to Virginia? I don't know, Jon, I have to think about it."

"Think away. As I said, I'll be back in about two weeks. We'll text, email and talk. I'll send you flowers and some kind of stuffed animal."

She looked at him, deeply, soberly. "Are you leaving on a top-secret assignment?"

"Yep."

"Something to do with aliens, no doubt?" Molly asked, teasing.

Jon moved in for a kiss. After he climbed back on top of her, she ran her fingers through his hair and kissed him again. "Hot boy, Jon Tanner. You get me all flamed up. You got time?"

"Come to Virginia with me, Molly Hutton. We'll be so cool together. I know it."

Molly's face melted into a sexy invitation, as she batted her long lashes. "In two weeks, Jon, I'll be packed. But I warn you, I have a cat. A big black and white cat named Harry. And I love him to death."

Jon leaned his head back, distressed. "But I'm allergic."

Molly flashed him a big grin. "Welcome to a real relationship."

CHAPTER 43

They were in the heated airplane hangar. Sally stood about five feet forward from Kara and Ayita. They waited in darkness, in dim overhead lights, and in the green glow of exit lights. The hangar door was partially open, and Sally stared ahead into the cold, unlit darkness that seemed to fall away into infinity.

"Is that where I'm going?" Sally muttered to herself, softly. "Into that darkness?"

"He's always on time, Sally," Ayita said. "How are you?"

"You said he'll speak to me telepathically, right? In my mind?"

"Yes," Ayita said.

"I've been thinking about that. But it will be in English?"

"You'll understand him. Just relax. He won't hurt you," Kara said.

"Well, I guess not, since they didn't hurt me before. At least, not on purpose."

A moment later, about ten feet in front of Sally, there was a flash, as if from a camera. Then another flash, and then the slow expansion of a pin light into a sphere that appeared as a bubble. It swelled. Sally swallowed away her dry throat, standing tall, mustering a courage she didn't have.

Within the blue bubble, a watery form appeared,

wavy and shimmering with a golden blue hue. And then he was there, the blue flame of a tall man with white-gold short hair, broad shoulders, and the peaceful face of a mannequin.

Sally had the impulse to step back, but she didn't. She felt his glowing eyes on her as if they were two distant headlights on a dark road.

"Sally Mason," the voice said in her head. It was clear and warm. It was deep and resonant.

Sally opened her mouth to speak, but nothing came out. She tried again and found her voice. "Yes. I'm... I'm Sally Mason," she answered, stammering.

"I am StrallVoss, a friend. Do not be afraid. I mean you no harm. I wish to be of help, if I can. Do you understand?"

"Yes..." Sally spoke audibly.

StrallVoss's glowing eyes found Kara and Ayita, and he acknowledged them. "StrallVoss is pleased to see you both once more."

StrallVoss returned his full attention to Sally. "Sally Mason, I have seen you before, one night when you were alone. It was many days ago. Do you remember?"

Sally recalled the night she'd left Bert's house to stroll in the backyard and, under the cover of trees, she'd seen a radiant being. "Yes, I remember."

"I attempted to speak with you, but my thought stream could not get through to you. Your fear blocked it. You do not have such fear tonight. That is good. You do not have to be fearful of me."

Sally cleared her throat. "This is... well, it is all

new to me."

"I understand, but all is well, and I have come to speak with you. I understand from Ayita Wells that you wish to return to your previous time and place. Is that correct?"

"Yes."

"And you have been informed of the risks?"

"Yes."

"It appears that in all places, and in all times, there are risks and choices to be made. This is how evolution succeeds, so I was told by my father when I was young. I understand you have children living in 1953?"

"Yes. A boy and a girl. I want to see them again. I want to see them young again, and I want to be there with them and help them grow up. I want to be a better mother and a better person."

StrallVoss's aura flashed orange, blue, and, finally, green. "I was told of your love for your offspring. I was sure you would choose to return, but I had to hear it from you before I approach my commanders with the request to send you back to 1953."

"Can you convince them, sir?" Sally asked, in an eager voice.

StrallVoss's image faded, then glowed violet, then flickered as if he were being projected from an old movie camera. "It will be for them to decide."

Kara spoke up. "StrallVoss, if you send Sally back in time, she will change the world. It won't be the same world just by her being there, and by the choices she makes. The world will be altered, perhaps only in small ways, but, who knows, she could also change it in dramatic ways that we cannot foresee."

"That is correct, Kara Gonne," StrallVoss said. "And it is important to acknowledge that. Consider this: every day, millions of people make choices, contributing to the constant renewal of Earth for good or for evil. The unpredictable nature of these choices is what we call learning, growing, and evolution. When Sally Mason returns, the Earth will undergo a subtle transformation, deviating slightly from the path it took when Sally vanished. While the change will be subtle and go unnoticed by most of your populace, individuals like Ayita might discern a slight shift. This will not be an easy decision for my commanders to make."

"But I didn't want to be sent into the future," Sally said, her voice pleading. "I didn't have a choice."

StrallVoss's blue aura shimmered. "Sally Mason, the one who sent you here is sorry for his actions. I communicated with him recently. He did not fully consider all the consequences of his choice, as we are taught to do. He was, as you would put it, quite young at the time, and he made the choice too quickly."

Sally took a step toward StrallVoss. "Sir, please don't punish him. I know he did it to save me from... well, from what would have happened."

StrallVoss lifted a feathery, white-fingered hand. "Sally Mason, if we choose to return you, what might have happened to you may still happen. It is possible you could also die. It is even possible that you might advance ahead from 1953 or retreat to a time before the year 1953. Much has happened in your world since you left it. Without your being there, choices have been made. Actions were taken that would not have been taken. In small ways, you have changed the fabric and the trajectory of time when you traveled ahead seventy years. And just like the flutter of a butterfly's wings across an open field is altered by a changeable wind, the currents of time have all been slightly altered by your being here in this time. Do you understand this, Sally Mason?"

"Yes, I think so."

StrallVoss gave her a direct gaze. "And you will not be the same person you were before. You have changed, and so the trajectory of time in that data stream will also be changed by your experience here in this time of 2023. Do you understand?"

Sally shifted her eyes. "Yes, it makes sense, but how can anyone know what those changes might be and how they will affect the past and the future?"

StrallVoss nodded. "Your thoughts are accurate. One cannot know."

"But I want to go back to my kids."

StrallVoss's shape dissolved for a time, and Sally perceived him as though he were a delicate, misty haze. Her mouth twitched, her pulse kicked, and she waited, thinking he might have gone.

Moments later, StrallVoss's form returned and solidified, shining golden. "Sally Mason, knowing all the risks that lay before you, and all I have shared with you, are you now prepared to be transported back to, or close to, the Earth year 1953?"

"I am. Yes. Yes, I want to go back."

StrallVoss's form became staticky, as blue flashes of electric lightning passed through him. "Sally Mason, do you have any final questions for StrallVoss?"

Sally took another small step forward. "Yes, sir. If I return to the past, will I remember everything that has happened to me here? Or will I forget?"

StrallVoss's mouth moved into what appeared to be a smile. "Sally Mason, StrallVoss likes your energy. In my world, we strive for authenticity of character and action. We strive for compassion. We have fought many wars to achieve these qualities over what you would call centuries. I tell you this because StrallVoss likes your authenticity, and your honesty, and your compassion. Therefore, I will grant you whatever you wish. If you wish to remember what has transpired in this time, you will. If you do not, it will be erased. Which do you prefer?"

Sally let her nerves settle before she spoke. "I want to remember," she said firmly. "I want to remember everything that has happened to me. I will be a better person and a better mother because of it."

StrallVoss offered her a little nod. "Yes, having a bigger picture of reality does help a being to expand their mind and realize there is more to the universe than one had believed possible. All right, Sally Mason, then it will be granted. That is, if you survive your time travel ordeal, and if your mind is not damaged, you will remember all that has taken place in this time. Also, please be aware that no decision has yet been made about returning you to 1953. My commanders must decide. I will have a conclusive answer in one of your days, and I will contact Ayita Wells. Then all the arrangements will have been made, and there can be no change of mind. Is that understood, Sally Mason?"

"Yes, sir. I won't change my mind."

"Then I wish you happiness, and I also offer our apology. We seldom, if ever, become involved in the affairs of peoples in other worlds. All beings must follow the natural course of their lives without interference. We must allow others the freedom to make their own choices, no matter where they may lead, to good or to evil. It is the way of things. We are all netted in this universe. All connected. Thus, we must learn to grow ourselves, and to be kind and helpful. Over many centuries and many wars, we have found this to be the best way. StrallVoss wishes you all peace."

CHAPTER 44

Two days after their visit with StrallVoss in the New Mexico hangar, Sally's 1951 Chevy Belair was flown in via cargo plane from Indiana, along with her purse, clothes, shorthand book, and steno pad. A day later, the vehicle was positioned on a runway at the airport, and Sally stood next to it, her hands shaky at her sides.

She wore the same outfit she'd had on in 1953: her floral-patterned dress, pink sweater, black pumps, green scarf, and pink headband. It was the first time she'd been outside the hangar in daylight, beyond the high garden walls. The sun was an orange ball, descending into the rusty western sky. In the distance was a mountain range, gilded in gold, as gray and blue shadows crept across the desert sand.

Sally noticed a heavily fortified control tower, two additional aircraft hangars, and a domed structure that blended in with the desert landscape. Kara said it held a radar installation and some communication equipment.

Kara also pointed to a series of silos designed for launching or testing advanced missile systems in utmost secrecy.

"You're seeing things, Sally, that most people will never see. And over there, about a quarter of a mile away, is the power generation facility. It's a power plant that provides energy to the entire secret complex. Beyond that... see that long, low, gray building?"

"Yes... It looks kind of like a bunker."

"It's a quantum computing center, which is an advanced computing facility dedicated to quantum research and simulations."

"I have no idea what that is," Sally said.

Kara smiled. "I know, Sally. I'm just trying to distract you while we wait."

Ayita approached. "Well, it won't be long now, Sally. How do you feel?"

Sally drew in a breath. "One part of me is calm, and another part is completely panicked, and I couldn't tell you where either of those parts is. My heart is kicking around like it's loose."

Ayita reached a hand and gently placed it on Sally's shoulder. "Keep positive. As I said during our sessions, keep imagining a positive outcome."

Sally gave Ayita a hopeful look. "Can you see into the past or the future? Do you have any idea how it might turn out?"

Ayita removed her hand and shook her head. "No, Sally."

Sally turned to Kara. "If I do leave, will you promise to tell Bert I'm on my way home?"

Kara nodded. "Yes, of course. I told you I would."

Sally looked up and searched the skies. "I don't see anything... any spaceship or anything like a spaceship."

Kara followed her gaze. "StrallVoss was very cryptic about that, so a spaceship might appear, or it might not. He just said to be right here, where we are standing, and they would do the rest."

Sally shivered as a breeze circled them and then died away. "Well, I'm ready. I just want to get this over with."

"It's time you got into the car," Kara said. "We're only five minutes away and we know how prompt old Strall is."

Sally's eyes held warmth. "Thank you both. I'll miss you."

Ayita gave her a little hug, and Kara shook Sally's hand.

"It's so weird, isn't it?" Sally said. "If I get back to 1953, neither of you will have even been born."

Kara winked. "But we will look you up, Sally. We'll find out all about you, and what happened to you, and maybe even visit you."

Sally looked at Ayita with wonder. "I'll probably be dead..."

Ayita shook her head. "You don't know that."

Sally cast her eyes to the orange glow of the horizon. "What does it all mean? What is life about, anyway?"

Kara crossed her arms. "I'll leave the philosophy to Ayita."

Ayita shrugged. "I look at it this way. It's a great big mystery, and who among us doesn't love a good mystery? Perhaps the mystery of life isn't meant to be solved, but only explored. Okay, Sally, off you go, and good luck."

Kara opened the Chevy door and Sally slid behind

the wheel, turned, and smiled. "I won't forget you both. I hope you have happy lives, and you should think about getting married. It's not so bad, really... Well, unless you marry the wrong guy, like I did. But how can I hate him? We created two wonderful children, didn't we?"

Kara shut the door, and then she and Ayita stepped back and moved more than fifty feet away, as StrallVoss had instructed them to do.

At exactly 4:55 p.m., Kara and Ayita saw something they'd never seen before. A beam of blinding white light flashed down from the heavens, engulfing the car.

They watched in stunned silence as the car broke into pieces and sparkled like broken glass in the setting sun.

And then the car and Sally vanished.

ΔΔΔ

The black asphalt road raced by, the white center line a blur. Sally Mason snapped out of her trance, both hands gripping the wheel, her eyes filmy, struggling to focus, breathing hard through clenched teeth.

In the lane opposite, two white headlights approached—two white points that grew into blazing suns as they raced past.

Sally squinted as another set of headlights sped by. Where was she? What had happened? Glancing at the speedometer, she saw she was speeding—

forty-five miles per hour—but she couldn't seem to slow down, as the world outside seemed a scary dream.

There were dark trees, a narrow dusty shoulder, a curve in the road ahead. Sally swept around the curve, maneuvering a tight corner, tires squealing, struggling to keep the car on the road. A horn blared, and Sally jumped.

She glanced into her rearview mirror to see headlights swing out into the opposite lane. A pickup truck roared by, the driver's fist raised. The pickup swerved back into the right lane, just as an oncoming car charged toward it. Horns blasted, and Sally saw the pickup had but one red taillight.

The night seemed a threat, the car unstable, and a foggy mist crept from the trees over the road. She had flashes of memory, but they were scattered and broken, and she couldn't piece them together. The past was the future, the present the past, a collage of melting distortions.

Faces slid in and out of her head—torn images —some ripped in half, some shouting as they were flung away into the rolling fog of her mind.

Suddenly, two glaring headlights rushed at her. With only seconds to react, Sally jerked the steering wheel right, through a burst of fog, aiming the car to the shoulder of the road, away from the attacking headlights.

But it was too late. The oncoming car sideswiped Sally's Chevy, and she screamed, losing control of the car. She grasped the steering wheel for dear life as the car skidded off the road, the momentum propelling the car forward. It went plunging down a ravine, pitching and bouncing, slamming into the trunk of a tree.

CHAPTER 45

Sally was vaguely aware of a flashlight beam sweeping back and forth across her face. She heard a knock on her window, and she squinted her eyes open.

"Hello? Hello? Are you all right?" a male voice called from above.

Her forehead ached, and the sharp smell of gasoline assaulted her nostrils. Coming to full consciousness, she thought she must have slammed her forehead into the steering wheel when the car plowed into the tree. Her first thought puzzled her. *Why didn't cars have seatbelts like they had in the future?* Then she thought. *Where had that thought come from?*

"Can you roll down your window?" the voice shouted.

Sally touched her forehead with two fingers and winced in pain. There was no blood, but it ached like the dickens. She focused on the windshield, noticing a large, jagged crack moving from left to right. Why hadn't the thing shattered on impact?

With a straining effort, she reached a hand and slowly cranked down the window, peering out into the bright flashlight beam.

"Can you lower that thing?" she snapped, in a surprisingly strong voice.

"Yes... Sorry. Are you all right, Miss?"

Sally heard the scream of a police siren and saw a flashing red light in her rearview mirror.

"Yes, I think so."

"The police are here. Can I help you out? Is anything broken? Do you need an ambulance?"

"No, I don't think so," Sally said, gently flexing her feet and legs. "I think I'm okay. My forehead hurts. I must have hit it on the steering wheel."

"Okay, let me see if I can open your door. I think I can pull it open."

A minute later, the door was open. "Take my hands. I'll help you out."

Sally reached, clasping his hands, her head pounding.

"Let's take it easy," the man said. "I'm just going to gently help you out. Can you swing your legs out first? Take it slow, and just swing them out and put your feet on the ground. Can you do that?"

"I'll try."

She did so, shifting her legs outward and placing her feet on the weedy brown grass.

"That's good. Very good," the man said.

"I think I'm all right," Sally said, lifting her head in amazement.

"You were lucky, Miss. I saw the whole thing. I was driving behind you when that car came at you in the opposite lane and crossed the line. He ended up in a ditch by the side of the road. I didn't stop to see how he was. I guess the cops are there now. Can I help you out?"

"No, I think I'll just sit here for a minute," Sally

said. "I feel a little strange, and my head aches."

"Yes, rest. I think maybe I should call an ambulance."

Sally put her face in her hands, white spots swimming before her eyes. "Yes… Maybe. Yes, maybe you should call one."

"All right. Hang on. By the way, my name is Mike Hansel."

Sally lowered her hands. "Thank you, Mike. I'm Sally Mason."

"Are you cold? You don't have a coat on."

Sally realized she was trembling. "Yes, I'm cold."

Mike slipped off his gray woolen coat and wrapped her shoulders with it. "That should keep you warm. Hang on. The cops are on their way. You stay here and I'll go up and tell them to call an ambulance."

Within minutes, Deputies Carter and Wysong clambered down the ravine, the beams of their flashlights searching. They found Sally sitting, holding her head.

"Hello, Miss," Deputy Wysong said. He was the younger of the two and had a long face and earnest eyes. He turned the flashlight beam to the ground. "There's an ambulance on the way. The man who found you said you'd hit your head?"

"Yeah, but it's not so sore now. I'm just a little dizzy, but I'm all right and I want to go home. My husband can call a tow truck and haul the car to a garage."

"Are you sure?" Deputy Carter said. He was a

broad, stern-looking man.

"Yes… I want to go home. Can you take me?"

"Yes, ma'am, but at some point, we'll need to write an accident report," Deputy Carter said. "And you'll need it for your insurance. Are you up to it now?"

Sally was distracted, still confused as to where she was. "How is the other man? The man who hit me?"

"I'm afraid he's drunk, Miss. May I ask your name?"

"Mrs. Sally Mason. You said he's drunk?"

The two deputies exchanged a startled glance. Deputy Carter straightened a little and adjusted his hat, while Deputy Wysong shined his flashlight beam over the car with a mounting interest.

"Did you say your name is Sally Mason?" Carter asked.

"Yes, that's right."

Deputy Wysong ran a hand across his mouth as he shifted his eyes from his partner, then back to Sally. "And your husband… would that have been Ronnie Mason?" Wysong asked.

Sally's mind was dull, but she certainly knew who Ronnie was. "Yes, that's right. Ronnie Mason, my husband."

Deputy Carter's expression darkened. "Ronnie Mason, who owns the construction company?"

"Yes… what's wrong? Has something happened to him?"

The officers exchanged another troubled glance.

"And you say you are Sally Mason?" Wysong asked.

Sally looked them over, confused. "Yes... Of course. How many times do I have to tell you? Yes, I'm Mrs. Sally Mason. What's going on? What's the matter? Is Ronnie okay? Are my kids..."

And then it happened. It was as though someone wiped clean a foggy window. Sally's memories of both the future and the past came rushing back in vivid clarity. Everything became clear, startlingly so, unbelievably so. The realization hit her: she had survived. The car accident hadn't killed or maimed her. She was alive and living in 1953.

Sally struggled to her feet, keeping a hand braced on the car. "I've got to get home."

Deputy Carter moved to help if she faltered. But she didn't falter. She stood strong and smiling. "Can we fill out that accident report later? I've got to get home and see my kids."

Deputy Carter's expression was strange and worried. "Mrs. Mason... I don't know how to say this exactly. Well, can you tell me where you have been for the last two years?"

Sally stared at him, not understanding. "What? What do you mean, where have I been? I... I mean..." Sally stopped, not finishing the sentence. "I just want to go home. Can you please take me?"

Deputy Wysong pocketed a hand. The police radio squawked from the police car up on the road, and then a siren wailed, approaching.

"Mrs. Mason," Deputy Carter said, searching for words, "you have been missing for two years."

Sally blinked. "What did you say?"

"Ma'am, you went missing two years ago, and if my memory is right, you went missing at around the same time of year. We searched for you for months."

The radiant, hopeful light left Sally's face, and she staggered. Deputy Carter seized her arm and helped her sit back down on the front seat. She stared, not seeing, not feeling.

"What year is this?" Sally asked.

"It's 1955, Mrs. Mason."

She repeated the year slowly, as if she didn't understand the numbers. Shaking her head, she muttered, "No, that can't be. No... I was supposed to come home. It was supposed to be 1953."

Deputy Carter had a hopeless look. Deputy Wysong puckered his lips and made a silent whistle.

The ambulance above screeched to a stop and then they heard excited voices.

Deputy Carter indicated toward the road with his chin. "You'd better get up there, Jim. I'll handle this."

When Deputy Wysong was gone, Deputy Carter offered his arm. "Mrs. Mason, I think you should go to the hospital and get a thorough examination. Later, we'll have to talk."

Sally kept her eyes down, an icy dread pooling in her stomach. "Do you know my husband, Ronnie?"

"Yes, ma'am, I know him."

"How do you know him?"

"It's a small town, Mrs. Mason. His company did some renovations on the courthouse and the police station about a year ago. We've had a beer or two over at O'Grady's."

"Do you know about our kids?

"I've seen them."

"How are they?"

"Fine, as far as I know."

Sally slowly raised her sad gaze. "And you say it's 1955?"

"Yes, Mrs. Mason, it most certainly is. November 8, 1955."

Sally hesitated before asking the next question. She didn't want to ask it. It hurt to ask it. "Where is Ronnie now? Do you know?"

Deputy Carter shifted uncomfortably, angling the flashlight beam to his right. "I guess I wouldn't like to talk any more about this, Mrs. Mason, until you've had the chance to be examined by a doctor, and until I can interview you in an official capacity."

"Please tell me. Where's Ronnie? Where are my children?"

Deputy Carter scratched his cheek. "Mrs. Mason, we tried to find out what happened to you. Ronnie searched everywhere. He hired a private detective, and we all did our very damned best to find you; to find out what happened to you. Ronnie did all he could to find you."

"Please tell me where my children are."

"They're with Ronnie. Mrs. Mason, a little over a year after you... well, after you went missing, Ronnie filed a petition for a divorce on grounds of abandonment. It was granted, and he has remarried."

Sally's head lowered by degrees until her chin was

on her chest.

"He married a nice girl. Linda Hughes."

She lifted her head slightly. "Okay. So, my kids are living with Ronnie and Linda?"

"Yes."

"And they're healthy? I mean, as far as you know, they're fine... my kids? I have to know that they're all right. I have to know that."

"Yes, Mrs. Mason. As far as I know, they are doing well."

They heard voices coming near them, but neither Sally nor Deputy Carter moved.

Finally, Carter asked, "Can I help you up?"

Sally's eyes were full of torment. "No, not right now. I can't move. I need to sit here for a while. You see, I'm lost. I'm just so lost."

CHAPTER 46

While Sally was taken to Rosemont Hospital by ambulance, Deputy Carter phoned Sheriff Tom Widmeyer. The two troubled men convened at the police station shortly after midnight. They had both been involved in trying to find Sally Mason after her disappearance in 1953. After much discussion of their options and the probable consequences of Sally's extraordinary reappearance, they decided to delay reaching out to Ronnie and Sally's parents until early the next morning.

Upon arrival at the hospital, Sally was examined by Dr. Anthony Stevens and his assisting nurse. Sally had encountered a series of jolts: an emotional shock from time traveling, a mental jolt upon realizing two years had elapsed, and a physical shock resulting from a car accident.

As a result, the answers she gave Dr. Stevens were vague. A stocky, mature man with a kind manner, he suspected that she had suffered more trauma than was initially apparent from the bruises and contusions on her body and face.

"You were very lucky, young lady, that your windshield didn't shatter and that you don't have any broken bones," he said. "But I want you to stay overnight, so we can observe you. I'll give you a mild sedative to make sure you sleep and don't wake up with nightmares."

Sally was too exhausted to protest, and the sedative soon put her into a deep sleep.

She awoke a little after 8 a.m. to a sore body, a dull mind, and a snowy November day. Nurse Jenny Moore placed Sally's breakfast on her over-bed table and rolled it toward her. Sally had no appetite.

"You should eat something, Mrs. Mason."

Sally looked at her through narrow, sleepy eyes. "I just want to sleep—to go back to sleep and sleep forever."

Nurse Moore's smile was practiced. "Sleep will do you good, Mrs. Mason. Sleep is always the best thing after a shock."

"And don't call me Mrs. Mason," Sally said sharply. "I'm not Mrs. Mason anymore. I'm Sally Anne Davis. Just plain old Sally."

Nurse Moore drew back, startled by Sally's outburst. "Pardon me, Miss Davis. I didn't wish to offend you."

Sally regretted her harsh tone as soon as the words left her lips. "I'm sorry, Nurse," she said, with the face of an apology. "I didn't mean to sound so harsh. I'm just not myself."

"I understand. A doctor will see you soon. But in the meantime, you do have some visitors."

Sally pushed the tray away and propped up on elbows, grimacing, ignoring the pain. "Visitors? Who?"

"Your parents and… Ronnie Mason. They've been in the lounge for at least an hour, waiting for you to wake up."

Sally collapsed back down, shutting her eyes, her head sinking deep into the pillow. "Tell them to go away. I don't want to see anybody. Tell them that."

Nurse Moore rolled the food tray away. "All right, Miss Davis. If that's what you want."

"And call me Sally. I'm just Sally. Just plain old Sally, who's out of her mind."

At that moment, the door opened, and Ronnie entered. He took a few steps toward the bed and stopped, the weight of the startling moment etched on his still-handsome face. His eyes widened with a mixture of shock and uncertainty as he gazed at his former wife, Sally—someone he'd believed to be lost forever.

He felt relief, confusion, and then a flicker of anger. As he started for the bed, he battled a surge of conflicting feelings, torn between happiness and suspicion.

Drawing nearer to Sally's bed, Ronnie struggled to speak. "Sally?" His voice was a mix of surprise and caution as he grappled with the reality of her presence. "You're here? It's you, after all this time?"

Sally slowly sat up, leaning back against her pillow. Her dry lips parted, but no words came out.

"I thought you were dead. I mean, I really thought you were dead, and yet, here you are. What the hell, Sally? You just left me, leaving me with the kids? I don't get it. What the hell?"

Nurse Moore lowered her head and left the room.

The former married couple locked eyes. Ronnie's

gaze filled with a fiery anguish, while Sally's opened fully to the realization that she didn't love him, and maybe she never had.

"Talk to me, Sally. I mean, come on. Talk to me. Tell me something. Anything."

Sally lowered her gaze. "How are Mary and Don?"

Ronnie flicked an irritated hand. "That's it? Not how are you, Ronnie? Not this is what happened, Ronnie, or I'm sorry, Ronnie? I ran off with some other man, Ronnie."

"I didn't run off with another man."

"No? Then what the hell happened to you, Sally? What?" he asked, pushing a hand through his thick, James Dean-like hair. "I searched for you all over the place. I hired two detectives to find you and spent thousands of dollars to find you. Half the damned town was out looking for you. So, don't just lie there and ask about Don and Mary. That's not making it with me, Sally, okay? I deserve some kind of explanation."

He gestured toward the door. "Your parents are out there, and they've been worried sick. You should see them. They look old, Sally. You aged them and you almost killed them. Your father had a heart attack, and your mother lost so much weight she had to be put in the hospital for a damned week. So don't sit in that bed and not say anything. You owe all of us an explanation, Sally."

Angry, he turned in a circle, ran his fingers through his hair again, and pointed to the window, where snow flurries drifted and scattered in the wind. "You want to know about Mary and Don? Well, they're happy now, that's what. I guess you heard I married Linda Hughes, right?"

Sally nodded. "Yes."

"Yes, you bet I did, and you know what? She's a better mother to those kids than you ever were, okay? Can you take that? Linda would never, ever, run away from me and those kids. She loves them just like her own. And you know what else, Sally Davis? Linda's pregnant, and in four months, she's going to have a baby. Now, have you got anything to say to me? Like, well, Ronnie, I ran off with this guy because he had money, a big house and he was going to let me go to work so I would never, ever, have to stay home and take care of my kids."

Sally straightened her back, the adrenaline bursting in her, the anger sharp and hot. "Shut up, Ronnie! For once in your life, just shut up. You always shoot your mouth off like you know everything. You don't know anything, and you never did. So, just shut up."

He surged toward her, his face hot with rage, his hands squeezed into fists.

She lifted her defiant face to him, daring him. "Go ahead, Ronnie, hit me. If you do, I'll scream for the doctor and I'll call Deputy Carter, and I'll have you arrested for assault. You'll be in jail, and I'll spill everything to the newspaper."

CHAPTER 47

Sally's and Ronnie's eyes clashed in the hostile air.

Sally spoke through clenched teeth. *"The Rosemont Chronical* will just love writing about you, Ronnie, local businessman. A nurse told me that the *Chronical* is anxiously awaiting my story. Won't it be a thrill for you when they splash your photo all over the front page with a bold headline like, 'Tragic Reunion: Local Woman Faces Assault After 2-Year Disappearance.' Or how about this one, Ronnie, 'Reunion Turns Violent: Woman Missing for 2 Years Assaulted by Angry Ex-Husband.'"

Sally glared at him. "So go ahead, Ronnie, hit me."

Ronnie backed off, staring at her warily, the rage melting into confusion. Her face was rebellious, her eyes hard. There was a strength in her, a conviction he'd never seen before. It wasn't the Sally he'd known. She was different, more confident, and fearless. It unsettled him.

Ronnie relaxed his fists and squared his shoulders. "Okay, Sally. Okay. Fine," he said in a milder voice. "So, can you just tell me where you've been for the last two years? Can you do that, at least?"

The night before, as she was drifting into sleep, Sally had created a story for herself. It wasn't a good story, or a believable one, but it's all she could come up with on short notice, and in her fuzzy state of mind.

Obviously, she couldn't tell anyone the truth. Most, if not all, would think she was out of her mind, and what if, once again, the government came for her? She wouldn't be able to go through all that again.

Sally stared Ronnie down and he lowered his gaze. "All right, Ronnie, you do deserve an explanation, not that you'll believe me. But, anyway, here it is. There is a thing called amnesia. I'm sure you've heard of it."

He looked at her doubtfully, his mouth a hard line.

"The last thing I remember in 1953 was leaving the high school, and as I walked down the stairs, I fell and hit my head. After that, things are fuzzy. I remember bits and pieces of things. I must have driven out of town. I remember an old man who helped me. I remember two women who were nice to me. I remember them asking me who I was, but I couldn't remember. I forgot about you, and Mary and Don, and my parents, and everything and everybody. It was as if I was someone else, completely."

Ronnie crossed his arms, unconvinced. "So, when did you... I don't know, wake up and remember who you were?"

"I guess it was a few days ago. I hit my head again, and I suddenly remembered. My mind cleared. I have no idea how or why, and then I remembered everything about my past life. So, I got in my car and

I drove here. And then that drunk man hit me and… Well, you know the rest."

Ronnie shoved his hands into his trouser pockets and Sally looked away, hiding her eyes from his scrutiny.

"So you're saying that for two years, you never thought to look in your wallet to see who you were, or look at the car registration in the glove compartment to see who owned it? You never did that? That's like, the first thing I'd do."

Sally was trapped, but she had to stand by her story because she had nothing else. "I can't explain it, Ronnie, I just don't remember. It happened, and that's just the way it was."

"So, now you're saying you have amnesia again, and now you don't remember anything from those two years?"

"I told you everything. Believe it or don't believe it, I don't care."

Ronnie stared out the window and shook his head. "And then you show up here with the same car, *my* car, with the same 1953 Indiana license plates?"

Sally shrugged. "What more do you want me to say? I told you what happened."

Ronnie looked at her and exhaled a snort through his nose. "Well, okay then," he said. "I'm not going to say I believe you, because most of me doesn't believe you, but I won't say I don't believe you because, you know what Sally? It's all water under the bridge now anyway, isn't it? I mean, everything is all messed up, and here we are."

"I want to see my kids," Sally said.

Ronnie gave her a long searching look. "You don't even look the same... and you don't act the same. What the hell happened, Sally?"

"Ronnie... Please, I just want to see my kids."

Resigned, Ronnie closed his eyes, pinched the bridge of his nose, and sighed. "All right. I'm not going to fight you on this, Sally," Ronnie said, opening his eyes. "I don't want Linda or the kids upset, and I know you're going to gab like a goose to that damned newspaper. I don't want my business to go down the tubes. And, besides all that, I don't want to go through anymore of the shit I went through two years ago. If you want to see Mary and Don, fine, we'll set it up all legal and right, then whatever the judge says, that's what I'll do. But that's it. I don't want to see you anymore than I have to. I'm going on with my life and you can get on with yours, whatever that might be."

Sally had little time to recover after Ronnie left. Her parents, Ruby and Herman Davis, rushed in, all tears, hugs, and gratitude. Her mother took Sally's face in her hands and studied her daughter. "Thank God you're here," she said. "You look the same, not a day older. My beautiful daughter."

Thrilled to see them again, Sally apologized and wept, observing that her parents *had* aged. She could imagine how they had suffered, just as she would have suffered if one of her children had vanished.

As Sally recounted her amnesia tale, both listened with unease and distraction. Neither seemed to care about the details of her story, whether it sounded plausible or not. They were tearful and joyful that their daughter had returned to them alive, and nothing else mattered.

CHAPTER 48

The *Rosemont Chronicle's* Morning Edition sold out quickly, and within two hours of the Afternoon Edition hitting the newsstands at the drugstore, the pool hall, and Van's Grocery, it, too, was completely sold out. It marked the second-highest sales in the *Chronicle's* history, the first being on December 7, 1941, when the Japanese bombed Pearl Harbor.

Local Woman, Sally Anne Davis Mason, Emerges After Amnesia Episode: A Baffling Two-Year Mystery Solved!

Rosemont, Indiana - November 11, 1955

In an astonishing turn of events, Mrs. Sally Anne Davis Mason, whose disappearance on October 5, 1953, baffled the town of Rosemont for two years, has re-emerged. Three days ago, the police responded to a report of an accident on Route 9, and they discovered Sally Anne in one of the cars, injured but awake. Her story stands as a living testament to the enigmatic nature of memory and time.

The mysterious vanishing of Mrs. Mason had left Rosemont in a state of collective bewilderment. Search efforts spanning many months yielded no trace of her, despite her husband, Ronnie Mason, sparing no expense in employing private investigators to unravel the truth behind her disappearance.

Sally's reappearance marks a miraculous twist in the tale. Residing temporarily with her parents, Sally has opened up about the tumultuous journey she embarked on two years ago. In a statement to this reporter, she said that the last memory she can piece together from 1953 was her departure from Rosemont High School, where she had attended an evening class in shorthand. She descended the steps, fell, and struck her head on something she does not recall. The days that followed became a blur of fragmented recollections, creating a disorienting mosaic of experiences.

Sally drove out of town that night and somehow found her way to New Mexico. She remembers an elderly man and two young women who helped her. Yet, as her mental landscape was shrouded in haze, she could not recall her own identity, her origins, or her family.

However, as fate would have it, a recent day in New Mexico served as a watershed moment. Sally Anne was hiking in the mountains and struck her head on a rocky over-hanging ledge as she was about to enter a cave. Her mind cleared like a storm dissipating, and her memory seamlessly stitched itself back together.

In a flash, and to her utter shock, she recalled her distant past in every detail. "It was as if I were in a waking dream, and I was an entirely different person," she remarked, highlighting the surreal quality of her journey. It is especially bizarre because now, she cannot remember any significant events from the two years she was away.

Sally Anne Davis Mason's story continues to captivate the imagination of Rosemont residents and beyond. Her experience serves as a poignant reminder of the boundless complexity of the human mind and the unforeseen journeys it can embark upon.

Upon Sally's release from the hospital, her parents drove her to Ronnie's house so she could reunite with her children. His wife, Linda Mason, wasn't home, and it was unclear whether she had left on her own or if Ronnie had asked her to leave. Regardless, Sally didn't care.

From the backseat of her parents' car, Sally leaned forward and checked herself in the rearview mirror, carefully examining her face. She'd applied makeup to hide the bruise on her forehead, not wanting to alarm the children.

Her parents watched anxiously as Sally strolled up the walkway toward the house.

Ronnie met her at the door, coldly, and escorted her into the living room. Being back in the house was both familiar and strange, like something Sally had once dreamed. All the furniture had been changed, the carpets were new, the curtains were new, and the walls were painted a mint green. It was the same house, and yet it was different, just as she was different.

She felt Ronnie's nerves and his conflict, and she felt a desperate hope and anxiety.

"They're waiting in the family room. I'll call

them," Ronnie said, and then he raised his voice in a firm command. "Mary... Don, come into the living room."

Mary led the way, entering cautiously, taking a few steps forward. As Sally caught sight of her, tears formed and glistened. The little five-year-old she once knew had blossomed into a lovely seven-year-old. She wore a soft blue dress with white lace trim, her curly hair crowned with a cute little blue bow. Mary stared at her mother with a mix of curiosity and fear. She took a step back, stuck a pudgy finger in her mouth, and lowered her eyes.

Sally swallowed away choking emotion. "Hello, Mary. It's me. It's your mommy. I've missed you so much, my darling. So very much."

The moment expanded as Sally waited for Mary to speak—prayed for Mary to speak—or to come to her.

"Go to your mother," Ronnie ordered. "Go ahead, now."

"It's okay," Sally said, gently. "Only come if you want to, Mary. But you must know I love you with all my heart."

In an unexpected burst of energy, Mary rushed to her, and Sally gathered her up into her arms, clinging to her, kissing her cheeks and hair. "I've missed you so much, Mary. Mommy missed you every minute she was away."

Sally held her daughter at shoulder length, blinking away the tears. "Did you miss me, Mary Sweetness? Did you miss mommy?"

Mary nodded, speaking in a pleading voice.

"Where did you go?"

"I had to go on a long journey. But I'm back now, and I'll never leave you again."

When Don didn't appear, Ronnie marched toward the family room. "Don, get out here. Now! Come and see your mother."

Sally cringed, wishing Ronnie hadn't been so forceful.

Don entered the living room, a shadow of the rambunctious young boy she once knew. He'd grown taller, but he was remote, with his hands stuffed into his pockets.

It was impossible for Sally to control her battering emotions of loss, guilt, and love. She stood up, still clasping Mary's hand, and slowly moved toward her son, pausing a few feet away.

"Hello, Don..." Sally said, vulnerable, her voice trembling. "You're nine years old now, and you've grown so much and you're so handsome. I've come home, Don."

"So what?" Don said, curtly.

"Hey, watch your mouth, Don," Ronnie snapped. "That's your mother you're talking to. You have some respect, or you'll get the back of my hand."

Don lifted his head, his eyes cold. "Yeah, well, where was she, huh? She ran out on us, Dad. That's what you said, wasn't it? You said she ran off and left us and she was never coming back."

Sally swallowed and then cleared her throat. "I'm so sorry, Don. I didn't want to go away. Please believe me. It was an accident. I would never have left you and Mary. Please, Don, believe me. I love you. Will you forgive me, Don? Please... please forgive me?"

"You're not our mother anymore, so what does it matter?"

Sally took a tentative step toward him. "I *am* your mother, Don, and I'll always be your mother. No matter what happens, I *am* your mother."

Sally felt Ronnie's eyes on her. Don stood his ground and didn't budge. Sally thought, *Don is a lot like his father. It will take time to win back his trust and his love.*

Mary looked up at her mother. "Will you come back and take us for ice cream?"

Sally kneeled down, face-to-face with Mary, smiling tenderly. "Of course I will, and it will be just like the old days. We'll go to town, and you can ride the coin-operated pony."

Sally looked at Don. "I'll buy you a new baseball glove."

"Dad already bought me one. I don't need two."

Sally maintained her loving gaze, recalling the stooped and bitter old man she'd seen in Fort Pierce, Florida in 2023. She was determined to change Don's life for the better. One way or the other, she'd help Don to have a happy life. "Okay, Don, then we'll find something else."

Ronnie clapped his hands. "All right. All right, that's it now. You two kids get back to the family room. I need to talk to your mother alone."

Sally watched them go, and the ache in her grew, and she swallowed it down.

Ronnie was generous. He told her no matter what the judge decided, Sally could see the kids whenever it was convenient for him and Linda.

"You just call me and we'll work something out. The weekends are good, and maybe one weekday night, depending on school and Linda's Tupperware parties."

Sally left the house in a pale despair. She'd lost her old life, and it would be nearly impossible to get any of it back.

CHAPTER 49

Sally sat at her desk in her childhood bedroom, staring apprehensively at her unopened purse —the black patent leather purse that had traveled with her seventy years into the future. There was no logical reason why she hadn't opened it, but anxiety seized her whenever she'd looked at the thing. She considered it a sort of Pandora's Box, fearing that once opened, it might propel her into the future, back to the New Mexico desert of 2023.

So it had sat on her desk or just under her bed for five days. When she finally mustered the courage to twist the silver clasp and open it, a little catch in her throat stopped her. She stole a glance out the window, postponing the event once again, allowing her mind to happily wander.

The delicate white lace curtains evoked memories of past sewing projects shared with her mother. That morning after she'd washed the breakfast dishes, she sat at the kitchen table, while her mother hovered at the stove and her father read the newspaper.

Sally thought it was good to be home again, seeing her parents in good spirits, her father whistling, her mother humming while she baked oatmeal cookies.

"I have to fatten you up, Sally. You lost weight," her mother had said.

"Just as pretty as always, though, Mother," her

father added. He'd called his wife "Mother" for as long as Sally could remember.

Sally had propped an elbow on the table, her chin in the palm of her hand, and her worried eyes went from one parent to the other. "I have to find a job."

"You will, Sally. All in good time," her mother said.

"I have no money and nowhere to go. I can't live here for the rest of my life, and I need money so I can buy things for Mary and Don, and rent an apartment so they can come for long visits."

"Don't you rush yourself now, Sally," her father had said, lowering the newspaper and speaking over it. "You take it easy for a while. I'll give you all the money you need until you can get back on your feet."

Her mother wiped her hands on her apron and gave her daughter a loving smile as she slid a sheet of cookies into the oven. "We're in no hurry to see you get your own place, Sally Anne. For heaven sakes, we haven't seen you in two years, and these cookies are your favorites. They have raisins and walnuts in them, just the way you like them."

"Mother is right, Sally. Don't be in such an all-fired hurry to leave again. You just relax here with us, and let the dust of all that amnesia business settle."

"By the way," her mother said, "I put your purse on your desk while you were taking a bath. I found it on the floor just under your bed."

Sally's attention returned to her desk and the purse she'd purchased on sale in 1952 at Maude Deaver's Women's Shop for $10.95, a real bargain.

Finally, resigned to the task, Sally carefully reached into the purse, withdrew her wallet, a tube of lipstick and a compact, placing them on her desktop. Next, she retrieved her address book and the half-pack of Kent cigarettes. Curiously, it was because of those two items that the police in 2023 had believed her alien time travel story.

When she noticed a bulge in the inner compartment of the purse, she unzipped it and reached her fingers inside. What was it? She removed the item, held it up, and let it dangle from her fingers, staring in a startled wonder. It was a necklace. A beautiful gold necklace studded with diamonds.

Her mouth opened in astonishment, then snapped shut. Where did it come from? It wasn't hers. She'd never owned such a necklace. She couldn't have afforded such a necklace, and only in her wildest dreams could she have owned such a necklace.

Turning it over in her hand, completely enthralled, Sally slowly rose from the chair and moved toward the window, holding the necklace up into the light. It dazzled, and the diamonds flashed in the late morning sun.

Her eyes didn't want to let it go. "What in the world?" she said aloud, unable to find more words.

As an afterthought, she returned to the purse, reached in, her fingers exploring, finding a small envelope. She removed it. Written across the face of the envelope in a beautiful flowing script was her name, SALLY MASON.

Sally opened the flap and removed a thank-you card. It was decorated with shimmering stars and a big yellow moon that dangled from a string, held by a gleeful girl about Mary's age, who gazed up at the stars. Sally opened it and read.

Sally:

StrallVoss wanted me to give this necklace to you, along with his apologies for your "many trials," as he put it. Don't ask me where he got it because I have no idea, and I didn't ask. He said, "When you view the diamonds, remember the beauty of the universe and the night sky." He also said, "Do not hesitate to sell it for money. We all love watching the stars while we dream of distant worlds, but we must be practical, too."

And then if you can believe it, StrallVoss actually laughed, though it was barely audible.

Love,
Ayita Wells

And then Sally laughed—laughed so hard her ribs hurt. She laughed so loud, her mother came to the closed door and knocked.

"Are you all right, Sally Anne? What's going on in there?"

"Sorry, Mom. I'm fine. Just fine."

For the next few minutes, Sally paced her room laughing, unable to stop. Who, in their wildest dreams, would ever believe that she, Sally Anne Davis, had received a diamond necklace from an alien from some distant planet, and his name was StrallVoss?

CHAPTER 50

A week after Sally returned from 2023, she was in her parents' living room, telephoning local Rosemont businesses, looking for a job. Her first choice was *The Rosemont Chronicle*, but she didn't dial the number, afraid of rejection. *They will never hire a woman, especially one with no experience. Never in a million years,* she thought.

The five businesses she called recognized her from the newspaper article, but none of them had any openings, and she had no real work experience except for a summer job as a ticket taker at the Rosemont Roxie Theater.

After lunch, and after stalking back and forth from the phone to the sewing room, Sally screwed up her courage, a courage she would never have had before she'd time traveled. She marched to the telephone, yanked up the handset, listened for a dial tone, and eased down in the easy chair. Recalling cellphones from the 21st century, she smiled as she placed her finger into the hole of the corresponding number on the rotary dial and dialed *The Rosemont Chronicle*.

The editor, Art Wright, answered the phone. Sally cleared her voice and said, "This is Sally Anne Davis, Mr. Wright. You were at the house the other day. I read your article about me. I... well, I mean, I thought it was good."

"Glad you liked it," Art said rapidly, impatient. "Helluva thing, Sally. Like I said, when I interviewed you, it was one helluva thing."

"I'm a good writer," Sally blurted out.

"What was that?" Art asked.

"I need a job, and I'd like you to give me a try. I can..."

Art attempted to interrupt her, but she persisted, speaking louder, talking over his resistant voice. "People know me, Mr. Wright. People all over town know me, especially after that article you wrote. People know me all over Indiana and beyond. And I can chase down stories, and I can write them. I wrote for the high school newspaper, and I've written short stories, and I wanted to go to college, but I couldn't. But I've always wanted to be a journalist. I couldn't when I was married, but now I'm not married so..."

She paused, catching her breath, scared Art was going to hang up on her before she could finish. "So, I'm looking for a job, and I'll work for nothing, at first. I just want to be a journalist. I want to write about people and... things. I know I can do it, Mr. Wright, if you just give me a chance."

Sally heard silence, but it seemed a small eternity. "Hello... Mr. Wright? Are you there?" she asked meekly.

"Yeah, I'm here, Sally."

More silence.

"So... Mr. Wright, you haven't hung up on me. Will

you give me a chance?"

She heard him exhale, and it whooshed into the phone. "Sally, do you know what the most important questions are in journalism? Did you learn that when you wrote for your high school newspaper?"

Sally didn't hesitate. "The five W's are, who, what, when, where and why?"

"You forgot one. A big one. How."

"I'm smart, and I'm a fast learner, Mr. Wright. Please give me a chance."

More silence.

When Art Wright spoke, he sounded doubtful. "Well, people do know who you are and they're fascinated by your story. No doubt about that. In fact, lots of people have been talking about you. That's a plus. The paper has received more letters responding to that article about you than any other, except for the time you disappeared back in 1953. And the bombing of Pearl Harbor. Anyway, I'll admit that you, Sally Davis, have sold many newspapers."

"I hope they were good letters?" Sally asked modestly.

"Most of them. You know how people are. A third like you, a third hate you, and the others don't give a damn—excuse my mouth, or don't excuse it. The point is, if you can write, even a little, you may have just given me a good idea. Okay, here's what we'll do. You write me two articles, you choose the subjects, no more than five-hundred words, and then you bring them to me. We'll see what you've got. If they show promise, I'll give you a column. If they don't, you're out. As you said, people know you, and I think they'll read a column by you, if you can write. Make the subjects provocative. You figure it out. How's that sound?"

Sally shot up from her chair, feeling tall with hope. "Yes, Mr. Wright. Thank you. Thank you so much. I'll be there tomorrow morning."

"And if I take you on, Sally Davis, you won't work for nothing. As Samuel Johnson said, 'No man but a blockhead ever wrote except for money.' It won't be a fortune, mind you, but, for a woman, it won't be so bad either."

Sally was giddy, feeling drunk. "Thank you, Mr. Wright. Thank you so much. I won't let you down. I promise."

"Hey, wait a minute. On second thought, make one of your articles about UFOs. Those always sell and they're big right now. People don't much believe in them, but they always read about them, and we get a lot of letters. Boy, oh boy, do we get letters, and subscribers love reading them, and then they respond. Everybody has a damn opinion about aliens and flying saucers. So, yeah, write a UFO article. Use your imagination, and it doesn't matter if it's 'way out there,' pun intended."

Then, as an afterthought, Art lowered his voice and asked, "Do you know anything about UFOs, Sally?"

CHAPTER 51

That same night, before dinner, and just as Sally was completing her article about UFOs, her father knocked on her bedroom door.

"Sally, there's a man downstairs. He wants to talk to you."

Sally glanced up from her Royal typewriter. "A man? What man?"

"He says his name is Mike Hansel."

"I don't know a Mike Hansel."

"He says you have his coat from the other night at the accident."

Sally straighten up in recognition. "Oh, yes. That's right. I do have his coat. Just a minute. I'll be right there."

When Sally entered the living room, Mike Hansel rose from the sofa with a shy smile. He didn't fit her recollection of him, not that she'd remembered all that much. He wasn't so tall, or so handsome, but his bluish-gray eyes held intelligence, his Roman nose added character, and there was a comfortable-in-his-own skin quality that Sally found instantly attractive.

"Hello, again," Mike said, with a gentle courtesy. "I hope you're well?"

Sally moved toward him, as her father stepped toward the gleaming fireplace, puffing on his pipe.

"Yes, I'm fine, thank you. I'm so sorry about your

coat," Sally said. "I couldn't remember your name. I hoped you'd come by."

Mike had a good, athletic build, a flattop haircut, and he was a bit bowlegged, which she found endearing.

"Well, I was going to stop by the hospital, but they said you weren't up to seeing visitors... So..." He lifted a hand in finality.

Sally said, "I would have seen you. You were the first person I saw after the accident, and you helped me. I would have told them to let you in. And you gave me your coat. That was so thoughtful. I was very cold and didn't even know it. I'm so sorry, what is your name?"

"Mike Hansel."

Sally thumped her forehead with her palm. "Yes, of course. I remember now. Well, Dad just told me a minute ago. I guess I'm still a little scatter-brained."

"I can imagine," Mike said. "You've been through a lot. I read the article in the paper about what happened. That was really something. No wonder you're mixed up.... No, I don't mean mixed up exactly," Mike said, struggling to recover. "What I mean is, there was an accident and..."

Sally laughed a little, breaking in. "... Mike, you're right. I'm mixed up, but I'm getting better. I'm much better, and maybe now I'm not so mixed up."

Sally's mother, Ruby, entered, carrying a plate of freshly baked oatmeal cookies.

"Hello, Mr. Hansel. My husband said you were here. I'm Sally's mother, and I've just taken these cookies from the oven, so you just sit yourself down and have some."

Mike's shy smile reappeared, and Sally liked it. "It's nice to meet you, Mrs. Mason, but I don't want to be any trouble or anything," Mike said. He glanced at his watch. "It must be near to your dinner time."

Sally noticed a kindness and respect in him and, after all she'd been through, she found them relaxing.

"Don't you fret about that, Mr. Hansel," Ruby said. "Cookies won't ruin anyone's appetite. They never have, and they never will. I also have some freshly made coffee. Sally, come and help with the cups and saucers."

A few minutes later, Sally and her mother were on the sofa, Mike was in an armchair, and Sally's father, Herman, rocked in a chair by the fire. They munched cookies and reached for their cups of hot coffee.

"What business are you in, Mike?" Herman asked.

"I own my own accounting firm, sir. I know it doesn't sound so exciting, but I enjoy the work and I have clients as far away as Chicago."

Sally held her coffee cup to her lips. "I think it sounds exciting. To own your own business like that, and it's a good thing to have a steady, successful profession."

Mike smiled at Sally with gratitude. "Well, I think so, and, as I said, I like the work."

"And do you have a family?" Ruby asked, as she blew the steam from her coffee cup.

Mike took another bite of his cookie. "These are

very good, Mrs. Davis. Really, these are the best oatmeal cookies I've ever eaten, and I love the walnuts and raisins."

Ruby beamed at him. "They're Sally's favorite cookies, too, aren't they Sally?" she asked, turning her encouraging eyes on her daughter. It was obvious to Sally that her mother approved of Mike, and she'd slipped into her match-making mode.

"Yes, Mom. They're very good."

Herman spoke up. "So, do you have a family, Mike?"

Mike softened his voice. "I'm a widower."

The room fell silent.

"I'm so sorry," Sally said.

"Thank you, Sally. Marsha passed away a little over a year ago. It happened rather suddenly. An invasive infection, the doctors said. Sepsis."

"My heavens, I'm so sorry to hear it, Mr. Hansel," Ruby said. "It must have been so difficult for you."

"I have a good family and friends, and they helped me through it."

"And do you have any children?" Herman asked, observing that Sally kept her eyes on Mike, studying him.

Mike nodded, his mood lifting. "Yes, I do. I have two boys, and they keep me hopping."

"What are their names?" Sally asked.

"The older boy is Albert, but we call him Bert. He loves to draw and play with colors. You give him a pencil and paper and he's good for an hour or two. I think he's going to be a famous painter someday.

My other boy is Hank. He just likes to play ball out in the backyard, and he wants to be a pitcher for the Cincinnati Reds."

Sally's mind shifted, an old memory resurfacing. "Mr. Hansel…"

"Please, just call me Mike. Even my clients call me Mike."

Sally glanced away, an eerie feeling rising. "Mike… Your son, Bert. How old is he?"

"Bert's six years old now. Yes, he turned six in late September."

Sally's mind went to work, calculating the years. If Bert was born in 1949, then in 2023, he would be seventy-four years old. Sally's eyes moved left and right. Was it possible? How old was Bert when she'd met him in 2023? She strained her brain to recall. Seventy-four. Bert was seventy-four.

Mrs. Davis looked at Sally with concern. "Is something wrong, Sally?"

"Have I said something wrong?" Mike asked.

Sally snapped out of it and her eyes connected with Mike's. "Mike… Can I see Bert?"

Mr. and Mrs. Davis traded a puzzled glance.

Mike smiled curiously. "Well… yes, of course, Sally. If you want to."

Sally rose. "Can I see him now? I mean, would that be all right?"

They all stared at Sally.

Mike slowly stood up. "… Yes, sure. The boys are with the babysitter, but sure, if you want to see Bert, we can go."

Ruby and Herman Davis pushed to their feet. "But what about dinner, Sally?" Ruby asked. "It's almost ready. Mr. Hansel, why don't you stay? There's plenty, and your coat's in the laundry room. I cleaned it and brushed it."

Mike was conflicted. He wanted to be alone with Sally, but he didn't want to be rude.

"I'll get your coat, Mike, and be right back," Sally said, starting off. "Mom, I'm sorry. I'll be home as soon as I can. I just have to see Bert."

After Sally withdrew, Mr. and Mrs. Davis and Mike Hansel stood awkwardly, staring down at the carpet.

Ruby Davis finally broke the silence. "Sally always did love kids... and, well, she missed her own kids so much."

In Mike's car, traveling toward his house, Mike glanced at Sally, his smile warm with invitation. "I was thinking, Sally. After you see Bert, would you like to go out for dinner?"

Sally wanted to rush back home and finish her articles for Mr. Wright, but she also wanted to have dinner with Mike. His energy was soft, his manner was easy, and she needed an escape from everything.

"Yes, Mike, I'd like that."

"Is Italian, okay? My mother was Italian."

"I love Italian," Sally said, rolling down the window to stare up at the stars. "It's a beautiful night. So many stars."

"We can take a walk after dinner, if you'd like."

Sally looked at him, happiness rising. "It's a good life, isn't it?"

Mike glanced at her with a new pleasure. "Yes, Sally, despite all the trials we go through, I believe that life is good."

"Thank you for lending me your coat."

He sat up a little taller and his smile widened.

Sally returned her gaze to the night sky. "Isn't life a great big mystery, Mike? I wonder how I'm going to change the future."

EPILOGUE

JANUARY 2024

Kara Gonne and Ayita Wells occupied adjacent seats aboard the Gulfstream G650, soaring through the skies at twenty-five thousand feet. They were only forty minutes from landing at DuPage Airport in Chicago.

"I'm nervous," Ayita said.

"You, nervous? The calmest person I know, nervous?" Kara asked.

"It's a first, isn't it?"

"Oh, yeah, it's a first all right," Kara said. "Sally Mason has taken us all on a lot of firsts. Poor Morgan. Stuck in Istanbul."

Ayita glanced over. "I thought you said he was in Africa."

Kara grinned and winked. "Right. But he could also be in Cuba, or Taiwan."

Ayita shook her head and eased back in her seat. "You people, with all your secrets."

"*You* people? What about the secret of Sally Anne Hansel? Isn't that one of your secrets, too?"

Ayita closed her eyes. "Okay, so we've watched the world go upside down."

"And right itself again, Ayita, although it ain't the same right side up. It's hard to believe that we were there, only last month, when Sally Mason vanished in that 1950s Chevy in New Mexico."

"I won't forget any of it. Ever. And maybe I shouldn't have come."

"Like you were going to stay home and not see Sally?"

"I keep seeing her car disappear. I have flashbacks of you and me running back inside that hangar to boot up your laptop and key-in her name."

Kara took a sip from her bottle of *Coca-Cola*. "It was as if some Harry Potter wizard waved a magic wand and—poof—we were living in a different world, and I guess we still are."

Ayita sat up. "As StrallVoss predicted, I felt it."

Kara shot her a curious glance. "You never said. Felt what?"

"Right after the car vanished, I felt a jerk, a glitch, or whatever you want to call it. It was only for seconds, but I felt it, inside."

"A glitch?" Kara asked.

"Yes, a glitch is the best way I can say it. A glitch, as in an unexpected snag in a system that can lead to unexpected outcomes."

"Why didn't you tell me this before now? We're about to see Sally."

Ayita shrugged. "I wasn't sure. I needed to meditate on it. Think about it."

"So what are you saying?"

Ayita looked directly into Kara's eyes. "Are you aware of the parallel universes theory?"

"I'm not a physicist or a philosopher, but of course, I know what that is. It has something to do with the possibility that the universe contains planets and galaxies similar to our own that may form a grand multiverse."

"Yes," Ayita said. "Parallel universes theory basically says that space is so big that it's probable that somewhere else out there, there are other planets exactly like Earth, and on some of those planets, the events that play out would be virtually identical to those on our own Earth, but there could be slight differences."

"Well, Ayita, I'm a practical, here-and-now kind of girl. I like things I can touch. I like facts, not theories."

Ayita considered that. "You saw Sally Mason vanish, Kara. That wasn't theory, nor was her time travel experience. Did you feel it? The shift? The glitch?"

"No, but then I'm not psychic like you. Anyway, I was too anxious to get to my computer to see if Sally had survived her trip back in time."

Ayita tilted her head, a little smile forming. "You say you're a practical, here-and-now kind of girl, but here we are living in a different world than the one we were living in only two months ago."

Kara pursued the thought, staring ahead. "Yes, I know, and I've had to acknowledge that with a lot of sleepless nights and not a few martinis. I've had to twist my brain around it, and I'm still not sure I have. Maybe when I see Sally again, things will just fall into place."

Ayita kept her eyes on Kara. "When we saw that Sally had survived, we knew she had changed the past, and thus, the future. And in small ways, ways we can't even measure, her kids changed things, too, and then *their* kids, and so on."

Kara drained the last of her soda, placed the empty bottle in the seat cup holder, and turned to stare out her window, into the darkness beyond. "After you went home, Morgan and I talked about it for hours. He drank too much single malt scotch and I smoked a half pack of cigarettes. We didn't sleep that night. We're much the same, Morgan and I, and we didn't want to accept any of it. Too much fantasy or science fiction for us. In his somewhat inebriated state, Morgan even suggested that maybe StrallVoss and his commanders created the Earth billions of years ago, and that's how they can manipulate it. I didn't go there."

"That's even a bit too far-out there for me, Kara."

Kara readjusted her seat to the upright position and turned to Ayita, her eyes narrowed. "You knew Morgan was hoping Sally would die in the accident, right? In his view, it would have been for the best. It would have restored the course of events to their natural progression before Sally was propelled into the future. He didn't want to send Sally back, scared that it could significantly alter the world to the point of unrecognition. Morgan even thought there was the possibility that the world could be jeopardized if she were sent back."

Ayita lifted an eyebrow, processing Kara's words. "Well, I was thrilled to read that Sally didn't die, she married again, had another child, and helped raise her first two kids. Her son, Don, had a happy marriage and became an engineer. Her daughter, Mary, by all accounts, also lived a happy life."

Kara nodded. "Yes. And so Sally did alter the world and she had one helluva career doing it," Kara said.

"And the world is still here, so Morgan must be pleased at the outcome," Ayita said.

Kara barked out a laugh. "Morgan pleased? No. Never. The last time we talked he was still worried, and he wants me to call him as soon as we leave Sally's place."

Ayita smiled. "When you called, how did Sally sound?"

"Her voice sounded youthful and happy. She said she seldom thinks about what happened all those years ago. And she emphasized that she'd kept the whole thing a secret."

Ayita grew circumspect. "You didn't want to send her back either, did you, Kara?"

Kara stared ahead. "No."

"Then why did you let her go?"

"You won't believe it."

"Try me."

Kara looked at Ayita candidly. "I was afraid that if she stayed, she would have slowly died of a broken heart. So I voted with you, and it was two against one. I chose the one over the many. Who would have ever believed it?"

Ayita sought to change the subject. "Did you and Morgan ever think of getting married?"

Kara threw up her hands. "Oh, God, of course not.

We had a fling once. 'Just one of those things,' as the song goes. It was fun, but there was nothing to it. We both like our work too much, and our freedom. Relationships are complicated and messy."

"Well, in the end, Sally had a good one, didn't she?"

"The second. Not the first."

"And her kids did well, much better the second time."

Kara nodded. "Yes, they did. It is a little sad that she outlived them."

Ayita studied her gold Aztec ring, twisting it as she contemplated. "All but Bert. The Bert you met is alive. Bert, the painter, who helped Sally escape to see her son in Florida. Now, isn't that quite the story?"

"Her stepson... Yeah, what a strange turn of events that was. And who could have imagined it," Kara said.

Ayita's smile held satisfaction. "I'm proud of her, Kara. Sally pulled herself up by the bootstraps and really made a difference in the world."

Kara nodded. "Yep, I'd say so. An internationally known journalist. A war correspondent in Vietnam. Yes, that's impressive."

"And she won the *Pulitzer Prize* for those articles on homelessness."

Kara turned to her window, gazing up into the night sky. "Do you know what I think when I look at all those stars? I think, was Sally Mason the only person to have ever been transported in time and then returned?"

Ayita considered it. "What did Einstein once say? 'The most beautiful thing we can experience is the mysterious. It is the source of all true art and science.'"

△△△

The next morning, Ayita and Kara arrived at Serenity Springs Senior Living in Oak Park, Illinois. It was modern, clean, and uplifting, with plenty of trees, quiet walking paths, and spacious public rooms with many windows that let in natural light.

Kara and Ayita entered through the glass doors, Ayita carrying a bouquet of fresh flowers, wrapped in floral-colored paper and tied with a lavish pink bow. They stopped at the reception desk, received their security stickers, and were escorted down a carpeted hallway by a pleasant young woman with long nails and high heels.

They reached Apartment 10, and a ring of the doorbell was soon answered. The door slowly opened, and Sally Anne Hansel stood before them, stooped, white-haired and smiling.

Her wrinkled face opened with joy, her eyes glowing. "Hello, Kara. Hello, Ayita," she said, in a soft, trembling voice. "Oh, my heavens, it's so good to see you both again. It's been such a long time, hasn't it? At least for me it has. I was such a young woman."

Ayita and Kara adjusted their surprise at seeing

Sally as an elderly woman, despite the recent photos they'd seen. Ayita met Sally with a hug, and when it was Kara's turn, she stretched a hand, and she and Sally exchanged a brief shake.

Inside the apartment, Ayita presented Sally with the flowers, and she accepted them with a warm smile.

"Thank you, ladies. I have the perfect vase for them," she said. "Come with me to the kitchen and help me arrange them."

Minutes later, they re-entered the living room and Ayita placed the vase on the coffee table.

"What an extravagant bouquet. I just love lilies and roses and daisies," Sally said. "I feel so special. Thank you both again. Are you sure I can't offer you something? I'm slow, but I can still open wine, bottled water and a can of ginger ale."

"We're just fine, Sally," Ayita said. "We've had breakfast and plenty of coffee."

Sally sat in a deep leather chair and the two young women sat opposite her, side by side on the sofa.

Ayita's gaze traveled the walls, and she saw framed awards for journalism, photos of a younger Sally standing next to Prime Minister Margaret Thatcher, Presidents Clinton and Bush, Nelson Mandela, Joe DiMaggio, and Dolly Parton. On an opposite wall were framed watercolor paintings of Florida sunsets and Indiana autumns.

"I'm impressed, Sally," Ayita said. "Look at all those awards."

"I've had a long life, and a good life, Ayita. And

don't forget, I gained two years when I returned to 1955 from 1953, so, technically, I'm only ninety-five years old. Still just a kid," she said with a chuckle.

"This is a nice place," Kara said, glancing about.

"Yes, it is. Bert found it for me. I told him I wanted a cheerful assisted living facility, and he searched for a month before he found this one.

He didn't want me to leave his house, but I told him that I wanted my freedom, and my own place, and he finally gave in. And then do you know what he did? He sold his house, and now he lives here, just a few doors down from me. He's in his 70s, so he fits right in. And he has been such a joy in my life. It was strange and wonderful for me to be his stepmother and to watch him grow into a good man, and a good husband and father.

Maybe when our little visit is over, I'll text him so he can drop over and meet you. He's giving an art class right now."

"But you've never told him about your other life, right?" Kara asked. "Or about StrallVoss?"

"Oh, my heavens, no. I didn't tell anyone, not even Mike, my second husband, or my children. It was my secret and my own personal experience that no one would have believed anyway. Sometimes, even I wonder if it really happened."

"Then I think it's better we don't meet him. Don't you agree, Ayita?"

Ayita looked to Sally, hesitated, then nodded. "Yes, I think it's best."

Sally folded her hands in her lap, studying them

with amusement. "Well, how would I explain the two of you, anyway? One a mystic, one a CIA agent who has contacts with extraterrestrials? Truly, ladies, you must admit that your professions are mysteriously eccentric."

Their laughter was easy, and then their chat elaborately conversational as they discussed Sally's awards and the famous people she'd met.

Kara asked, "And your second marriage was a happy one, Sally?"

Sally's eyes warmed. "Yes. God bless him. Mike was so good to me. I traveled a lot after the kids were in high school, and he never complained. I loved him dearly."

"I have to ask," Ayita said, leaning forward. "Do you still have the necklace StrallVoss gave you?"

Sally gave them a ghost of a smile, and her eyes grew distant. "Yes, I still have it. Over the many years, whenever I needed help; whenever I was stuck and needed help with a difficult decision, I would take the necklace out and gaze at it. Within minutes, I got a flash of inspiration, and I was off to the races, as they say. I have thought about StrallVoss many times, and I still do whenever I gaze up into the night sky."

Sally leaned back in her chair and pinned them both with a penetrating stare. "Do you know, ladies, that I visited you both when you were little girls? I watched you on playgrounds, and as you walked to school or played outside. I was quite the stalker."

Kara's pulse jumped, and Ayita was as still as a

shadow.

"You visited us?" Kara asked.

"Yes... Several times when you were growing up. And I sent you both Christmas presents from time to time and labeled them 'From Santa.'"

Ayita's face lifted in amazement. "Those presents were from you? My parents couldn't figure it out. The paint set, the amethyst rings, the bracelets?"

Kara swallowed back emotion. "I don't believe it. The dolls? The bicycle?"

Sally grinned from ear to ear. "Yes, ladies, they were from me, and I had so much fun buying them for you. I knew someday I'd see you both again when the time was right."

"But why?" Kara asked.

"Why?" Sally responded with a glowing smile. "Because you both helped to give me a second chance at my life, and it was the life of my dreams. I wanted to give something back to you and, as you know, I love children. And let me say that you were both the prettiest little girls, although, you, Kara Gonne, could be pouty and moody."

A long startled moment later, Ayita rose from the couch, went to Sally, crouched, took her hand, and looked her fully in her beautiful, lined face.

"Thank you, Sally."

Kara got up and crossed to Sally. "Sally Anne Mason Hansel. Please stand. I want to give you a big hug, and hugging isn't easy for me."

Ayita and Kara helped Sally to her feet. After hugs, the three of them stood holding hands, silent.

Finally, Sally released their hands, clasped her hands together, her smile expanding. "All right, enough of all this excess female emotion. I have a chilled bottle of Chardonnay in the refrigerator, and I think we should drink a toast."

After she'd opened the wine, poured three glasses, and handed one to Ayita and Kara, Sally laughed a little. "I have looked forward to this since 1955."

Sally's face brightened, her eyes twinkled, and she seemed to grow young again as she raised her glass. "Let us toast to love, and the wonderful mysteries of life, and to the miracle that has brought us back together. What an adventure it has been. Cheers!"

Their glasses touched, and chimed.

THANK YOU!

Thank you for taking the time to read *Time Lost – A Time Travel Novel*. If you enjoyed it, please consider telling your friends or posting a short review. Word of mouth is an author's best friend, and it is much appreciated.

Thank you,
Elyse Douglas

Other novels by Elyse Douglas that you might enjoy:

The Christmas Diary (Book 1)

The Christmas Diary – Lost and Found (Book 2)

The Summer Diary

The Other Side of Summer

The Christmas Women

Time with Norma Jeane (A Time Travel Novel)

The Christmas Eve Letter (A Time Travel Novel) Book 1

The Christmas Eve Daughter (A Time Travel Novel) Book 2

The Christmas Eve Secret (A Time Travel Novel) Book 3

The Christmas Eve Promise (A Time Travel Novel) Book 4

The Christmas Eve Journey (A Time Travel Novel) Book 5

The Lost Mata Hari Ring (A Time Travel Novel)

The Christmas Town (A Time Travel Novel)

The Summer Letters

Time Change - A Time Travel Novel

Time Visitor – A Time Travel Novel

Daring Summer - Romantic Suspense

The Date Before Christmas

Christmas Ever After

Christmas for Juliet

The Christmas Bridge

Wanting Rita

www.elysedouglas.com

Editorial Reviews

THE LOST MATA HARI RING – A Time Travel Novel
by Elyse Douglas
"This book is hard to put down! It is pitch-perfect and hits all the right notes. It is the best book I have read in a while!
5 Stars!"
--Bound4Escape Blog and Reviews

"The characters are well defined, and the scenes easily visualized. It is a poignant, bitter-sweet emotionally charged read."
5-Stars!
--Rockin' Book Reviews

"This book captivated me to the end!"
--StoryBook Reviews

"A captivating adventure..."
--Community Bookstop

"...Putting *The Lost Mata Hari Ring* down for any length of time proved to be impossible."
--Lisa's Writopia

"I found myself drawn into the story and holding my breath to see what would happen next..."
--Blog: A Room Without Books is Empty

Editorial Reviews

THE CHRISTMAS TOWN – A Time Travel Novel
by Elyse Douglas
"The Christmas Town is a beautifully written story. It draws you in from the first page, and fully engages you up until the very last. The story is funny, happy, and magical. The characters are all likable and very well-rounded. This is a great book to read during the holiday season, and a delightful read during any time of the year."
--Bauman Book Reviews

"I would love to see this book become another one of those beloved Christmas film traditions, to be treasured over the years! The characters are loveable, the settings vivid. Period details are believable. A delightful read at any time of year! Don't miss this novel!"
--A Night's Dream of Books

Editorial Reviews

THE SUMMER LETTERS – A Novel
by Elyse Douglas
"A perfect summer read!"
--Fiction Addiction

"In Elyse Douglas' novel *The Summer Letters*, the characters' emotions, their drives, passions, and memories are all so expertly woven; we get a taste of what life was like for veterans, women, small town folk, and all those people we think have lived too long to remember (but they never really forget, do they?).
I couldn't stop reading, not for a moment. Such an amazing read. Flawless."
5 Stars!
--Anteria Writes Blog - To Dream, To Write, To Live

"A wonderful, beautiful love story that I absolutely enjoyed reading."
5 Stars!

--Books, Dreams, Life - Blog

"The Summer Letters is a fabulous choice for the beach or cottage this year, so you can live and breathe the same feelings and smells as the characters in this wonderful story."

ABOUT THE AUTHOR

Elyse Douglas

Elyse Douglas is the pen name for the husband and wife writing team of Elyse Parmentier and Douglas Pennington.

Some of Elyse Douglas' novels include: "The Other Side of Summer," "Time Stranger," "The Christmas Eve Series," "The Christmas Diary Book One and Two " and "The Summer Diary."

They live in New York City.

www.elysedouglas.com

elysedouglass@gmail.com

PRAISE FOR AUTHOR

"The Christmas Town" draws you in from the first page, and fully engages you up until the very last. I would love to see this book become another one of those beloved Christmas film traditions, to be treasured over the years!

- A NIGHT'S DREAM OF BOOKS BLOG

"This is a five-star read! 'Speakeasy' by Elyse Douglas is a stunning and enveloping novel, that whisks the reader back to a time of flappers and gangsters."

- CELTICLADY REVIEWS

BOOKS BY THIS AUTHOR

Time And Tide - A Time Travel Novel

Will Gillian rewrite history or surrender to destiny?

In 2023, newlywed heiress, 27-year-old Gillian Woodruff, and her husband, Richard Woodruff, are honeymooning on their private yacht. Richard is hiding secrets and is not all he seems. When the boat encounters a strange, violent storm, it is struck by a towering wave, and Gillian is hurled into the sea, washing up on a rocky, deserted Massachusetts beach, close to death. She soon learns it is 1900.

Time Passage - A Time Travel Novel

Can Cindy Survive the Past to Find Her Future?

In 2022, Cindy Downing, a 25-year-old woman with a troubled past, kills her billionaire boyfriend in self-defense and flees, boarding an Amtrak train headed for Chicago. While passing through a tunnel, the train plunges through a burst of light—into another time and place.

Time Visitor - A Time Travel Novel

In 1944 a Squadron of Navy Planes Disappears off the Florida Coast. One Lands in 2005... In Ohio.

Printed in Great Britain
by Amazon

40580628R00209